BLACK ICE...

SO WE MEET AGAIN

V. BROWN

Published by:

G Street Chronicles
P.O. Box 1822
Jonesboro, GA 30237-1822
www.gstreetchronicles.com
fans@gstreetchronicles.com

Cover design:
Hot Book Covers, www.hotbookcovers.com

ISBN: 978-1-9384423-0-8
LCCN: 2012950152

.

Join us on our social networks

Facebook
G Street Chronicles Fan Page
The G Street Chronicles CEO Exclusive Readers Group

Follow us on Twitter
@GStreetChronicl

Special Edition

Part 1 - Broken Promise is included!

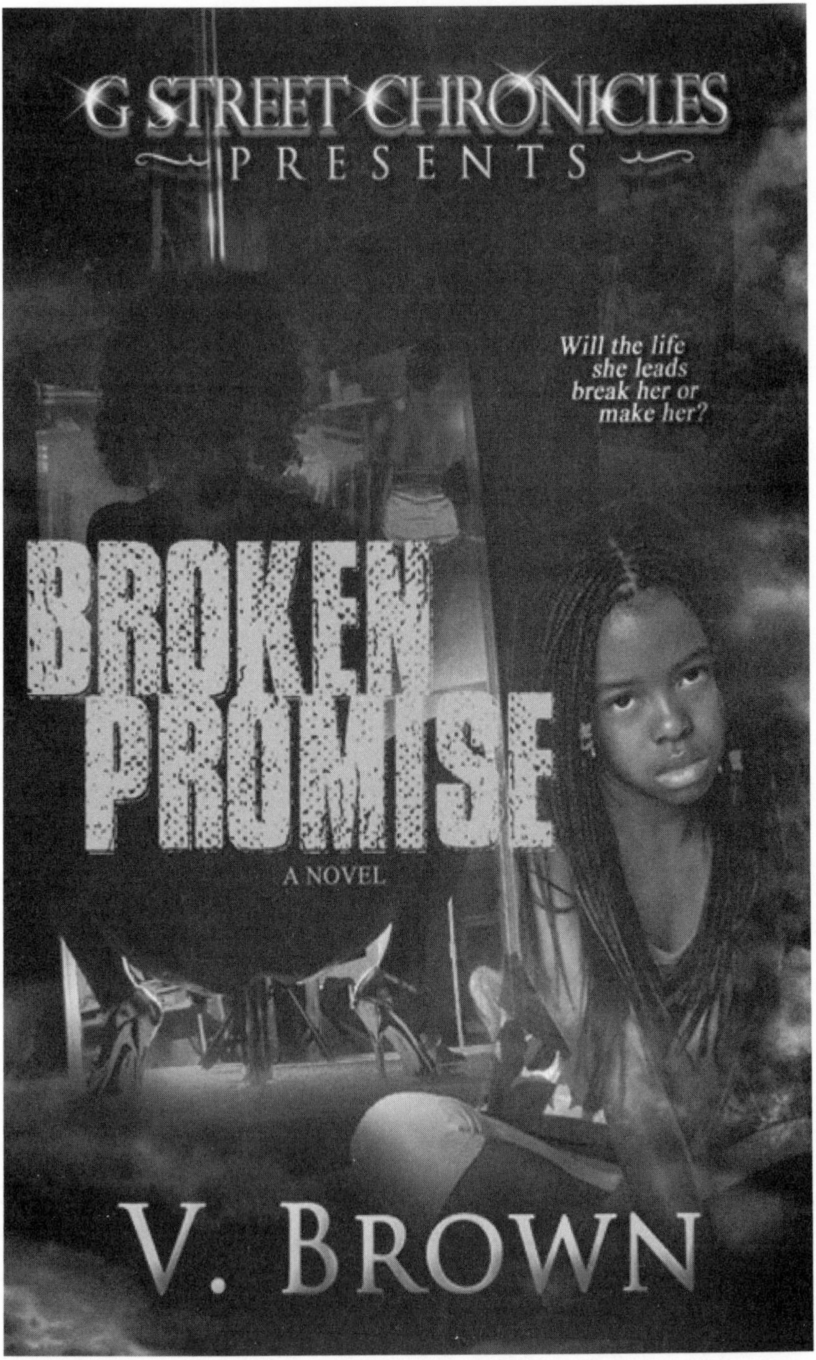

Acknowledgements

First and foremost I want to thank God for blessing me with the gift to tell stories that may either take a person out of a bad mood or touch a person in more ways than one.

I would like to acknowledge my mother Vadia and my father Ted, though we might not always see eye to eye I thank y'all for being there the times you were. I love you!

I want to thank my sister's Vatia, Tamara aka Bam, Marquessa and Marquetta for supporting and encouraging me when I felt I didn't have any support.

Thank you to my brother's Lorenzo, Michael, Ted Jr. Courtney, Aj and my nephews Jarvis Jr. aka Mook, Lil Zo and Zion…y'all give me the strength to keep pushing.

To my Godmother Dot for being the one person who always believed in me. If it wasn't for the laptop you gave me as a birthday gift a couple of years ago I wouldn't be able to type these amazing stories. Thank you!

Thank you to all of my Aunts, Uncles and Cousins when you need family I smile because I can count on y'all in one way or another.

Thank you to all of my close "Real" friends who keep it real with me. Y'all do more for me then y'all can imagine. If you're questioning if you're in this category that means you're not because my real friends would never question it.

The picture of me on the cover was taken by a great photographer by the name Kedric Lajuan. Check him out on Facebook. He's a beast with the camera. Thank you for capturing me in a different light.

To all of my readers that 1-clicked my first book Broken Promise and didn't even know me from a can of paint, but were willing to take a chance on me and my story I say Thank You. Your support means the world.

To the Facebook groups that I'm a part of, starting with The G Street Chronicles CEO Exclusive Readers Group! Divas and Goons I love y'all because y'all go so hard in pushing me to keep that heat coming. A Day Early Publishing Book Club ran by Tiffany Byers, thank you for supporting me and being the first person to interview me after the release of my first book.

You give new authors a platform to stand on. Kindle Reading Club, Black Faithful Sisters and Brothers Book Club, United Sisters Bookclub, Let's Talk Relationships & Books!!! Y'all all show me a lot of love and any book club that I didn't mention I apologize, but thank you as well.

Last, but definitely never least Thank You to the company and people behind the company that made it all possible, y'all made my dream a reality. G Street Chronicles CEO George Sherman Hudson and VP Shawna A., I'm rocking with y'all while we float to the top, past all the naysayers.

To everyone that was mentioned, know that you are near and dear to my heart. Thank y'all and I love y'all. Alright now, let's get on to this juiciness I know y'all can't wait to begin reading. Enjoy!

BROKEN PROMISE

STREET CHRONICLES

Broken Promise is dedicated to everyone who truly believed in me from day one!

Prologue

"This drug game ain't no joke, Biggs. I been yo' right-hand man in this empire since you started it ten years ago, hustlin' on the co'ner," Toni said.

"Toni, man, I feel you on that. This shit gettin' crazy, nigga. Seem like the mo' money I make, the mo' problems come my way," Biggs replied.

"Speaking of problems, there go them West Side boys right there. Niggas think they can come 'round here and show face. Biggs, them the same mu'fuckas that robbed the spot last week. Told you we was gon' catch them fuck boys slippin', didn't I?"

Toni never got a response. Biggs was on his way up the block, dressed in all black, moving like a silent ninja in the still of the night.

Without thinking twice, Toni moved right along with his boy, ready to buss if he bussed and kill if he killed. That's just how they were with one another.

Then came a *Bam! Bam! Bam!,* followed by a loud, gut-wrenching howl. Biggs had just hit one of his targets, but he didn't see the young'n coming from behind a midnight-blue Chrysler, about to give him the same treatment he'd given his homie. Too bad Toni was already on the job by the time the young'n touched his chrome Beretta; it was lights out for him. *Boom*! Toni put one to the back of his head, and li'l dude never had a chance.

Biggs turned around and grinned at his partner in crime, then walked up on him and said, "Nigga, you always there when I need you. Li'l nigga woulda caught me sleepin' on 'im and probably dead me on some vengeance-type shit."

"Yeah, he almost had you, but that shit wasn't going down on my watch. Next time, warn a nigga before you go spaz out and start bussing niggas," Toni replied, chuckling at his homie.

"Man, next time I'm gunning for the whole crew. This shit here," Biggs said as he pointed to the dead bodies, "this is a message sent to all gangs. E'rybody gon' know you don't rob Biggs and keep yo' life."

"Robbing you is like robbing me, and I ain't too fond of that," Toni replied.

* * *

"Aye, bay, where you at, girl? A nigga been out bussing my ass all day in these streets, and you can't even be waiting for me at the door butt naked?" Biggs belted as he slammed the front door.

"Nigga, don't be walking in here slamming my damn door. I been taking care of our daughter, handling your business, making sure all the money from the spots on 34th, 26th, and Main Street are accurate, paying bills, and grocery shopping. And after all that you expect me to be waiting, butt naked in some stilettos, ready to get my brains fucked out? I think not," Sweet Pea said with a bewildered look on her face.

"Come here, girl. See? That's why I love yo' ass, 'cause you hold a nigga down. You gon' be my wife one of these days. You know that, right?" Biggs asked while grabbing an ample amount of her ass.

"Yeah, yeah, nigga. You're only saying that 'cause you want some of this hello kitty. Go ahead and put it on me, Daddy, while we have a moment, 'cause you know Promise. She'll wake up crying any minute. I'll be glad when she turns six months and starts sleeping through the night."

That was all Biggs needed to hear before he untied her robe and saw all of her succulent nakedness. *I'm about to fuck the shit out of her*, Biggs thought.

Chapter One

How It All Began

April 16, 1994

Sitting in the living room watching different people come in and out of her mommy's apartment was a normal thing. Promise's mother, Taniqua "Sweet Pea" Brown, cooked crack, sold dope, and did hair out of the same apartment they lived in, so there was never a quiet, dull moment in their home.

Promise Sa'Miya Brown was only eleven years old at the time, and she didn't understand that what her mother was doing was wrong. No, the woman didn't have a regular 9-to-5 like all her friends' mothers, but she got plenty of money and spoiled Promise to death with the finer things life had to offer. In Promise's eyes, they were 'hood rich.

The girl's daddy, Dontae "Biggs" Brown, was that nigga in the streets, the king of a drug empire that stretched through the city of Tampa and some surrounding areas. Nobody could mention Biggs's name without hearing about his murder game. The niggas he had working for him feared him, but at the same time, behind his back, they carried jealousy and larceny in their hearts.

Biggs's best friend, who Promise called Uncle Toni, was arrested on the other side of the projects earlier that day. Dudes had been stopping by all day, telling Biggs that the feds had knocked Toni. Toni was Biggs's right-hand man in his empire, so Biggs knew someone had turned snitch; he also knew them alphabet boys would be coming for him next.

He sat across from Promise stressing, sweating, and rocking back and forth. She'd never seen her father act like that before, and he'd been in the game since long before she was born, ever since he was twelve years old.

Promise's mother, on the other hand, seemed unfazed by the sudden news. Sweet Pea just picked up the phone and calmly called their lawyer, Billy Wright. She told Billy to find out what was going on and to get back to them ASAP.

"That's what we pay his ass good money for—to be on top of shit and jump when we say, 'Jump!'" she told this nosey lady named Shirley from around the way.

"Sweet Pea, you a damn fool," Shirley replied, laughing. *This bitch thinks she's got it so good with her beautiful daughter and rich husband,* Shirley thought. *Shit, they the only family in the drug empire who live in the projects as a cover-up and have a big-ass mansion over there on Bay Shore. I can't wait to see Sweet Pea and Biggs fall flat on their asses. Boils my blood just sitting there listening to them. Ugh!* Shirley seemed to always be at their apartment, whether she was getting her hair done or just shooting the breeze with Promise's mother.

Promise grew bored watching her daddy stress, and since *Sister Sister*, her favorite show, was over, she decided to get a snack from the kitchen. As she was shutting the cabinet, she heard the front door crash open with a loud *Boom!*

At least fifteen officers bum-rushed through it, yelling, "FBI! Everybody get down! Nobody move and keep your hands where we can see them!"

The girl just froze, right there in the middle of the kitchen, unable to move—so scared, in fact, that she dropped her freshly poured cup of Kool-Aid.

One of the officers grabbed her mother, threw her to the ground, and roughly slapped cuffs on her wrists. Sweat Pea tried to resist arrest, telling the officer, "Wait! My daughter is right there. Don't do this in front of her." Then she turned her attention to her little girl. "Promise, go to your room! You don't need to see this shit these fuckin' pigs are doing to yo' daddy and me."

As Promise turned to go to her room, a red-headed white lady with wide-frame glasses blocked her path. "My name is Nicole Scott. I'm a social worker, and I need you to come with me," she said.

Promise, not knowing what to do, turned for confirmation from her daddy, but by then, Biggs was yelling at the officers, "Y'all ain't taking my baby nowhere! Not my Promise." Then he rushed the lady to get her out of her way so Promise could make a run for it.

Promise could have sworn time stood still in that moment, as she heard about seven or eight shots ring out. The girl watched helplessly as her daddy fell to the floor.

With his eyes still on Promise, Biggs stuttered, "Know…that…I…love…you…Promise." Then he made a gargling noise before his body twitched and went limp.

At witnessing the death of her man, Sweat Pea started hysterically screaming and crying. "You fuckin' pigs! Why did you have to shoot him? He was just trying to protect our baby girl. Is that a fuckin' crime? Shit!" She tried to get up, but since she was cuffed and face down, with the knee of a taller, muscle-bound officer in her back, that wasn't going to be an easy task. Promise knew her mama wasn't going to be able to help her, and so did her mama, who finally gave up and just lay there, sobbing uncontrollably

For some reason, Promise could only cry silent tears, but she was shaking like a leaf on a cold fall night. She couldn't believe what was happening right in front of her . She had gotten up that morning thinking she'd spend the day shopping with her mother, but things had taken a turn for the worst. After that day, her life would be changed forever, and that was something her young mind almost couldn't process. As the girl walked sadly out of her front door with Ms. Scott, she took one last look at her mother.

Sweet Pea tried to assure her, "I promise this is all a misunderstanding, baby. I'll be there to get you as soon as…" She looked away and then continued, "As soon as I get things sorted out." She sobbed, and Promise knew she was lying. Promise's mother had always looked her in the eyes and told things to her straight, because she loved seeing the hazel and specs of green in her daughter's beautiful eyes, but this time, she couldn't make eye contact with Promise because she was making a promise she didn't know if she could keep. *Lord, what am I gonna do? I know I'm going down. Biggs is dead, so the FBI is gonna try take me down, especially if I don't tell them what they wanna hear. I love my daughter, and I have to get her back. Fuck!* Sweet Pea thought.

That was the last time Promise saw her mother before she was hauled off to become another statistic in the system…and the broken promises were just beginning.

Chapter Two

Things Just Weren't Going Right!

Promise had been in and out of three different foster homes, and it seemed like every one she was sent to was worse than the one before. The first foster home she moved into, she never really got a chance to stay there because of her allergies; they had two dogs and a cat, and it just wasn't going to work out. She lived there for about a month, until Ms. Alice grew tired of hearing her sneezing and coughing all the time.

Next, she was sent to live with Anna Mae Jenkins, a mean, stocky, sixty-seven-year-old woman. Anna Mae had a scowl plastered on her face at all times. She wore a pink and white pinstriped housecoat around the house every day, and her hair was never taken out of rollers. Anna Mae also had three children of her own: two of them—eighteen-year-old Shawn and twenty-year-old Renee—still lived with her. Her oldest son, Alex, was twenty-six, and he lived in New York.

When Promise first arrived at the Jenkins home about a week after she was taken from the other place, she was still shell shocked. She was told she would be moving to her new house with a new family because there was nobody to take care of her on her mom's or dad's side of the family.

When Ms. Scott and Promise drove up the driveway, the girl's nerves started to take over. It looked like a nice family home, nothing out of the ordinary. There was clean-cut grass, a basketball goal, and two basketballs at the end of the driveway.

Promise got out of the car and didn't even notice herself taking the few steps to the front door. She was scared out of her mind, and when she saw the mean-looking old lady, she knew her troubles were not over. In fact, she was pretty sure they were just beginning.

"You must be Promise. I'm Anna Mae Jenkins, but you can call me Anna Mae," the old woman said as she opened the door and looked down at Promise.

Promise got this eerie feeling when the woman touched the side of her face.

"Miss Jenkins," Ms. Scott said, "I'm just going to show Promise to her room, and then I'll be on my way."

The whole time, Promise was focused on Miss Jenkins. She didn't notice the tall boy staring at her from the other side of the room.

"Oh yeah. This is my son Shawn. Shawn, this is Promise, and she'll be living with us from now on."

Shawn gave her a warm but mischievous grin. He was a cutie, about six feet tall, with butter pecan skin, the deepest, almond-shaped, dark brown eyes, and always sporting a fresh Caesar haircut. He was also the star basketball player at his high school.

"Nice to meet you."

Promise was sure something wasn't right about him, but she wrote it off as just being nerves.

Ms. Scott walked Promise to her room.

Anna Mae shouted, "You'll meet my daughter Renee sooner or later. My oldest son, Alex, will be visiting from New York at the end of the month. You'll meet him then."

Promised sucked her teeth and stormed into her new room, a would-be prison. Promise's new twin-sized bed. It couldn't even compare to her full-sized bed with satin sheets that she had when she lived with her mother and father. Promise stood and just stared at the bare, dark gray walls. There wasn't even a window to look out of.

Ms. Scott set her things down by the sorry excuse for a bed. "Well, Promise, this is your new foster home. I promise you'll like it here, and I'm sure you'll fit in just fine. I must get going, but I'll be by to check on you after you get settled in," Ms. Scott said.

Promise didn't say anything. She just simply plopped down on the bed. When she heard Ms. Scott leaving, she sighed and let one single tear roll down her cheek. As she wiped it away, she looked up and saw Shawn standing in her doorway, still staring at her, as if he was admiring her or something, and his gaze made her feel uncomfortable.

Promise's daddy had always told her that she was the most gorgeous little girl he'd ever seen. "You look just like your mama with them dimples, hazel eyes slanted slightly, and that long, wavy hair." He often told her, "Baby, you're a mixed breed—black, Creole, and Cuban. Hold your head up high and don't ever let anybody put you down."

Shawn walked up to her. "You're not gonna like it here. The old bird, my mama, is a lot to deal with. She can be very…mean."

Promise's heart started racing 'cause she knew all that polite shit had been just a front for Ms. Scott.

He put his hand on the side of her face. "I'll try to protect you from her wrath that she unleashes from time to time."

She nodded her head up and down, looking into his eyes.

On cue, Anna Mae walked toward her room. She could hear the woman's heavy feet stomping down the hallway.

Shawn jumped up off Promise's bed quick and removed his hand from the side of her face.

"What are you doing back here?" Anna Mae asked as she stormed into the room.

"Uh, well, I...I was just making sure Promise is settling in good," he tried to explain stammering over his words.

"Go get that meat out the freezer and put it in the sink for me. We're having baked chicken, yellow rice, and string beans for dinner," Anna Mae said. "You ain't no vegetarian, is you? If you is, that's too damn bad, 'cause we're havin' chicken, and you're gonna eat what I give you. Now get up and get these clothes out of this suitcase. You can put them in this here dresser. Put your shoes in the closet, and line 'em up neatly. I ain't got room for no slobs in my house. When you get done with that, wash your ass up and get ready for dinner."

"All right," Promise replied with some attitude in her voice.

"Don't you 'all right' me, missy! It'll be 'yes, ma'am' when you're speaking to me," Anna Mae demanded.

"Yes, ma'am," Promise said, not wanting to get into it with the woman on her first day in the house. She got up and started doing what she'd been told.

Dinner was good, but quiet, and the family didn't eat at the table together. Instead, Shawn took his plate in his room so he could eat and continue playing his Xbox game, Anna Mae sat in her rocking chair with her plate on her lap and a beer by her feet, and Promise sat alone at the table, just her and her thoughts. So far she didn't like her new foster home, but she hoped meeting Renee would change that.

After eating, Promise brushed her teeth and went to her room so she could try to get some sleep, but she could only toss and turn. She hadn't really been able to sleep since her father's shooting and her mother's arrest. That night, she had her first nightmare...and it was only the beginning.

Chapter Three

Things still weren't getting better!

February 8, 1998

Promise had been living with the Jenkins family for two years, and her life was hell. She'd finally met Renee, a month and a half after she moved in, and Renee showed little interest in her. She did decide to inform Promise that they would be cool as long as she stayed the fuck out of her room and didn't touch any of her shit around the house.

Promise always wondered why Anna Mae never said anything about Renee's behavior, coming and going whenever she pleased, but she didn't have to wonder for long. One day when Renee came home, she handed Anna Mae a stack of money and went to her room. Anna Mae just counted the money and stuffed it in her bra.

Promise met Alex, whom she liked to call AJ, two months after meeting Renee. He was cool. He didn't talk much and mostly kept to himself when he came to visit. He didn't even stay at the house; he always got a room not too far away. The only time he stopped by was to eat dinner and chill for a little while.

Anna Mae was always gone, out playing bingo or cards with her friends. For an old woman, she got out of the house a lot. Renee was rarely ever home either. That girl was a wild, outgoing, club-hoppin' type of chick, so Promise and Shawn were left home by themselves a lot after school. Over time Shawn began to get very close to Promise. On the night when he kissed her, she felt a feeling she wasn't sure she should have felt. She was only thirteen at the time, and she felt like it wasn't right, like it was taking away her innocence somehow. From then on, she tried to keep her distance from him. She stayed at school late, ate dinner in her room, and only came out of her room to do her chores and use the bathroom.

The day before her fourteenth birthday, Anna Mae told Promise that she had planned her a surprise party 'cause she hadn't had to yell at her in a while, so she thought she would do something nice.

Promise was so excited she couldn't go to sleep that night. As she lay in bed with her back facing the bedroom door, she just stared at the clock. As the clock struck midnight, she smiled. *It's my birthday!* But that smile quickly disappeared when she heard her doorknob being turned.

In walked Shawn, and she felt his weight shift her bed. He tapped her on her shoulder and whispered, "Promise, you 'sleep? Wake up."

Promise didn't move or respond and tried to pretend she was asleep and didn't hear him.

But Shawn wasn't going for it. He shook her again.

Finally, having no other choice, she finally started acting like she was stirring in her sleep and then opened her eyes. When she turned over to look at Shawn, she saw him staring at her with that look that made her uncomfortable—the same one he'd worn on his face the day he kissed her while rubbing on his rising pole.

He smiled slightly and said, "Hey, birthday girl, I've got a gift for you."

That brightened her spirits a bit, and naïvely, she thought he had a nice surprise in store for her. "Really? What you got for me?'

Smiling, he leaned in and kissed her. "It's me, Promise. I'm your gift, and I'ma make you feel something you ain't never felt before." He rubbed her chest that was growing rather quickly for her age.

She was paralyzed with shock and fear—fear of what was happening and was about to happen. There he was, a grown man who'd been nice to her. He'd given her treats, talked to her from time to time, and checked her homework. And now? Now he was touching her inappropriately. It made her want to cry.

Shawn kissed her again, using his tongue. He then slid his big, callous hands up her legs till he got to her special spot. He began to massage her down there, staring in her eyes the whole while.

She shut her eyes tight. She felt sick, but for some reason she was too scared to scream. Tears began to run down her face.

He wiped the tears away with his free hand. "Don't cry, Promise. I promise I'm not gonna hurt you." Then he slid a finger into her hole.

It hurt like nothing she'd ever felt before. "Please stop! It…that hurts," she whispered, barely audible.

"Sh…I'ma make it feel good, baby—real good. Just bear with me. Don't you know I love you, Promise?" he said as he slid under her covers.

She tensed her legs up tight, and that must have angered him, because he forcefully snatched her legs open and yanked her cotton panties off, then kissed her treasure. Promise felt like at any moment, she might throw up, but as he went on doing what he was doing, the feeling got better and better. Promise actually started to enjoy it and even became a little moist—something else that had never happened in her life. She couldn't understand why that was happening to her. *What did I do to deserve this?* she wondered to herself.

When he got up to leave her room he said, "Damn, you taste so good and pure." He continued wiping his mouth. "Don't tell anybody about this—not your friends or teachers and definitely not Anna Mae. If you say a word, I'll make sure you end up on the streets homeless. Happy birthday, Promise." With that, he left her room and shut the door behind him.

Chapter Four

Why Promise?

Shawn continued to visit her room at least once a week. It got to the point where she was scared to fall asleep, sure that if she did, his hands would be feeling her up. He went from just using his mouth and fingers to even trying to use his pole. When he tried the first time and it didn't fit, he forced it, even though there was no moisture down there. He ripped and tore her hole, causing extreme pain, but Promise didn't scream out, for she was fearful of what might happen if she did. She just lay there crying silent tears, numb to her surroundings.

When Promise got up one morning after one Shawn's nightly visits, she screamed at the sight of blood in her panties.

She heard Anna Mae stomping down the hall toward the bathroom that was across from her room, yelling, "Promise! What the hell you in there screaming 'bout, child?"

Promise opened the door and told Anna Mae she believed she was dying.

"What? What's wrong with you?" Anna Mae asked, eyeing her like she was crazy. "What makes you think yer dyin'?"

"I'm…well, there's blood. I'm…I think I'm bleeding from my secret spot… down there," Promise said shamefully, pointing at her crotch.

Anna Mae started laughing, and Promise couldn't understand why, since she didn't think it was funny at all. "Gal, you becoming a young woman. That's just your rag coming on. Nowadays, y'all call it a menstrual cycle or a period or some technical shit, but back in the day, we called it the rag. Hold on, chile. Lemme see if Renee's got some pads in her room." A minute later, she came back with a pack of pads. "Now you go on and take a shower, then use one of these," she said as she showed Promise how to position the pad in the seat of her panties.

Promise stayed home from school for the next couple of days. The cramps from her period were so excruciating. During those few days, she got to know Anna Mae on a different level; she wasn't being the old mean woman she'd always been. Anna Mae even talked to Promise about her own life, what she'd been through that had made her such a strong woman. Promise was so comfortable talking to her, and she felt like Anna Mae had become the mother figure that had been missing from her life for what felt like forever. Sitting across from Anna Mae in the living room, Promise just blurted out, "Shawn has been coming in my room for at least two years, touching me and doing things to me that I don't think are right." *Why did I go and say that?* she had to wonder, as the next thing she knew, she felt an open-handed slap coming across her face at high speed. Her face felt like it was on fire.

"You little bitch! Why are you lying on my baby? You trifling little bitch. You want my son, but don't you know he can have any of them gals at the college? What would he want with yo' young, orphan ass? He's got a future in playing ball, and here you are trying to ruin it with these nasty little lies you makin' up in your crazy head."

Promise cried out, "I'm not lying! He's been doing those things to me for a while. Till now, I've just been scared to tell."

Anna Mae stood, towering over the girl, and began hitting her with the same open hand repeatedly "Just stop it! Stop the fuckin' lies! I can't deal with this shit. You gon' get the hell outta my house. I hope I still have that social worker's number so she can come get your sorry, lyin' ass, or else I'ma throw you out on the damn street myself. No little orphan bitch is gonna come in here fuckin' up my baby's life with lies!" she ranted as she went and got a folder with all of Promise's information in it. It didn't take long for her to find Ms. Scott's card among the paperwork.

Promise hadn't seen Ms. Scott in over a year, and seeing her walk through the door didn't excite her. Nevertheless, she was still packed and ready to go back to the group home. She was ready to get away from mean old Anna Mae and her pervert son.

* * *

When they left the Jenkins home, Promise thought sure they'd be heading back to the group home, but thirty minutes later, they pulled up to a duplex. She saw two little kids playing in the front yard. They got out of the car and Promised asked, "Who lives here...and why are we here?"

"When Miss Jenkins called me, I was at this duplex approving it for a foster home for a teenager, so I thought this would be a good home for you. I promise this will finally be the home for you—a place you can stay."

Instead of responding to the lie she'd just been told, Promise just stared straight ahead.

Her time in that foster home didn't last long 'cause she quit doing what Shantell asked her to and started doing what she wanted to do. Shantell would demand that she clean the house and wash the car before Promise could even do her homework. She taught her how to cook and put the girl in charge of making sure her kids ate breakfast in the morning before she went to school and dinner when she got out of school. Promise was miserable beyond belief.

Before long, there was Ms. Scott again, showing up to collect the state's no-good problem child. This time, though, there wasn't a new foster home for her to go to. As they rode to the group home, Ms. Scott asked, "What happened back there?"

"I'm not gonna be nobody's slave," Promise responded.

Chapter Five

Running Away May Be the Best Option!

Two Years Later

Promise had been at the group home for two years. During that time, she'd been in six fights and was separated from the rest of the girls and put in isolation. Half of those fights happened because her things kept coming up missing; Promise went to the known thieves and confronted them without the slightest bit of hesitation.

Then there were the main haters. She could be minding her own business in the mess hall for breakfast, lunch, or dinner and she would hear someone say, "That bitch thinks she's all that 'cause she got long hair." The ring leader of the group would say, "She always walking around batting her hazel eyes like they all that, just 'cause they got those little green flecks in 'em." The bitch who wanted to be just like Promise would say, "That bitch ain't shit."

But Promise always let their little slick remarks go, She always thought talk was cheap, and they didn't try to put their hands on her.

One day Keisha, the ring leader, got a little too bold though. She walked past Promise and pulled some of her hair; it was a big mistake.

Since Promise had been living in the group home, she'd developed quite a temper. Without a second thought, she jumped out of her seat and yelled, "Bitch, you really done fucked up now, putting yo' damn hands on me."

Keisha turned around and asked, "What chu gon' do about it, you Pocahontas wanna—"

Before that ho could even finish her sentence, Promise rushed and tackled her to the floor. She must've knocked the wind out of Keisha, 'cause she just lay there, looking shocked. Promise wasted no time putting in work, punchin', clawin', slappin', and chokin' the shit out of her ass. All she saw was red, and at that very moment, she was gunning for pure blood. The girls Keisha ran with saw Promise beating the shit out of her, but they didn't dare jump in. The next thing she knew, Patricia and her aid who watched over the quad pulled Promised off of Keisha just in time.

That was the moment, while Promise was being held back, when one of the li'l weaklings Keisha ran with felt the need to defend her friend's honor. Laketta said in a threatening tone, "I'm gonna fuck you up for doing my homie like that." She was right, too, because Keisha was fucked up bad; her eye was swelling more and more as the minutes passed, blood was leaking from her nose, and her lip was split to the white meat.

Promise didn't give a fuck though. She was acting out from all the shit she'd been through in her life.

That day, they took her to the isolation block, which she expected since she'd gotten in fights before. In fact, Promise spent most of her time in isolation. They wouldn't even let her out to eat in the mess hall with everybody else, and the first time they gave her any free time outside with everybody else, just three weeks later, she escaped.

Promise just ran right on out of the back gate. She knew it would be unlocked because she always watched them take out the trash, and they never locked the door behind them. The gate led to the front yard, so just like that, Promise was free, determined to make it on her own.

Chapter Six

A Master Plan

Promise's mother and father had been hustlers, and she knew she'd have to quickly follow in their footsteps. After all, she didn't have any money and no place to go, and she knew without that, she'd not make it out on the streets.

When she left the group home, she started to run. When she felt like no one was following her, she slowed her pace to a walking stride. She knew she needed to come up with a plan…and quick. Her stomach was starting to growl.

She wasn't far from the 'hood she used to live in with her parents, so she decided to keep walking until she found some familiar places. The only reason she returned to the projects was 'cause she didn't know where else to go.

Promise turned the corner on Main Street by the hair place and the corner store, she walked right into her mom's nosey friend Shirley. She wasn't paying attention, though, 'cause she was too wrapped up in her thoughts, tryin'a come up with a plan. She didn't even see the woman.

Shirley popped her gum and eyeballed Promise up and down. "Damn! Excuse you! Watch where the hell you going," she complained. Then she squinted at the girl. "Wait…you look familiar. Do I know you?"

"Hey, Shirley. It's me, Promise," she said, laughing to lighten the mood.

"That is you, all grown up! Hey, girl. How you been?" Shirley responded. *Damn! Where the fuck did she come from, and how the fuck did she wind up back in the 'hood? Once I told the officers she had no other family, I thought that'd be it for her, but now she's back. Shit,* Shirley thought.

"I've been okay. Just trying to make it out here, ya know," Promise responded as she ran her hand over her hair. She hadn't had her hair done professionally in years, but she made it a priority to keep it washed and her ends cut. She'd become very independent over the years and had learned to do a lot of things for herself.

"Girl, come here and give me a hug. You know, I used to be like your auntie back in the day. Me and Sweet Pea was close, like sisters. I know she'd be happy to know you're okay. You're all she talks about."

"You still hear from my mama?"

"Sho' do. I hear from her every couple months. I try to keep her on the up and up about what's going on out here in these streets. Even in prison, Sweet Pea can't stay away from the gossip of the 'hood."

"Shirley, I wanna talk to her," Promise said, her eyes wishful. She hadn't talked to her mother in damn near eight years, and she longed to hear her voice.

"Well, she'll probably be calling at the beginning of the month. She knows that's when I get my SSI check so I'll finally be able to pay the damn phone bill," Shirley said.

While they stood on the corner, Promise filled Shirley in on some of what she'd been going through and how she'd run away not even an hour ago.

"Girl, you're gonna be fine. You're like my niece. You can stay with me."

"Thank you, Shirley. I don't plan on living with you long, and I'll find a job so I can pay you some money."

"How old are you now anyway?" Shirley asked as she laughed about Promise's last statement on finding a way to make some money.

Promise put her hand on her hip with much attitude and replied, "I'm seventeen, almost grown. Just give me a couple more months, and I'll be an adult."

"Boy, time sure has passed. If only Biggs could see his baby girl now…" Laughing hard she continued, "That man would have a heart attack for sure. Come on, girl. Let's go to my apartment so I can cook you some good ol' home-made food. I know you ain't had none in a long time."

Promise wasn't even thinking about the fact that she hadn't had a homemade meal in a long time. She was thinking about how Shirley looked like she'd been living well at thirty-eight years young, sporting a long ripple deep wave sewn in black with blonde highlights, jeans so tight Promise woulda thought she'd hung them on a clothesline and jumped out a second-floor window just to get in them, and a shirt cut so low her breasts were sure to pop out. *At least she don't look all rundown like she used to.*

Chapter Seven

Hooking up with Shad on a Money Tip

Promise had been staying with Shirley for the last past four months. She was getting antsy just sitting around the house. She wanted to get into something, to get out and make some money.

That was where Shad, Shirley's nephew (who could pass as her son any day) came in. Shad was twenty-four. He wore his hair in dreads, with fiyah-red tips that went well with his complexion. He would have made a fine-ass runway model. Shad was in the drug game, and getting money was second nature to him, although he wasn't getting nearly as much money as Promise's dad used to when he was living large.

One Saturday morning, Shad came strolling into Shirley's apartment and went right to the kitchen. He looked in the stove and in the refrigerator.

Promise figured he was looking for some food. She chuckled to herself. *Sooner or later, he'll figure out there ain't shit to eat in there.*

"Damn. Where breakfast at, Promise?" *Shit, I don't remember Promise being so gorgeous,* Shad thought.

"Shit, yo' guess is as good as mine. I don't think Shirley's food stamps came yet," Promise replied.

"Well shit, money ain't nothing but a thing. If Shirley gon' cook, I'll pay for the groceries," he said as he pulled a big bank roll from his pocket and pulled off three crisp $100 bills. "Ay, yo, Shirley!" Shad called into the back room.

"Nephew, what you in here doing all that yellin' for? What's up?" she yelled, walking down the hall toward the living room.

"Man, Auntie, don't you wanna cook a nigga something to eat? Shit, I'm hungrier than a bitch. I'll pay for the groceries if you just get em' and cook em'," Shad said.

"All right. You got yo'self a deal! How much you gon' give me?" Shirley asked.

Shad held up the $300 with a smile.

Shirley snatched the money happily. "Shit, nephew. This how you rollin', let me go slip on my sandals so I can run to the grocery store," she said.

"All right, Auntie. I'll chill here with Promise till you get back."

When Shad sat down on the couch across from her, Promise couldn't help looking at the fine specimen of a man. His swagger turned her on. She couldn't figure out if it was the long-sleeved plaid Nike shirt or the pair of distressed jeans that sagged just enough to make it sexy. She knew it wasn't the White Forces; they were crisp and new and all, but she was caught up in the jewels he sported. Around his neck he wore a black diamond. The shit was nice, and it went so well with the black diamond presidential Cartier watch; the black diamond pinky ring wasn't to be overlooked either. *Shit, he lookin' just like money, and money's what I been striving to get plenty of.* She got straight to the point. "How can I make some money, Shad?"

She could tell she'd caught him off guard 'cause he ran his hand over his freshly twisted dreads and replied, "Oh yeah? You tryin'a make some money, huh? Well, I might know somebody who can get you a gig."

"That's cool and all, but I'm not looking to make no petty cash. I wanna make some real money—not that play-play shit I could earn flippin' burgers and saltin' fries at some fast food joint. Shit, if you can, put me on to some work with you. I won't disappoint."

"Naw, baby girl, this life I live ain't for you. I know you, and you ain't built for this shit. Like I said, I might be able to line up a gig for you, but first I need to see if you'll be able to handle it. Stand up let me see what you're working with."

Promise stood. She was very confident. Even though her worn-out clothes weren't nearly up to par, she was still sure her figure could compete with any twenty-something woman's.

Shad licked his lips, admiring her body. "Give me a full turnaround."

She did as he said, but she made sure to turn extremely slowly so he could take in every inch of her.

"Okay, you tight, ma, but can you dance?"

"Well, I don't dance much, but I'm sure I could put it down like a seasoned video vixen if I had a good beat," Promise said with a sly smile.

Again, that sexy, crooked grin appeared on his face. He nodded his head in approval, and under his breath she heard him utter, "Damn, she done grew up… and well at that."

"What did you say?" Promise asked Shad.

"Nothing. Just thinking out loud, that's all."

They talked for a little while longer before she said, "I wonder what's taking

Shirley so long. She must've gone somewhere else besides the grocery store."

"Yeah, well, you know how Shirley is. Anyway, let me get going. I gotta meet up with my homie Tre. He's the one who'll be setting up the gig for you, so just trust me on this. Tell Shirley I'll be back in a li'l while for my breakfast."

About thirty minutes later, Shirley came strolling in the door with a bunch of bags from Walmart, Shoe Connection, Papaya, Wet Seal, and Body Shop.

Promise shook her head and laughed. She'd known all along that Shirley would be out doing more than grocery shopping.

Chapter Eight

Getting Prepared for Her New Job Position

A couple weeks after Promise stepped to Shad about making some money, he called Shirley's house. "Yo, be ready in an hour."

"For what?" Promise asked.

"I'm taking you shopping to get you a couple new outfits for your interview later on tonight."

An interview? At this hour? What kind of job is this anyway? Promise wondered. *I guess I really don't care as long as I'm gonna be making that gwap.*

* * *

An hour later, Promise was in Shad's car, on her way to the mall. She'd never thought of herself as someone who dwelled on fashion, but Shad said, "Today were bringing out the big guns, changing and upgrading your whole look." Promise was down for it since she'd just been rocking a tank top, worn jeans, and a pair of raggedy hard-shell Adidas, along with a high ponytail.

Their first stop as soon as they hit the mall was the D&G store. She fell instantly in love as soon as they walked in.

Shad smiled as he saw her face light up. "Try on anything you want. Money ain't a thang. We're gonna choose the best from here, and then it's on to the next store."

After trying on a few pair of fitted jeans and a lavender D&G top with a plunging neckline, she noticed the lust that started to appear in Shad's eyes. The next little number she put on was a Red D&G corset dress that clung to every curve like it was specially designed for her. When Promise walked out of the dressing room, Shad swiftly stood up. "That's it. That's the one for you. Damn, Promise. Red's definitely your color."

While they stood at the register, she just had to look at the price tag to see how much the dress was. She knew it wasn't cheap, but she never imagined it would be $500.

Once all of her items were paid for, they headed off to the best heels store ever, Step Up, which carried all the top designer shoes. She fell in love upon entering. There was everything from stilettos to pumps and ankle boots. She was immediately drawn to a pair in the display window, so she called the saleswoman over and asked, "What kind of shoes are those?"

The snooty saleswoman looked at Promise with a scowl, as if she was way out of her league.

Promise caught an attitude and was about to tell the bitch to check that stank look before she chin-checked her, but Shad came over cleared his throat and asked, "Is there a problem?"

The saleswoman's whole demeanor changed when she checked out the ice Shad was rocking. She turned to Promise and answered, "Those are the newly released fall edition Jimmy Choo peep-toe ankle booties. We just got them in this morning."

"I'll take a pair of those in an eight and a half, thank you."

When the saleswoman reappeared behind the register with the shoes, they headed over so Shad could pay for them. Promise nearly fainted when she realized the damn shoes were $1,700. When Shad brought the black card out, she knew she had no worries.

"You know what? On second thought, go ahead and add the white strappy Prada heels over there in the display window. I saw you eyeing those, Promise. Also, those nude pumps…and the leopard print ones."

"Oh my God, Shad! How did you know? You're so sweet. Thank you." She turned to the saleswoman and said, "You heard the man. Ring em' up, and sweetie, close your mouth. I would really hate for something to fly in there," she said snobbishly. When they walked out of the store, she told Shad, "I bet that bitch'll be all up my ass next time I step foot in there."

Shad laughed and winked at her. "I bet she will."

Promise couldn't thank him enough.

Their next stop was at a salon called 813 Sho' Stoppers Beauty Salon.

"Yo, what's up, Nina? This is Promise, and she's going to be getting a full makeover with makeup lessons. Make sure they give her the works and take care of her."

Promise wondered how Shad knew the receptionist's name, and she figured they must have had some dealings in the past; the way Nina was looking at her with envy in her eyes confirmed that.

"Promise I'm gonna leave you with my black card. Get whatever you need. Don't hold back or worry about any expenses." A tear rolled down her check, but he caught it before it could fall. "Don't worry about nothing. Just make sure you make me proud at this job interview. Only certain women are chosen to work there."

"I promise, Shad. I'm gon' make you proud, and when I get the job, I'ma do it to the best of my ability."

"That's all I need to hear. Now go on and get made over."

* * *

Six hours later, Promise walked out of the salon, looking priceless, carrying a bagful of MAC products. She strutted up to the front of Shad's Range Rover and struck a pose.

Shad jumped out of the truck, eyeing her up and down. "Damn, ma! You done officially graduated to grown and sexy, looking like a million bucks. Go 'head, shawty." He would have loved for Promise to be his, but he was sure she wouldn't want no 'hood boy. *God, she's gorgeous though. Any man would love to make her his wifey.*

The stylist had done wonders on her hair; she cut highlighted and layered it. Promise's only request was that she get the Aaliyah bang. Her makeup was flawless: just a touch of moisturizer, foundation, shimmer eye shadow, and some MAC lip gloss to cover her perfectly shaped full lips. She felt like a superstar.

Chapter Nine

Will She Get the Job?

Promise decided to get ready for her interview. Her nerves were beginning to get the best of her, so she figured keeping busy would help her keep her mind off it for a while. When Shad had picked her up, he'd surprised her with some goodies from Victoria's Secret, one being the whole set of Amber Romance products. Promise used the bath wash, along with a touch of oil, lotion, and perfume. She dressed in her best, slipping into the red D&G corset dress with the Jimmy Choo booties. With her makeup she went for a smoky eye and black eye liner and kept her lips light with MAC lip gloss.

When she stepped out of her room, Shirley was amazed. "Damn, Promise! Girl, you sure do clean up well," she said, seemingly staring enviously at her. "Where are you going anyway, looking like you just stepped off of the red carpet? Let me find out you in them people stores stealing they shit. You might think you grown, but I'll still put my foot off in yo' ass."

"Shirley, chill out. Calm all that down. I didn't steal shit. Shad took me shopping so I can be prepared for my interview."

"Okay, but what kind of interview do you got this time of night?" Shirley asked, staring suspiciously at Promise.

"I don't know. Shad is hooking me up with the gig," Promise replied.

"Mm-hmm. Well, just be careful, Promise," Shirley said.

As soon as Shirley said that, Promise heard Shad beeping his horn in front of the apartment. "Well, I gotta get going. I'll be careful. Hopefully I'll get the job so I can start paying you for living here and someday finally get my own spot."

As soon as Promise got in Shad's truck, he started up. "That's what I'm talking 'bout. You look drop-dead gorgeous."

As they pulled off, she smiled at him, slightly blushing.

* * *

Forty-five minutes later, they pulled up to the Sweet Spot Gentlemen's Club.

Promise was young, but she wasn't no fool, and she simply asked, "A gentlemen's club? Shad, you want me to be a stripper? I'm not taking off all my clothes for a bunch of horny old strangers."

"Now hold on, shawty. Before you knock this shit, give it a try. This ain't just any strip club. It's owned by my homie Tre, and it's a top-of-the-line, high-class, A-list entertainment club."

Promise was sure Shad wouldn't knowingly put her in any sour situations, so she checked herself. "All right, Shad. Lemme give this thing a try."

They got out of the truck, and Shad grabbed the duffle bag from the back seat. They proceeded to the front door, bypassing the long line of men and women; Promise found it surprising that ladies were also wanting to get in.

At the front door, the tall, muscular security guard said, eyeing Promise, "What's up, Shad?"

"Ain't nothing, Mark. I'm just bringing a possible new dancer in to talk to Tre about an audition interview."

Promise stood there, scared shitless and not saying a word.

"Oh yeah. Well, from the looks of her, she's hired," Mark replied with a smile and not even a second thought.

"If only it was that simple. Now move this rope so we can get this show on the road."

Mark complied.

As they walked in, Promise took a deep breath to calm her nerves.

She heard Mark say, "Damn! She got a phat ass to go along with that pretty face."

Everything in the club looked vintage, including a classy black and white color scheme. Looking around, Promise noticed that there was no carpet on the entire 1st floor. She looked up and noticed three more floors, and from the looks of the first one, she couldn't wait to see the second or third.

All the dancers were brown-skinned, some darker than others.

"This is what they call the chocolate room, with all the chocolate-colored chicks," Shad answered, as if he'd read her mind.

"They're all so…so beautiful," Promise said out loud.

Shad grinned that sexy grin. "Aren't they?"

"Yes. They look so, so…exotic. Every one of them has something that sets her apart—eyes, breasts, ass, thighs, hair..."

Finally the man of the hour arrived, and as he walked up, Promise could tell he was taking in all of her curves and definitely checking her out. "So, is this my new top dancer you were telling me about, Shad?" Tre said as he gave Shad dap.

"Yeah, Tre, this is her. What do you think?"

Tre turned to speak to Promise directly. "You're a bad bitch—real bad—but a gorgeous face, thick thighs, and a phat ass ain't gonna get you the big bucks. The question is, can you dance?"

With her confidence at an all-time high, Promise put her hand on her hip and said, "With the right song, I'll have ya money falling right out of your pockets." She then moved closer to Tre and whispered in his ear, "I'll have your dick at attention, too, just begging to hit all this." Promise didn't know what had gotten into her, as she'd never said those kinds of things before. But ever since she was fourteen years old and Shawn had molested her over and over again, she'd had a sexual appetite that hadn't been fulfilled in years. *I wonder if Tre will be the one to fulfill that desire,* Promise thought.

Tre smiled and said with excitement, "Man, Shad, where did you find this one? She's something special!" Then he turned again to Promise. "Get dressed and be ready to go in an hour."

Chapter Ten

Officially a Stripper

Promise chose a sexy all-red cut-up bodysuit from the duffle bag. When she put it on, she noticed that it had a crotchless part that would show off the see-through thong that disappeared into her ample ass every time she stood up. The breast part was also see-through, and it tied behind her neck like a halter top. She walked over to the floor-to-ceiling mirror and checked out herself out. "Damn, I look good," Promise said out loud.

"Sure do. Hey. I'm Black Ice. You may not know it yet, but I'm the best dancer up in this bitch. Thing is, I'm quitting tonight, and it looks like you're gonna take my place, as long as you can dance as good as you look."

Smiling, Promise replied, "Thanks. My name is Promise. I don't have a stripper name yet. Got any suggestions?"

Black Ice grabbed Promise's hand and spun her around. "Girl, with them cakes and the fact that red is most definitely your color, you should call yourself Red Velvet. As a matter of fact, show me some of your dance moves."

Promise showed Black Ice her favorite dance move: She dropped it down to the floor, popped her ass, came back up, and made her ass tick-tock, making her left ass cheek and then your right ass cheek jump simultaneously.

"Okay, okay. Looks like you working with a li'l something. I mean, shit, I ain't seen half the hoes in here do no shit like that. We might have to call you Honey Dip the way you dip that ass."

Before Promise had the chance to respond, a bouncer came down the stairs. "Promise, they'll be ready for you in ten."

"Okay," she responded. "Oh, and can you tell the deejay I'm going by Red Velvet?"

"Sure thing," said the bouncer over his thick shoulder as he climbed the stairs again.

"Black Ice, I'm so nervous. I don't know what to do."

"Oh, girl, don't worry about it. I got something that'll take the edge off for ya if you want it. Just take this and drink the rest of my drink. By the time you hit that stage, you'll be feeling so good that you'll blow them rich niggas' socks off."

It sounded good to Promise, and she needed to calm down—at least this first time—so she popped the pill, sat down in Black Ice's chair, and gulped down the drink as fast as she could. "Now, tell me what I just took," Promise asked.

"Oh, just some X. You'll start to feel it in a couple minutes. If you need another drink, just go to the bartender and ask for a Dat's It. Make sure you drink water periodically through the night though, so you don't get sick."

"Dat's It, huh? What's in it?" Promise asked.

"Well, it's a mix of top-shelf liquor like Ciroc, Goose, Nuvo, a shot of gin, and a splash of pineapple juice."

"Well, damn, whatever's in it, that shit's good. It wasn't strong, just smooth. Let me reapply this lip gloss before they come get me."

For some reason, Promise started to feel woozy. the food she'd eaten earlier felt like it was trying to come up, and the next thing she knew, she was bent over a toilet in the bathroom right outside the dressing room.

Black Ice was holding her hair back. "Let it out, girl, but don't be so loud. See, Tre has a no drugs policy for all his strippers, his adult entertainers, as he likes to call us."

After throwing up her insides, Promise gathered herself and stood up. She looked in the mirror. Her eyeliner was starting to run and her lip gloss was completely gone, but she felt much better. All warm and tingly inside. As she was fixing and reapplying her makeup, the same bouncer came back down.

"Promise, er…Red Velvet, they're ready for you."

"All right. Thanks for your help, Black Ice. Now let me go out there and do my thang."

"You're welcome. I'll go make sure DJ Flip gets your name right. Oh yeah… what song you wanna jump that ass to?"

"Um, I don't know. You choose for me. I can dance to anything."

* * *

Promise waited patiently, feeling so sexy before it was time for her to go onstage. She kept getting the urge to touch herself. Her heart raced when she heard DJ Flip announce, "All right, I know y'all got plenty of money. Shit, to be up in here, you gotta have stacks on stacks on stacks, so y'all show some love to this next sexy-ass lady. She's new to Sweet Spot, so y'all treat her right and make it rain! Coming to the stage, it's Red Velvet."

As soon as Promise heard the beat drop to Silk's "Freak Me," she knew it was time to shut the whole club down. Slowly, seductively, she walked onstage, licking her succulent lips. She turned away from the crowd of lusting men and began to wind all the way to the floor. Popping her ass slightly, she bent over in a doggy-style position. She used her right hand to spread her ass cheeks apart so the crowd could see her G-string that disappeared when her ass cheeks were together. She trailed down the string until she got to her pussy; she patted it soft and then hard. "Mmmm," she moaned, even though she was the only one who could hear it. She was putting on a show, and the crowd loved her already.

She turned over on her back, closed her eyes, and spread her legs in a wide V. As she wound her legs up and down, she slid her hands to her hardened nipples and pinched them slightly. Her hand roamed down her stomach and into her G-string. She didn't know what was coming over her; she felt so turned on. She circled her clit in some kind of daze. With each drop of the beat, her juices began to flow.

Promise then sat up, opened her eyes, and removed her hand to see the whole club at a standstill. All attention was on her and the show she was putting on. Crawling to the man at the end of the stage with a fly-ass suit on, she took the same finger she had just taken out of her pussy and rubbed it across his lips. To her surprise, he licked, then sucked her entire finger into his mouth. She winked at him as she stood and untied her top, as if she was gonna take it off, teasing the men that stood before her. Promise could tell they were trying to contain themselves, so she did the unthinkable and took down her halter top, exposing her beautiful, perky breasts. She chose the sexiest man in the crowd and dropped her top in his lap, then waved at the crowd and exited the stage.

* * *

"Bitch, you put it down on that fuckin' stage!" Black Ice yelled as she walked into the dressing room. "You had the whole club stuck."

"I tried, girl. I don't know what came over me. I just felt so…so horny."

"Yeah, that was the X that got you feeling like that. I guess it's working."

"Whatever it is, it's got me feeling hella good, but I'm real thirsty. I need some water."

"Okay. I'll be back."

Before Black Ice walked out the door completely, Promise couldn't help but stare at her ass.

Black Ice turned around suddenly, making her jump. "Girl, don't worry about it. I'm used to males and females staring at my ass."

Promise put her head down, embarrassed.

Black Ice walked back over to Promise, lifted her head up, and kissed her passionately.

Promise didn't know what to do or say. *I've never been kissed by a female before...but I kinda like it,* Promise thought

"I was going to tell you before I walked out the door that the bouncer who came and got you for your show will be bringing you your bagful of money. His name's Bear. The stage was covered with fives, tens, twenties, fifties, and hundreds. From what I hear, you're already being requested. I'll be back. Let me go get you a bottle of water. I don't need you passing out because after work, I'm going to take you out to eat and give you the rundown on everything—the rules of the club, who to trust, and who not to trust."

All Promise could do was nod her head in agreement, still stunned.

As soon as Black Ice left, Bear walked in with a bagful of money.

Promise couldn't believe she'd made so much money. She thanked Bear for collecting her money off the stage and pulled out two $100 bills and gave them to him. She got dressed in the dress she'd worn to the club.

Black Ice walked back in. "Here ya go," she said, handing Promise the bottle of water.

"Thanks Ice."

"No problem, hon'. What are you about to get into, 'cause I'm ready to blow this joint?"

"Lemme check in with Shad and Tre and see what they talking 'bout, then hopefully we can be out." All Promise's things were packed up, and her money was in the duffle bag, so she left the dressing room and walked right into Tre. "Hey, Tre. What did you think about my show?"

"I think you did hella good up there, ma."

"So that means I'm hired?"

"Hell yeah, you're hired. Shit, I gotta feeling you're gonna be our number one requested adult entertainer. Shit, you're getting requests already, and you didn't even work the pole."

"Thanks, Tre. I won't disappoint you, and once I get the pole down pat, I'll be sliding up and down it with expertise."

"Okay. Dat's a bet, ma. I'm not trying to hold you up, though, so take the rest of the night off. Be here by 8:00 tomorrow if you can but no later than 9:00. I don't play that late shit. I'm serious when it comes to my money, and you should be too."

"I got chu. Where's Shad?"

"Over by the bar."

"Okay, thanks." On her way to the bar, which was halfway across the club, she was pulled five different directions by men asking her if she was Red Velvet. "Yes," she said. I am Red Velvet, but I'm off for the rest of the night. Catch me tomorrow." She walked up behind Shad and flicked him on the back of his neck to get his attention. "Well? What did you think about my set?"

"Man, Promise that shit was off the chain. I didn't know you could dance like that. Where the fuck did you learn that shit?"

"I practiced."

"You practiced? When?"

"Naw, I'm kidding. I really don't know what came over me. All of a sudden, I was in this sexual mood." She didn't think it would be such a good idea to tell him about the X she'd popped, or he might flip. "Me and Black Ice 'bout to go get something to eat."

"What? You cool with Black Ice already?" Shad asked with a shocked expression his face.

"Yeah, she's nice. She's the one who helped me get ready for my set."

"Damn, that's crazy."

"Why?"

"'Cause Black Ice don't fuck with none of these bitches up in here."

"Well, I'm not none of these bitches. I'm Red Velvet."

"What's up, Shad?" Black Ice said as she walked up. "You ready to go?" she asked Promise, putting her arm around the new dancer's waist.

"Yeah, I'm ready. I suddenly have a huge appetite. I feel real hungry. We 'bout to get up out of here for a bite then. Talk to you tomorrow, Shad. I'll have Black Ice drop me off at Aunt Shirley's," Promise said.

"Yo, Shad, did Velvet and Ice just walked out of here like some old-time friends? Is Velvet gay? You know how Black Ice gets down," Tre said, watching the two dancers leave the club together.

"Naw, she ain't gay that I know of, but shit, Ice is fine as fuck. If they fuck each other, that'd be two bad-ass bitches getting down. I'd wanna be there to see that shit."

"No shit! Ice is Puerto Rican, Irish, and black with that long, curly hair, blue eyes, phat ass, and juicy titties. Then she got that flawless skin that looks like silk or some shit. Man, you're right. That would be a sight to see," Tre said, thinking what it would be like to get with Black Ice.

"Don't forget about them legs. She's what, five-nine? And she's got them legs that'll make you wanna get on yo' knees and act like a midget and climb em'," Shad responded.

"True shit. All I'm saying is if they fuck, I wanna be there to watch—or at least record that shit and get paid in the process. You know how much niggas would pay to see that shit?"

"Man, you wild as fuck. I'm up though. I gotta go pick this money up from a spot over in Temple Terrace. Hit me up in the morning," Shad said, dapping Tre up.

Chapter Eleven

Who to Trust

P romise went to sleep thinking about her talk with Black Ice. "Don't be naïve," Black Ice had told her. "In this world of stripping, you can't really trust anybody. Everybody is out for him or herself, so you have to be too. Don't be friendly with those bitches at Sweet Spot. At the end of the day, they're just trying to take your spot. No matter how friendly they act, they'd throw you under in a heartbeat if it meant them getting on top. You're now the head bitch in charge there. No one has ever done an audition like the one you did. Just go in there, make your money, keep to yourself, and leave. I've been working there ten years and never had a problem. Sometimes you're gonna need something to get you through the night, so here's a bag of them X pills like the one you took earlier. Don't take them every night. Just use 'em on nights when you need that extra push and you feel like you can't make it through."

* * *

Sitting up on the couch, Promise felt like her head weighed a ton. *Where the fuck did this banging headache come from?* she asked herself. She got up feeling dizzy and began frantically looking for her duffle bag. She didn't remember too much from last night after they left the club besides their talk. Promise didn't even remember getting back to Shirley's apartment so she started to panic. "Where the fuck is my bag? Ugh!" she said out loud. She found it in the corner by the front door, looking rather flat. Once she opened it, she saw that damn near all her money was gone, but there was an envelope with a note attached to it:

Velvet…
By the time you read this, I'll be long gone, and yes, I took your money. You're just getting started in this stripping game. Like I told you, you gotta learn the ins and outs of the business. People

are always out for self, and tonight you simply got, got! I could tell when I saw you walking into the club that you are young and that this experience is all new to you. As sexy as you are, I knew you were going to make a mint. When I saw you go into the dressing room, I stood in the doorway and watched you get ready for your audition, you was so nervous you didn't even notice me standing there. As I looked upon your naked, toned body, I almost didn't want to set you up for the okie dokie, but it's all a part of the game. I'm in love with money, baby. Shit, it's my motivation, and that's what motivated me to do what I did. After we ate breakfast at Perkins, we stopped by my hotel room for a li'l while. By the way, I enjoyed you, and if circumstances were different, maybe we could've been more. On our way to your Aunt Shirley's house, you fell asleep. Once we got there, I used your key to get you in the house, then went back to my car to get your duffle bag, but before I brought it in the house, I took most of the money out and left you $1,000. Be easy and keep your head up, baby. Trust no one

The Infamous Black Ice
P.S. Make that money and don't let it make you!

Promise couldn't believe that shit. "That bitch got all my money!" she said in shock, talking out loud to herself. "And what the fuck did she mean, she enjoyed me in her hotel room? Did I do something with Black Ice? What the fuck went on last night?" Promise yelled to herself. She ran to get the cordless phone off of the kitchen counter. "Ah!" she screamed in frustration because she couldn't even think straight.

Shirley came walking into the kitchen, jollier than usual. "What's wrong with you?" she asked.

"The bitch who brought me back here last night, that stripper bitch, stole all the money I made!" Promise yelled, furious.

"Oh shit. Sorry to hear that, Promise. She paid me $500 to make up for waking me, what with all that noise she was making bringing you in."

"*She* didn't pay you nothin', Shirley! That was *my* $500, money *I* worked for. Fuck this shit! I'ma go find that thieving, lying bitch and demand my money back." Promise dialed Shad's number.

He picked up on the third ring. "What's up, Auntie?"

"This ain't yo' auntie, Shad. It's Promise, and I need you to get over here now!"

"You sound pissed, girl. What's up?"

"I need you to take me to find that bitch Black Ice. She stole the money I made last night and left me with just $1,000 in the fuckin' duffle bag. I'ma kill her, Shad. I'ma body that bitch, you hear me?" she yelled into the phone.

"Hold up, Promise. You say she stole yo' money from last night? How? What exactly happened?"

"Just get over here, and I'll fill you in while we go and try to find this bitch."

Thirty minutes later, Shad arrived.

Promise was dressed to kill—literally—in her True Religion jeans, Guess top, and Louis Vuitton pumps. She pulled her hair up into her typical high ponytail and hopped into Shad's truck. She handed him the letter, and they pulled off as he read it.

"What the hell? This bitch must be stupid. Promise, that bitch is got, you hear me? I'm gon' touch that bitch myself. You don't pull no fucked-up shit like that on nobody. I felt like something was off when y'all left last night but I wrote it off as me being overprotective."

"Yeah, she tried to make it seem sweet, but the bitch was actually plotting against me the whole time."

Shad put the pedal to the metal, growing angrier by the second. They arrived at the club within twenty minutes flat. "I already put Tre up on game that something happened between you and Black Ice," he said as they got out of the car.

Once they were inside, Promised saw Tre sitting at the bar. "Tre, where is that bitch Black Ice?" "Whoa! Chill out. First, I need you to tell me what the fuck is going on," Tre replied calmly.

"Show him the fucking letter, Shad," Promise said.

When Tre began to read the letter, his expression changed from relaxed to angry. "Yo! Red Velvet, baby, when she comes in tonight, we gon' handle this shit. I don't play shit like this."

"Tre, don't you get it? She quit, and whatever money she saved from working here plus my money she stole is what she's plannin' to leave with," Promise replied, her blood pressure rising.

"Well shit! Let's go over to her house right now. She lives over in Town 'n' Country," Tre stated matter-of-factly.

"Let's go! Shit, I'm ready to get my money back. Once I do, I'm putting my foot in her ass," Promise said, hyped at the chance of getting to Black Ice.

"Eh-yo, Bear, keep an eye on things till I get back," Tre told his most trusty bouncer.

* * *

They pulled up into Black Ice's driveway. The first thing Promise noticed was a car in the driveway, but it wasn't the car she and Black Ice had ridden around in the night before.

Shad pulled up his shirt. "I'm strapped. If a bitch pull some funny shit. I'm blasting 'em, straight up."

They hopped out of the car and walked up to the front door, which was open.

"Hello. Are you guys here to look at this house? You wanna rent it?" some geeky-looking white dude asked through the screen door.

"No. We're actually here to visit a friend. We thought she was renting the place," Tre said.

"Oh, you must be referring to Ms. Stevenson. She turned in her keys two days ago and informed me that she was paying her last month's rent and moving away. If she's a friend of yours, as you say, I'm sure she would've informed you guys that she was planning to move."

Promise thought steam was about to start coming from her ears at any second. "That's okay. That bitch set this shit up knowing she was going to move," she said, feeling like a little fish in a shark-filled ocean. "Y'all know what? Fuck this shit! I'm gonna find that bitch, and when I do, it's a wrap. You can bet on that shit," she wailed, heated.

"Let's go. I'm hungry, and I know Tre has to get back to the club so he can get ready for tonight. Who did you say is going to be there?" Shad asked as they pulled out of the driveway.

"A couple of the Orlando Magic players are gonna stop by after their game, and Buffy the Body is supposed to be the host," Tre replied.

"Word. I know the club gon' be on swole tonight. Shit, I need to go pick up something to wear."

They pulled up in front of the club.

"All right. Hit me up later. Red Velvet, baby, don't worry bout that money. You'll be making plenty more," Tre said.

"Thanks, Tre. I'll see you tonight around 8:30," Promise replied.

* * *

Promise and Shad drove off and stopped at a fast food joint.

"Aye, Shad, do you know if Shirley's talked to my mom lately? I really want to talk to her."

"I didn't know Shirley and your mom were still in contact. She's never said anything to me about it. How 'bout I find out where your mother is locked up, and we'll take a trip there for you to see her? You just can't tell Shirley."

"Aw, thanks, Shad…and I won't say a word." Promise replied.

"All right. Let's finish up here, and I'll drop you back off at Shirley's and pick you up later for a ride to work."

Although Promise's day had been shitty so far, she was ecstatic just knowing she would be able to see her mother soon.

G STREET CHRONICLES
A NEW URBAN DYNASTY
WWW.GSTREETCHRONICLES.COM

Chapter Twelve

A Visit with Mama, Ten Years Later

Promise lavished in the money she'd been making the past two weeks, starting the weekend when the Orlando Magic players and Buffy the Body hosted at the club. People came out in swarms, but only a select few got in. Promise ended up making more than $20,000 that night alone.. She bought a cell phone and went to look for an apartment with Shad. Next, she went to the DMV to take her driver's license test. "I passed, Shad! I passed."

"What? Quit playing, shawty," Shad replied.

"I did! Look at my license," she said proudly, showing it to him.

"All right. I see you, ma. Let's go. I'm gon' buy you a brand new car, any one you want."

"Thanks, Shad, but honestly, I wanna buy my first car with my own money. I don't even care if it's used. Just knowing I worked hard for it is all that matters to me."

"I respect that, girl. Let's go get your car then," Shad said.

* * *

Promise paid Shirley $3,000 for letting her stay with her for that short amount of time—even though she knew she hadn't used that much electricity or water or overstayed her welcome; shit, the girl was rarely even there. *I don't know why I gave her so much money knowing she only pays $15 for rent and only has a phone and cable bill. She loves to brag about the luxury of living in the projects. The bitch should be a damn spokesperson for it. Everything else is government living, from the food stamps to the first-of-the month check,* Promise thought as she pulled up to Shad's mini-mansion off Bay Shore Boulevard.

Shad looked sexy walking out of his front door, and he was dressed nice. Shit, he could have been wearing a tank and some sweatpants and still look edible. "You ready to go?" he asked.

"Of course," Promise replied.

"Get out of the car and let's get this show on the road. We got a long ways to go to Pulaski County, Georgia," he said.

Once they were on the interstate, Promise asked, "You mind if I ask you something Shad?"

"Naw, go ahead, shawty."

"Why are you helping me through all this, even though you're not getting anything in return?"

"Well, truth is, I remember when you were ten years old and the FBI ran up in your mom and dad's spot. They shot yo' dad, took you away, and locked your moms up. That shit wasn't cool. You was like my li'l sister—a fine-ass little sister, but my little sister all the same. I used to walk you to the store and home from the park, just watch over you."

"You're so crazy, but yeah, I remember everything. I just wanna thank you for it all. It really means a lot to me. I haven't seen or talked to my mother in damn near ten years, and you're the one making it happen for me."

"No problem, Promise. I don't mind doing this for you. I set up a li'l business meeting for while you're visiting your mama, so while you're there, I'll be handling business."

* * *

"Are we there yet? We've been driving for twelve damn hours," Promise complained like a little kid.

"Almost. It's the next exit," Shad replied.

By the time they pulled into the prison parking lot a few minutes later, Promise was a ball of nerves. She checked her makeup in the visor mirror.

Her heels clicked on the tile floor as they neared the first floor checkpoint. After two more checkpoints, she walked through a door. There was a woman sitting across the room, her mother. She looked worn and tired from everything she'd suffered, but she was still a beautiful sight to Promise's eyes. Promise remembered her mother as a strong woman who wouldn't let much if anything break her, but the woman before her was broken. The walk across the room seemed like it took an eternity, though it really only took a couple of seconds. When mother and daughter embraced, it felt like the longest, strongest minutes of Promise's life. She could feel the love between them, and tears began to run from her eyes. She felt like that little innocent girl she'd been all those years ago, when her mother and father were taken away from her.

Her mother kissed her forehead, cheeks, eyelids, and nose and continued to tell her how much loved and missed her.

"Mom, let's sit down. I feel weak and overwhelmed," Promise said.

"Okay. Let's have a seat then," Sweet Pea replied.

Promise just sat in silence. There was so much she wanted to say, but nothing would come out.

"Promise, you look so beautiful, like my little goddess. I see you've been doing well for yourself."

Promise smiled. "Thank you, Mom," she replied.

"Well, baby, I wanna get down to the nitty gritty. I know you didn't come all this way just to sit in silence. Almost ten years ago, you and your father were taken from me. I never thought I would see you again. Nevertheless, I never gave up hope, and I've been keeping my lawyers busy, trying to make appeals," Sweet Pea said.

"I wanna help you, Mama. I wanna get you some new lawyers. I wanna get you an appeal, a new case or something—anything but this," Promise said raising her hands and pointing around the room.

"It's okay, baby. I just want you to take care of yourself. Things will happen for me sooner or later," Sweet pea said with hopeful eyes.

"I am taking care of myself, Mama. It's not the best work, but I do what I have to do, and it pays good money. I just moved out of Shirley's apartment and got my own…" Her words trailed off as she saw her mother's whole demeanor change at the mention of Shirley's name. "What's wrong, Mom?" Promise asked.

In a low, raspy voice, almost a growl, Sweet Pea replied, "Shirley's the bitch who's responsible for getting me locked up in this hell hole. She's the reason your daddy isn't living anymore, and she's also the reason you were sent away. That bitch sat up in our apartment for years, talking to me the whole time with a hidden agenda, watching the moves your daddy made. She knew when shipments came in and when money was exchanged. I thought she was my friend. Your daddy told me to keep people out of our business, but I thought I could trust her."

"What, Mom? What are you sayin'? I don't believe this," Promise said, bewildered.

"Believe it, baby. That ho used to do the drop-offs and pick-ups on packages sometimes. One day she was high and drunk after picking up a big shipment, and the police pulled her over for swerving. Once the police smelled weed in the car, they placed her under arrest. In searching the car they found ten kilos of coke. They took her down to the station and told her she either had to roll over on who she worked for or go to federal prison for the rest of her life. As you can see, the bitch is out scot-free, while the rest of us—me, Toni, and all of our crew—are on lockdown."

"I can't believe this shit! Mom, she was there the day the feds kicked in our door. Now that I think about it, she was too cool, like she knew what was about to go down. She told me you've been calling her every couple months to keep in touch and keep your ear to the streets."

"Baby, I haven't called that bitch in damn near seven years. They kept her big mouth a secret, but someone investigated it for me and found out how the FBI got inside info on your daddy's empire. When I found out Shirley was the bitch behind it all, I cut all ties. She probably only asked you to move in with her 'cause she felt guilty about everything that happened."

"But I paid her 3,000 damn dollars for letting me live with her. Ma, I'm gonna handle that bitch, straight up, real talk," Promise said, .38 hot.

"First of all, watch your mouth! I'm still your mother young lady. You leave all that get-back at Shirley up to me, Promise. I'll take care of this situation," Sweet Pea replied sincerely.

"Fuck…er, I mean forget that, Ma. It's been almost ten years since that happened, and you haven't moved on her yet because you're…well, incapacitated, locked up in here because of that bitch runnin' her mouth. It's time Shirley got, got—literally and figuratively. It ain't like she's untouchable. She *can* be touched, and I'm going to be the one to touch her," Promise said very matter-of-factly.

Before Sweet Pea had a chance to reply, the guard stepped up. "Time's up. All inmates to the left, all visitors to the right."

Promise turned to her mother and mouthed, *"I love you."*

Sweet Pea mouthed back, *"I love you too."*

Promise walked back to the truck in a daze. She just wanted to get home and let her thoughts take over. She began talking to herself. "Who can I really trust? Is Shad in on this too? Shit, Shirley's his auntie. I don't know what to think. This shit is just too much for me."

Chapter Thirteen

Who Can Be Trusted?

Promise was glad to be home. She had a severe headache and was physically and emotionally drained.

For the whole ride back to Tampa, all Shad had done was ask question after question, "What happened? Did your mom say something wrong? You were so excited before you went in to see her, but now you seem upset. Is there something you wanna talk about?"

Promise didn't even hear him or answer him. She was too engrossed in thinking about what her mother had just unveiled to her and all the bullshit that Shirley had been feeding her.

Now, back at home, she looked at the clock on her nightstand; it was little after 10 o'clock in the morning, so she decided to get some rest before work later that day. She wrapped her hair up and set an alarm for 5:00 p.m.

* * *

"Shit!" Promise said as she heard her phone going off, pissed that she hadn't put it on vibrate. "Look at these missed calls!" Shad had called twice, and Shirley had called once. Clicking out of the call log, she noticed a couple text messages:

"Whenever you ready to talk, I'll be here, ma. I got chu," wrote Shad.

The next text message was from Tre: *"I got something I need 2 discuss w/u on this money tip, so find me when u get here. Be on time!"*

Tre's text brought back a little joy for her after all the shit she'd been going through. She texted him back, *"OK. Will do. :)"* Then she threw her phone in her Michael Kors bag.

Since she had been rudely awakened early by her phone, she decided to have a soak in the tub, cook something to eat, then pack a couple of outfits to wear tonight. *Gotta pack my happy pills too,* she reminded herself. *I got a feeling it's going to be a long night.*

* * *

Promise parked her car in her favorite spot, right in front of the club. Being the top-paid dancer had its perks. The other bitches had to park in the back, behind the club, and they sure hated that shit. Since she'd been working at the club for a while now, she and security had developed a sister/brother relationship. There was no more open lusting for her, but they all had their secret crushes. "Yo, what's up, Brus?" Promise said to Mark, the front door bouncer.

"Shit, can't call it, sis. Just working hard, tryin' a keep these broke-ass niggas on the other side of this here rope."

"I hear ya. Keep it up," Promise replied, attempting to walk past Mark.

But he stopped her in her tracks. "Hold up. Let me tell you now before you go inside and get caught off guard. Tre is walking 'round the club snappin' on any- and e'rybody 'cause a you. Says he's tired of you comin' up in his spot late like you runnin' shit."

Damn! she thought when she looked at her diamond Rolex and realized it was already 10:45 p.m. "Man, let me go on in here and catch the raft of the boss man. Thanks for the heads up," Promise said, ready to get the talk over with.

"No problem. Be easy, li'l sis," Mark said, moving out of her path.

When Promise walked through the club, she couldn't find Tre anywhere, so she headed up to his office.

Two seconds after her hand made contact with the door to knock, he snatched it open and stood there glaring at her with bloodshot eyes.

Damn! Has he been doing some type of drugs? Why the fuck is his eyes so red? Promise wondered as she stared at Tre, who was staggering back and forth. "Tre, let me explain. I had to—"

Before she could even finish, Tre cut her off mid-sentence. "I don't give a fuuuuck what you had to do. You wasn't here making me no monnnnney," he slurred, continuing his rant. "You know yo' established clients and new clients come here every night requestin' you, but you show up late all the damn time. It's like you're basically sayin', 'Fuck them! Their money don't mean shit,'" Tre said.

"That's not how I want them to feel, Tre. I was just—"

"Shut the fuck up, Velvet. I'm still the boss 'round here, in case your high and mighty ass has forgotten that," Tre said, spinning around. "I run this mu'fucka, and you wouldn't make half the money you make here over at the spot on Nebraska Avenue—or anywhere else, for that matter. Now, take yo' ass downstairs, get dressed, find yo' clients, and make that money." That said, Tre slammed the door in her face.

Promise was so bewildered that she felt her happy pill wearing off, so she took another one from her purse.

Unbeknownst to her, an envious stripper by the name of Jelly was watching her from the corner of the hallway as she popped the pill in her mouth and swallowed it. Jelly was heated about Promise being hired in the first place. As far as she was concerned, Promise hadn't put in any real work, but Tre still put her on a pedestal. Jelly had been there just as long as Black Ice, and she was sure she'd be next in line once Black Ice left, but Tre gave Promise—an unknown—that honor instead, and that pissed Jelly the fuck off. *What does she got that I don't?* Jelly had asked herself many times, growing ever more jealous every time Velvet stepped onstage.

As Promise made her way to the stairs that led to the dressing room, she saw Jelly coming up them. "What's up, Jelly? Hey, if you're going to see Tre, take it from me, he's not in the best of moods."

"Thanks for the heads up, but I'm sure I can make him feel better," Jelly replied with much attitude dripping from her words.

"Suit yourself," Promise replied with a shrug. *There really ain't no point being nice to these envious hoes,* Promise thought.

But Jelly had thoughts of her own. *That dumb-ass bitch think she can tell me about Tre. Her young ass better recognize I been there and done that,* Jelly thought as she fumed, her envy boiling over.

Dressed and ready to get her night over with, Promise walked up to her favorite client, Dezman Turner, who just so happened to play ball for the Boston Celtics, her favorite basketball team. Dezman was a cool, laidback, down-to-Earth, big-spender type, so he kept her attention. She'd met him on her seventh night working at Sweet Spot. Unlike his teammates, who were celebrating their win against the Miami Heat by drinking, hooting, and hollering at the other dancers, Dezman had stood out because he was sitting back chilling, zoned out. They'd connected a couple times outside of the club, and they even chatted on the phone every now and then. He had even flown her out to an Atlanta Hawks game, but it was only a one-night sleepover since he was traveling with his team. After the game, though, instead of going out to celebrate with his team, he joined her for dinner. She'd woken up the next morning in his presidential suite to breakfast in bed and a note on his pillow that read: *"Red Velvet...until next time! D.Turner"*

Snapping back to her dance, she noticed that Dezman had showered her with plenty of $50 bills. "Thank you, baby." She kissed him on his cheek and then went on to her next customer.

After a hard night's work, a set onstage and over ten A-list clients, Promise was deadbeat tired. She sat at her vanity drinking yet another bottle of water.

Bear walked up to her. "Boss man wants to see you before you leave."

She sucked her teeth and replied, "What now? Did I not dance fast enough for him?"

"I don' know, Velvet. Just go see the man before you leave," Bear said.

She threw all her shit in her bag, dreading what she knew would be a one-sided conversation. Promise took her time getting to Tre's office, and when she got there, the door was cracked open. Instead of going in right away, she decided to tap on it.

"Come in," Tre said.

"You wanted to see me?" Promise asked.

"Yes. First, how much did you make tonight?" Tre asked.

"Around $4,500, and I've already paid the house fee," Promise replied.

"You're going to give me half of that. Maybe that'll teach you about coming in late," Tre said, sounding much more sober than he had earlier that night.

"Man, this shit is un-fuckin'-believable." She handed over the money. "Is that all you wanted?" Promise said, pissed the fuck off.

"No. You have a lot of A-list celebrities as your regular customers, and a lot of them have come to me asking if you date outside of the club. Some of them just wanna take you out to dinner, and some of them want more, if you know what I mean. They're all willing to pay the price."

"Let's cut to the chase, Tre. Tell me what you're asking of me," Promise demanded, not in the mood for him beating around the bush.

"Since you put it that wayyy," he slurred, suddenly sounding drunk or high again, "how would you feel about being a top-paid escort?" Tre asked.

"When you say top paid, how much is the minimum you're thinking?"

"The minimum will be $10,000, just to be their company and nothin' physical. They want that extra shit, they'll pay more."

"Shit, that sounds good to me," Promise said, imagining the piles of money she could make.

"I will be getting a cut since I'll be the one doing all the behind-the-scenes work, setting it up and everything."

"How much of a cut are you talkin'?" Promise asked.

"I'm thinking 30/70. You get to keep 70 percent of your take."

"That's what I'm talkin' 'bout! Cool! When do I get my first client?"

"Your first date will be tomorrow at 8:00 p.m. Take this Nextel, but it is to be used strictly for business. You are to have this phone on at all times, and when I chirp you, you chirp back ASAP. Got me?" Tre stated.

Promise took the phone and asked, "So who is my first date with?"

"I'm supposed to keep that a secret, but I will tell you he's an artist, CEO and owner of a certain record label based out of New York. He's flying you out to New York early tomorrow afternoon. Your only requirement for taking this position is that you must show up for work here twice a week."

"That's fine. I guess I'll see you Sunday then," Promise replied. *Shit,* she thought as she left Tre's office, *it's already 4:30 a.m. I gotta head straight home, take a shower, and pack a light bag since I should be doing some shopping while I'm in NYC.*

Chapter Fourteen

This Is the Life!

A fter a stressful night and a nervous plane ride, it felt good to be back on the ground. Since Promise had only brought a carryon bag, she didn't have to stop by baggage claim. After looking around, she noticed an older Italian-looking man holding up a sign that read: *"PROMISE BROWN'S DRIVER!"* She smiled. *Whoever the mystery artist CEO is, he got me my own driver. This is what I'm talkin' about!* she thought. "Hey, Frankie, is it? I'm Promise."

"Hi, ma'am. The car is right this way. Mr. Johnson will be happy to know you arrived on time. How was your flight?" Frankie said.

"It was fine. My first time flying, so I was nervous, but still okay," she answered. In the car, she checked her makeup and rolled down the divider and asked, "Does this Mr. Johnson have a first name?"

"Yes, but I'll let him reveal it to you. As a matter of fact, once you see him, you'll know exactly who he is, I'm sure," Frankie replied.

Promise didn't say another word and sat quietly as he drove her to the fancy Four Seasons.

"You have a room here. It's already taken care of, so just go to the front desk and give them your name," Frankie directed.

Promise was in awe at how beautiful the décor of the hotel was. After receiving the keycard for her room, she took the elevator up to it. Once inside her room, she realized she would be staying in a presidential suite. *This trip keeps getting better and better! Damn, this is the life.*

On the counter sat a fresh bouquet of red roses and an envelope. Promise opened the envelope and read the letter:

Hi, Red Velvet!
I hope you like the flowers and the suite. As you can see, there
is $5,000 here. Please use it to buy a sexy dress to wear to

my album release party tonight. Also, visit any salon you like to get your hair, nails, and feet done if they're not already done to perfection. If you go over the $5,000, I'll hit you with whatever you had to spend out of pocket. Be ready at 9:45 p.m. Frankie is your driver, and he'll be waiting downstairs whenever you're ready to go shopping and whatever else you need to take care of. See you soon.

The Mystery Man!

Promise was overjoyed and ready to hit the top stores. She put her carryon bag down and left without a second thought. "Hey, Frankie, I'm ready to go shopping. Can you take me to Dash, Bloomingdale's, and Saks Fifth Avenue?"

"Okay. I believe two of those shops are on Fifth Avenue. Let's go to those first since they're the closest."

"That's fine," Promise said.

Her pussy got wet as she walked through the doors of Saks Fifth Avenue. Ever since she'd started working, she'd developed quite a shopping addiction. She demanded the finer things in life, and she was finally going to get them.

"Welcome to Saks. Let me know if you need help with anything."

The first dress she came across was a royal blue Versace mid-thigh with a plunging neckline. It was hot and would be just right for the party. *Okay. That was easy. Now all I need are some hot heels to set this shit off,* Promise thought. On the other side of the store she found some six-inch Gucci sling-back heels.

When she approached the counter to check out, the cashier told her, "I don't know if you're interested, but we have the Gucci clutch to match these heels over there in the black case."

"I'll take it," Promise replied.

"Okay. That'll be $7,900.98. And how will you be paying today?"

"Cash!" Promise replied proudly and reached into her Hermés Birkin bag to hand the woman $8,000. "Keep the change." She chuckled to herself at the thought of the two cents change. She grabbed her bags and was on her way.

When she got back in the car, she yawned. She thought to herself, *Since I got up this morning and got my hair, nails, and feet done before I caught my flight, I should just go back to the room and get some rest.*

"Where to next?" Frankie asked, pulling away from the curb.

"You can take me back to the hotel. That plane ride has me exhausted," Promise replied.

"Okay," Frankie responded.

It felt good for Promise to be back in her suite. She kicked off her platform pumps, peeled off all her clothes and got into bed naked. It felt amazing as her body sank into the California king bed. She looked at the clock and saw that it was 6:00, which was perfect because she could sleep until 8:00 and then get up and get ready for the album release party, where she'd finally meet the mystery man.

* * *

Promise was dressed and ready to go, looking good enough to eat. Then came a knock at the door. "Who is it?" she asked, looking through the peephole, but she couldn't see the person's face on the other side of the door due to a huge bouquet of flowers.

"Delivery for Promise Brown."

Promise opened the door and noticed that the deliveryman was dressed in a Hugo Boss suit. She didn't know any deliveryman who dressed like that. "Sit the flowers over there on the counter, next to the roses…and thank you." She opened her clutch and pulled out a $10 bill to tip him, but when she turned around, her mouth dropped open, and time stood still.

Standing before her was owner, famous producer, and top-selling artist of the Turnt Up record label.

"J-Sean Johnson," Promise said in awe.

"That would be me! You looking damn good in that dress, Promise. We're gonna look fly together at the party."

"You mean to tell me you're my client? Wait…how did you find me? I've never seen you at Sweet Spot," Promise asked shocked.

"So many questions! First, yes, I am your date, and you're right. I've never been to Sweet Spot while you've been working there. I have been there before, though, and my dancer of choice at the time was Black Ice. I don't know if you've met her before, but when I have special events, I usually fly her out to be my date since I'm not dating anyone officially," J-Sean replied.

"Okay, but that doesn't explain where you heard of me."

"Well, I called Tre to book Black Ice for this event, but he informed me that she's no longer working there. I told him I didn't want to take a celebrity friend 'cause the press would have a field day with speculations and rumors and be reportin' all kinds of bullshit. Tre told me you are the most gorgeous top-paid adult entertainer he has on staff, but I wasn't really persuaded, truth be told—not until he said you're even better looking than Black Ice. That was what sold me on you…and I can see now that he was right."

"Wow. I can't believe this. I'm honored to be your date for your party,"

Promise replied, kinda uneasy.

"Okay. After you then," J-Sean said as they left the room.

Forty minutes and a couple glasses of Moët later, they arrived at J-Sean's release party.

Walking up to the red carpet, Promise was bombarded with questions from reporters and media people from various entertainment and music industry magazines and newspapers. "Are you and J-Sean exclusive?" one reporter asked, shoving a mic in her face.

"Who are you?" another reporter asked.

"Where are you from, and how did you and Mr. Johnson meet?" a reporter from *The Wendy Williams Show* asked. "Are you the new luck lady in J-Sean's life?

"Whoa, whoa, whoa! Chill out with all the questions. We're just mutual friends, out to enjoy a party together," J-Sean said as he ushered Promise away from the press and paparazzi.

"Thanks for saving me back there. I'm not use to all that flashy, in-your-face stuff," Promise said.

"It's cool, ma. You keep fucking with me, you'll get used to it. Next time, I'll have my security with us," J-Sean replied.

The weird thing about walking into the party with J-Sean was that every actress, actor, model, and artist that Promise saw was dressed in all white. She leaned over to J-Sean and asked, "Is there something you forgot to tell me?"

"Naw. I told you everything," J-Sean replied, looking around the party.

"Why are we the only ones wearing different colors? Everyone else is dressed in white, like they're all getting married or something," Promise asked, feeling a little uncomfortable.

"Well, it's my party, and I don't go by the rules. I look good in my Hugo Boss suit with Gucci dress shoes, and you look damn good in your Versace dress and those Gucci heels."

Promise watched J-Sean as he walked around the club, mingling with his peers. She noticed the sexy dimple that showed up on his left cheek every time he smiled. He was a 6'6", dark-skinned, low-cut-wearing smooth brother. He would make any chick's panties get soaking wet. She turned her attention back to the party as Mary J. Blige and her husband walked in. J-Sean was talkin' business with Lil Wayne about them doing a record together or possibly collaborating on a remix track. Lil Wayne was way shorter than Promise imagined he would be.

Chapter Fifteen

Is This How Sex Feels?

When the party was over, Promise could barely contain herself. J-Sean had been giving her the eye, rubbing on her thighs, grabbing her ass, licking his lips, and whispering the freakiest things in her ear. Promise hadn't ever fucked anyone before, but she decided she was going to put it on J-Sean like she was an expert porn star, and she planned to get things started in the limo.

"You know my dick been throbbing for you all night. The way that dress fits you like a glove makes me wanna bend you over and fuck you doggy style. Shit!" J-Sean said.

Promise, loving a challenge, placed her hand on his pole and began to massage it through his pants. It seemed to grow a little more from her touch. She unzipped his pants and released his member through the slit in his boxers. She wrapped her warm mouth around his dick.

"Damn, girl! Shit!" J-Sean said and then groaned.

Flicking her tongue on the slit of his dick, she licked up the pre-cum that dripped from the head. Promise got into a rhythm and began to deep-throat him, taking his balls in her hand. She massaged them and hummed on the tip of his member, all at the same time.

"Damn, girl! You 'bout to make me bust already. Fuck!" J-Sean said.

Promise could see on his face that she was putting down the best blowjob he'd ever had in his life. "Don't cum yet, baby. I wanna ride this dick all night. This is just the beginning. We'll finish this up at the suite." With her tongue she trailed down all nine inches to his balls and sucked them into her mouth.

"Fuck! Where you been all my life?" J-Sean asked, his eyes rolling to the back of his head and pleasure dripping from his voice.

Promise hadn't sucked a dick in her life, but she'd learned a lot working at the club. "That should hold you till we get to the suite, huh?" Promise asked.

"If that was just the beginning, I can't wait to see what's to come. It's gonna be a long night," J-Sean replied.

"It sure is, 'cause I want this dick in every position possible," Promise said.

Back in the room, J-Sean wasted no time ripping at her clothes.

Promise had already taken one of her get-me-through-the-night pills, so she was past ready to fuck his brains out.

His eyes lit up when he saw her hardened nipples.

When his mouth covered her breast, she let a moan escape her lips. It felt so good. "Shit!" Promise said as cream flowed down her inner thighs.

Laying her down, he kissed her inner thighs and then buried his face in her pussy. He ate it like it was the best forbidden fruit he'd ever tasted.

His lips tasting and exploring her treasure made her legs began to quiver. She locked her legs around his head, refusing to let him go. The feeling was so intense. "I'm…about…to…cum. Oh shit! I'm about to cum!" Promise yelled out in pure pleasure.

"Cum then, baby, right in my mouth. You like that? Huh?" J-Sean asked as he slid a finger inside her.

That sent her over the edge, and she erupted all over his finger and mouth.

"Damn, girl! This pussy tight as hell. Shit!" he said, massaging his dick that was now positioned at the opening of her pussy.

"Do you have a condom?" Promise asked, not willing to be stupid and end up pregnant.

"Yeah," he said. He opened the foil wrapper and smoothly rolled the rubber down his massive dick with expertise, like he'd done it a thousand times before. "I wanna feel every bit of this pussy," J-Sean said as he dipped the head of his cock in and out of her, teasing her into a frenzy.

Promise couldn't take it anymore; she wanted more. She started rotating her hips, trying to get more of his length inside of her.

He finally gave her what she wanted and plunged into her pussy.

It hurt like hell, but she would never admit it. Promise met every thrust, even though it felt like she was being ripped apart.

"Man, I'm about to bust."

"No, not yet! I want more! Give me more!" Promise said, almost begging, as the pain turned into pleasure.

There was one last, long stroke, then he stiffened, lingered inside her, and fell on top of her, drenched in sweat.

That's it? That's all I fuckin' get? I didn't even get to cum again. Shit, Promise thought. She was too through. She wondered what happened to the sheer pleasure people had always talked about. *What about the climax and multiple orgasms?* She had experienced none of that.

"I laid the dick down, huh? You got some tight, sweet-ass puss, Red Velvet. You should call yo'self Sweetness, sweet as that pussy is," J-Sean said.

Promise laughed and got up. "I'm 'bout to get in the shower. Wanna join me?" Promise said, secretly hoping he'd refuse.

"Naw, I'm good. I'm beyond exhausted, and I have a meeting in the morning," J-Sean replied.

"Suit yourself. You're loss." She smacked her ass and seductively made her way to the bathroom. After showering, drying off, and slipping on a nightie, she crawled into bed. She noticed J-Sean was in bed, already knocked out. *I guess I wore him out,* Promise thought and smiled to herself.

* * *

It felt like she'd only been asleep for fifteen minutes, but the sun was already peeking through the curtains. She turned over and noticed that J-Sean wasn't there anymore; in his place lay a thick envelope with a letter attached to it. I'm getting tired of finding envelopes with letters attached to them. Last time I read a letter like that, a bitch stole my money, Promise thought. She opened the letter and read it:

> If you're reading this, sleepy head, that means you're finally up. I just wanted to write you a li'l something so you didn't think I just jetted on you. Last night was amazing. You have a goldmine down there, and if you continue seeing me, I'm gon' bless you. Originally you were just supposed to accompany me to my album release party and get paid $25,000, but I had no idea you would look that damn good. In the envelope you'll find $50,000. Enjoy it. You deserve it, ma. I'll be in touch.
> J-Sean

Promise snatched the envelope open with lightning speed and a bunch of $100 bills spilled out. She picked up the money and put it in her bag, then began to get dressed. It was 9:50 a.m., and her flight was scheduled to leave at 11:15. *Time to head home,* Promise thought.

Chapter Sixteen

Getting Things in Order

A fter arriving home $50,000 richer, Promise started handling her business. She stopped by the club to drop off Tre's cut. They chatted for a while, and then she was off to her next destination.

She pulled up to the lawyer's office, the one Shad had recommended to her as one of the best criminal defense attorney's in the state of Florida. "Hi. My name is Red…er, Promise Brown. I have an appointment to see William Spenser." *Damn. I've really go to get a grip. I'm starting to call myself Red Velvet outside of the club.*

"Okay, Ms. Brown. Please have a seat, and Mr. Spenser be right with you," the receptionist said.

"Hello. Nice to meet you, Ms. Brown. I'm William Spenser. Please follow me back to my office," William said.

"Nice to meet you as well," Promise said, following him back to his office.

"So how can I be of service to you?" William asked. He pulled out a notepad to take some notes.

"I'm here today to see what can be done on my mother's case and also to see what your fee would be to become my mother's lawyer. I want to know what your thoughts on my mother's case are, so I gathered all the information I could," Promise said, handing him the file.

"I'm going to take this file and look through all the information, but I will also do my own research on your mother's case to see what else I can find out. We'll set up another appointment to discuss fees and how we can go about helping your mother," William replied.

"Thank you, Mr. Spenser," Promise said as she stood to leave.

"Please call me William," William replied, standing to walk her back to the lobby.

* * *

Promise was finally home and exhausted. She started to unpack her luggage, and as she did, she thought about her mother again. It was nothing new, for ever since the day she'd gone to see her mother, she'd been dwelling on how she might be able to get at Shirley and make her suffer the same way they had, being ripped apart like that. Promise remembered what her mother said about leaving it up to her—that she didn't want her to get involved. Little did Sweet Pea know, though, that her daughter was already involved, because it boiled her blood just to think about what the bitch had done to her family.

Her phone began to ring, jolting her out of her thoughts. She checked the caller I.D and saw that it was Shad. "Hello!" Promise said.

"What's up, Promise? How did your trip go?" Shad asked.

"Nothing much is up. Just got done unpacking. My trip went great, and I'm actually ready to go on my next one," Promise replied.

"I hear ya. That money looking right, huh?" Shad said as he chuckled.

"Yeah. We need to meet up, though, 'cause there's something I need to speak to you about. I don't know how you're going to take it or feel about it," Promise said.

"You know you can talk to me about anything, girl, so whenever you're ready," Shad replied.

"Okay. In that case, let's meet at the Hip Hop Soda Shop over on Fowler Avenue, around 7:30 p.m." Promise said.

"You bet," Shad said, and they hung up.

Not even a minute later, her phone began to ring. She didn't even look at the caller I.D. before she picked up. "Hello?" Promise said tiredly.

"What's up, Red Velvet. This is Tre. Remember the actress Angela Richardson who hosted at the club a few weeks ago?" Tre asked.

"Yeah, I remember her. I gave her a private dance that night," Promise replied.

"Well, she must have really liked it, 'cause she's requesting you to accompany her for her birthday weekend in two days. You'll be flying out to L.A.," Tre said.

"Is that right? What time is my flight?" Promise asked, smiling to herself.

"Yep, she got in touch with me personally to request you. Shit, I wonder if she's gay. Anyway, your flight leaves at 12:15 p.m. Be ready to go," Tre replied.

"All right. I'll be on that flight. See you tonight," Promise said ignoring his question even though she was wondering the same thing. Angela had been quite hands-on that night.

* * *

As Promise parked in the parking lot of the Hip Hop Soda Shop, she noticed Shad's Range Rover was already there, so she made her way inside and found Shad sitting in a corner booth. "I see you beat me here," Promise said as she walked up.

Shad stood and gave Promise a hug, then replied, "Yeah. You always late."

"No I'm not! Have you ordered yet?" Promise asked.

"Naw. I was waiting on you. Let me get the waitress so we can get our orders in."

After they put their orders in, Promise felt like it was time to get the main reason why she asked him to meet her. "Look, Shad, I know Shirley is your auntie and all, but she's part of the reason my father is dead, my mother is in prison, and I was tossed around in that damn state foster care system. Straight up, I want Shirley dead," she said bluntly. Once she broke the news to him, she just sat there and waited for his facial expression to change, but it never did. "You don't have anything to say to what I just revealed to you?" Promise asked, getting annoyed by his silence.

"Yeah, I got something to say. I'm just blowed that the bitch done fucked up more than just one family. I'm going to tell you something doesn't too many people know. Shirley is the reason my ol' head is in prison for life, you could say," Shad revealed.

"What? I thought said your dad was dead?" Promise replied in disbelief.

"Naw. My ol' man been locked up for about twenty years now. Let me tell you the story my moms told me," Shad said. "One day, Aunt Shirley needed to run some errands, and since I was sick with the flu, my mom had to stay home and take care of me. It was my dad's off day, so she didn't want to bother him with the task of taking care of a sick child. My dad was sitting on the couch, doing what he loved to do. Man, how that man loved to watch basketball, particularly the Boston Celtics against the Lakers. His favorite team was the Celtics, so there was no way he was going to move from the TV. Anyway, Aunt Shirley called the house and asked my mom if she could take her to run her errands. Moms told her she had to take care of me, but she would see if Big Shad would take her. She went and asked my dad, and although he was reluctant and didn't really want to leave the game, he would have done anything for my mama, so he told her he'd go get Shirley when halftime came. When he picked Shirley up, their first stop was your house. She came out carrying a duffle bag—the same one she'd taken from her house, only this time it wasn't empty. She stuffed it in the trunk. My dad didn't speak on it 'cause it wasn't his business. Then Shirley told him she needed to go to Walmart, so that was their next stop. At the store, she bought sandwich bags, plastic wrap, some little baggies, and a couple of different scales. Looking at his watch, my dad realized halftime would be over at any minute, so he put the pedal to the metal and ended up running a stop sign where an officer was sitting."

The waitress came back with their orders, so Shad and Promise stopped the conversation momentarily, though both of them were interested in finishing the stories rather than eating. They hurried their waitress off, and Shad got right back into the story.

"The police officer asked my dad for his license and registration, but when he'd rushed out of the house to pick Shirley up, he forgot to grab it, so that gave the police cause to search his car. The fact that he'd run the stop sign, paired with the way Shirley was acting, made them even more suspicious. My dad told the officer he had no problem with him searching his car because, as far as he knew, he had nothing to hide. As my father got out of the car, he apologized for speeding and for running a stop sign. He told the officer he was just trying drop his sister-in-law off and get back home to catch the second half of the basketball game. After the officers searched the car, they appeared with Aunt Shirley's gym bag and the bags from Walmart. They put cuffs on my dad and Shirley and took them down to the station to be questioned. Shirley ended up telling the officers that all her paraphernalia and drugs belonged to my dad, and she claimed she was just a passenger in his car and knew nothing about any of it. They charged my dad with possession of cocaine—a felony amount—possession with intent to sell, and trafficking. They also added some other knickknack charge just because they felt like it. When he went in front of the court, he told the judge the stuff wasn't his, but my daddy was a black man living in poverty, and that was all they saw. They sentenced my innocent father to forty-five years to life. Forty-fuckin'-five years to life, man!" Shad said finishing the story with a shake of the head and an angry expression on his face. "Just like you, Promise, I've been trying to figure out how I'm gon' get at Shirley. I want real revenge, some shit she'll feel. She robbed me of having my dad there to watch my games and cheer me on. Why you think I didn't go to college on a basketball scholarship? I woulda been a number one draft pick coming out of college. Everybody wanted me to go, but what was the use if my ol' man couldn't be there to go all the way with me?" Shad said in an almost hurting tone.

"I'm shocked. I mean, I don't know what to say. It's crazy that she's torn up more than one family and ruined so many lives. She got my mama locked up and my daddy killed! I'm on some bang-bang, shoot-her-up-type shit. I already got it planned out, but now that I think about it, that plan might've just changed. You down or what, 'cause I'm ready to make it happen?" Promise said, excited about the revenge that would soon fall upon Shirley.

"Shit! I'm down. When you tryin'a get it done?" Shad asked, ready to put his murder game down, this time for a good reason.

"Well, I leave for L.A in two days. Money first, but when I get back, we'll set my plan in motion," Promise replied. "That bitch is gonna pay."

Chapter Seventeen

Who Knew She Would Like It?

Promise could tell things were going to be different than they had been during her visit with J-Sean. When she arrived at the airport, Angela was there to pick her up in her royal blue 645Ci convertible. *Hmmm...definitely impressed,* Promise thought. *This car doesn't even hit the market until next year.* She wasn't going to stay at a five-star hotel; instead, she would spend her days in Angela's mansion, a beautiful place with a very artistic design, different colors and patterns all worked together perfectly.

"I can feel you staring at me," Promise said out of the blue, while she continued to look around the mansion. She'd felt Angela's eyes on her ever since they'd left the airport.

"I'm sorry. It's just that you're so beautiful. You could have a career doing anything you want. Why are you a stripper, if you don't mind me asking? You're not like the around-the-way girls I usually see in strip clubs," Angela said.

"Well, since you asked, I needed a job fast, and it was the first one I found. The pay isn't anywhere near bad, especially not with this side hustle I have going on," Promise replied, feeling kinda uneasy with the personal questioning. "Since you asked me an uncomfortable question, it's only right that I ask you one. I've never read or seen anything on TV or in magazines about you being gay. Are you a lesbian?"

"Yes. I've always been one, of course, but my agent feels it would ruin my career if the world found out the truth about that. Then I wouldn't be the it-girl of Hollywood. I would be just another new actress trying to get my career going, and that's not what I want," Angela replied.

"That's understandable. Your career is important. I mean, it's your livelihood," Promise said.

"Maria, go ahead and take Ms. Brown's bags up to her room," Angela said to one of her maids.

"Is there anything you would like to do while you're in L.A., Promise?"

Angela asked.

"Whatever you wanna do. It's your birthday weekend, right?" Promise replied.

"Okay. In that case, go ahead and get changed. We'll go to dinner and hit the club up afterward. Tonight, when we get back here and get behind closed doors, I don't know if I'll be able to keep my hands to myself," Angela said, massaging Promise's pussy through her Juicy jogging suit.

"Keep it up and we won't be going to dinner. I'll be your dinner, and you'll be my dessert," she said smiling as she turned to follow the maid to her room.

Promise couldn't believe the words coming out of her own mouth. She'd never been with a woman before. Not only that, but it wasn't just any woman—Angela was the Hollywood it-girl. She was beautiful and reminded Promise a lot of LisaRaye in looks, skin complexion, and body type. She was mixed, black and Asian, about five-eight, with a gorgeously toned body, legs for days, long, jet-black, wavy hair cascading down her back, and those slanted cat like eyes. Simply put, she was a downright gorgeous woman, but for some reason, Promise just couldn't stop thinking about Dezman. The last time they'd talked, he was back in Boston preparing for a home game. That was about a week ago. She couldn't deny that she was really starting to like him on a more romantic level. Her thoughts were broken by a buzzing sound. Realizing it was coming from an intercom, she went over by the door and pressed the button. "Um… hello?" Promise said.

"Are you ready to go, or do you need some more time?" Angela asked through the intercom.

"Give me about five more minutes. I was enjoying this bed," Promise replied, halfway telling the truth.

"Okay, no problem. Take your time," Angela replied.

Shaking the thoughts of Dezman out of her head, she resumed getting dressed. Promise opted for a sexier look—a feathered, tight Valentino Haute Couture dress with a pair of Louis Vuitton booties. She kept her accessories simple, just some diamond-encrusted hoop earrings.

When she walked down the spiral staircase, she saw Angela, who must've gotten the sexy memo 'cause she went for a revealing Rachel Roy mini-dress and the new Prada heels. Promise had the same shoes on order, but Angela looked amazing in them.

Angela looked amazing. "You look fierce, Promise. I can't wait till we get back from the club tonight. It's gonna be on," Angela said, looking lustfully at Promise.

"You look great as well, and what do you have planned for us when we return from the club?" Promise asked as they walked out of the door hand in hand.

"How about I leave that pretty little mind of yours wondering?" Angela said, smiling with that one-of-a-kind smile.

They got into the Hummer limo, and the driver asked, "Where to?"

"Do you like Japanese food, Promise?"

"Never had it before, but I'm up for trying it," Promise replied.

"Okay. David, take us to the Geisha House," Angela said.

After they finished their delicious dinner, they sat and talked for a while, enjoying each other's conversation. Promise learned a lot about Angela and, feeling comfortable, she told Angela a lot about herself.

The lounge they hit up was called Lounge 1020, a cool, laidback party atmosphere. They partied in the VIP area. Promise had brought some of her happy pills with her and sneaked off to the bathroom to pop one. She started to feel in the mood to have a good time almost immediately. That pill plus the four glasses of wine from the restaurant and three cups of Incredible Hulk had her on another level.

Everybody in the VIP area had their attention on Promise. She swayed back and forth, hypnotizing all the men and women with the flow of her hips to Trey Songz' newly released song, *Scratchin Me Up*.

After a minute or two, Promise felt a set of arms wrap around her waist from behind. She was so immersed in her own movement that she hadn't even noticed Angela get up. "What happened to keeping the fact that you're gay behind closed doors?" Promise asked.

"If anyone questions this, I'll just have my publicists tell them we were just two drunk party girls having a good time for my birthday," Angela replied.

* * *

Promise felt so free being around Angela. She had this presence about her that just put Promise at ease. Although it was only her second encounter with the actress, the way Angela touched her, gazed into her eyes, told her she was the most beautiful woman she'd ever seen, and listened to her problems made her feel like she truly cared for her.

For once, she looked at her paying customer as more than that. Angela wasn't just someone who'd pay for her company and her services. She was someone she cared about.

"I'm about to get in the shower and wash away all that sweat from the dance floor. Do you wanna join me?" Promise asked.

"How 'bout instead of the shower, I set up a bath for two?" Angela asked.

"Okay. Go ahead. I'll back in a second," Promise replied. She then went back in the room to take off her clothes and pin her hair up. She noticed her phone lighting up on the bed, so she picked it up and saw that there was a message from Dezman a smile crept across her face as she read it: *"Hey, baby cakes...just seein' how U R doin'. Sorry u haven't heard from me. Busy with practice, road games, charities. I miss u though."*

To Dezman she texted, *"It's okay, Dez. I understand. I miss u more. I'm in L.A right now on a job, but I'll B headin' home in a couple days."*

As Promise got up to head back over to Angela's master bedroom, her phone beeped with another message from Dezman: *"Damn, that's crazy! I'm in L.A. too! We play Lakers 2morrow. You should come to the game, I'll leave some tickets for you at the box office."*

She replied, *"We'll see. I have to go. MUAH!"*

She made her way back to Angela's room. The door was cracked open, and she saw flickering lights, so she pushed the door open and noticed at least fifty tea-light candles placed throughout the room, creating a path that led to the master bathroom. The sounds of Jodeci's "Freek'N You" cascaded through the entire room. That, mixed with the smell of the candles, was enough to turn Promise on. Sitting in the heart-shaped sunken-in spa tub that could easily fit five or six people, Angela looked so sexy with bubbly water running down her body.

Promise couldn't believe what was going on. Besides Black Ice, she'd never looked at another woman, but there she was, far more than a little attracted to this woman.

Angela stood up in the tub and helped her down into it.

"Is this Amber Romance body wash?" Promise asked. "I'd know that smell anywhere."

"Yes. It's my favorite. Something else we have in common I see," Angela responded. "Come over here. Why are you so far away?" Angela asked as she pulled Promise on top of her lap. Angela touched Promise's breast, and her nipples instantly hardened. Turning Promise around on her lap, Angela uttered, "I've wanted you since the first time I met you." With lust in her eyes, she took Promise's breast into her mouth. She sucked and probed Promise's nipples, sending waves of pleasure from her pussy to the tips of her toes and back up her spine.

Promise bit her bottom lip to keep from moaning out Angela's name. She couldn't resist touching Angela's creamy wetness, intensifying the pleasure even more.

"Let's get out and go in the bedroom. I wanna taste you," Angela whispered in her ear.

Promise lay on the bed with her legs open. Her clit was swollen and throbbing, ready to be devoured.

Crawling on the bed, Angela kissed her from the tip of her toes, up her legs, to her inner thighs, teasing her with gentle touches and kisses.

"Mmm, baby. Don't tease me," Promise moaned.

"Oh? You want me? How bad?" Angela asked.

"Real bad," Promise panted.

Finally, Angela went for what she knew. She wasn't just amazing at acting. The girl could eat pussy like her life depended on it.

With every lick, it felt like Promise got closer to the clouds. She pulled her hair, scratched her back, and quivered all at the same time. The pleasure was intense. "Your tongue should be illegal. Damn!"

"Your pussy tastes so sweet, like freshly picked strawberries. Mmmm, I could eat you all night," Angela whispered.

Promise began to buck her legs, throwing her pussy on Angela's tongue. "F-u-u-u-c-k! Shit! I'm…I'm about to cum. I'm about to…cum. Ahhh… yessss!" Promise yelled as she released her juices into Angela's mouth.

"Angela, I wanna taste and please you now. This will be my first time, so work with me. I know how I like to be pleased, so I'll start there," Promise said. Taking her time, she kissed and gently bit Angela's thighs. She sucked her pearl out of its hidden oasis. She flicked her tongue up and down, around and around, while sticking two fingers inside her wet slit; they slid in with ease.

"Oh shit. Right there, baby. Right there. That's…my…spot. Mmmm… Fuck! I'm cumming!" Angela yelled with pleasure.

Promise devoured her delicious cream, sweeter than any candy she'd ever tasted.

They lay in bed in each other's arms, spent from their euphoric sexcapade, and fell asleep with thoughts of each other roaming through their mind.

Chapter Eighteen

Figuring Things Out

They slept through the morning and finally made it up that afternoon. They felt some shopping was in order. Shopping Rodeo Drive was great for Promise. There was every shop she could think of: Chanel, Cartier, Gucci, Banana Republic, Dolce & Gabbana, Fendi, Jimmy Choo, *Louis Vuitton*, Michael Kors, Tiffany, Valentino, Versace, and Yves Saint Laurent. It felt like they'd died and gone to retail heaven.

"I sure wouldn't mind living out here. I would probably go bankrupt though," Promise said as they sat down at a bistro for a little something to snack on.

"That's why I keep so busy with work, auditioning and shooting. Every time I set foot on Rodeo, I spend over $10,000. See all the bags? And those aren't even counting the ones we dropped off at the car earlier," Angela responded.

"You know, I really enjoy your company, Angela. How would you like to go to the Celtics/Lakers game tonight at 7:00? I have a friend who'll get us courtside seats," Promise said.

"Aw, that's sweet, Velvet. You know, my all-time favorite NBA team is the Lakers," Angela said, smiling her unique grin once again.

"Well, I suppose that's where we differ. I love the Celtics myself," Promise shot back jokingly. "We've got to get Celtics and Lakers jerseys for tonight," Promise said.

"Perfect! We can to the game and stop by my house after to shower and get ready for my birthday party," Angela replied.

"Sounds like a plan. Let's do it!" Promise said.

The last couple of days of her life had been the best days she'd had since before the tragic day when her father was shot to death in front of her and she was taken from her mother ten years ago. Promise and Angela had gotten to know each other on more than one level, and she liked her, but Promise had to wonder if that meant she was a lesbian. It was a question she didn't have the answer to.

* * *

Promise was glad to be back home. She couldn't help thinking back to yesterday's events. After they'd watched the Celtics beat the Lakers by twenty-five points, Dezman had come over and invited them to go out for a victory celebration with him. Although Promise wanted to, it was Angela's birthday, so she had to let him down easy. "Sorry, Dezman. It's Angela's birthday so were going to her party tonight to celebrate it," Promise said.

Before he could even say anything back, Angela interrupted, "Dezman, is it? Why don't you come out to my birthday party and have some fun with us?"

For some reason, Promise didn't like the way she said it, so lustfully and seductively.

"Fo' sho. Where's the party gon' be?" Dezman asked.

"At a club called My Studio. Come dressed to impress," Angela responded.

"Bet. I'll even bring a couple of my teammates," Dezman replied as he kissed Promise's cheek.

The events that followed after the party still bothered her. They arrived at the black-tie affair and took their place in VIP. Everything was top shelf, Rémy Martin, Ciroc, Nuvo, merlot, Cabernet Sauvignon, vodka, and the list went on. Halfway through the night, they were lit.

When Dezman showed up, he started drinking and dancing letting loose like Promise had never seen do before. Before she knew it, they'd made a sandwich, with Promise in the front, Dezman in the middle, and Angela in the back, slow dancing to every song, even the fastest ones.

They left the party thirty minutes early. In the limo, things seemed to take a turn for the better.

Angela had been giving Promise fuck-me eyes all night, and her hand began riding up Promise's leg. She then swept it across her thigh and started massaging her clit.

Damn, she knows how to work those fingers! She knows how to please a pussy—my pussy especially, Promise thought.

It obviously turned Dezman on, 'cause he's started to massage himself through his pants.

Promise's pussy was aching to get sucked and licked on by Angela, but at the same time, it was throbbing to get pounded by Dezman. *Fuck it. Why can't I have the best of both worlds?*

That was the last thing Promise remembered before waking up next to a stretched-out Dezman and a cuddled-up sleeping beauty Angela. *What the fuck happened last night?* Promise asked herself.

Promise had been thinking about that night all day on her plane ride home; she didn't even take her usual nap.

Pulling herself out of her thoughts she heard her cell phone ring, and she recognized the number as the lawyer who was now representing her mother.

Chapter Nineteen

Revenge Is A Dish Best Served HOT!!

"Hey, William! Please tell me you have some good news for me," Promise asked, hoping for the best.

"Well, actually I might. In going through your mother's case, I see that when the feds interviewed her she kept asking them what it was all about. She said over and over again that they didn't show her any paperwork or even read them their rights and that they shot her husband, who was just trying to protect his daughter. 'They placed me under arrest and didn't even read me my rights. Y'all have some fuckin' nerve!' Those were your mother's exact words. Promise, the fact that your mother said that helps her case tremendously, and it might be the thing that gets her off. It's against the law for them to arrest her without reading her the Miranda rights," William said. "Yes, it's a technicality, but it's an important one. It's the law, and they broke it."

"This is music to my ears, William! When can we get the ball rolling?" Promise asked.

"I'm going to draw up the proper paperwork and get things in motion first thing Tuesday. I must warn you that it's not going to be easy, but we'll make it happen," William said.

"All right. Thank you so much. You don't know how much this means to me," Promise responded.

"No problem. You can show me how much it means to you with that retainer fee," William said in a joking tone, but Promise knew he was serious.

"Gotcha," Promise said, finally releasing a sigh of relief, happy that things were coming full circle.

She needed to go see her mother soon, but first she had to deal with her so-called auntie. Promise texted Shad: *"Meet me @ Blue Martini tonight around 9:00. We'll have drinks and get the ball rollin'."*

Minutes later, her phone beeped, a message from Shad: *"Bet! I been waitin'!"*

* * *

A couple days after their meeting at Blue Martini, where they discussed all the details, it was time to set their plan in motion.

It was 12:45 a.m. on Wednesday, a hot summer night. Shad, Mark (the bouncer from Sweet Spot), and Promise parked an old 1995 Toyota Camry by Riverfront Park. Shad and Promise got out of the car dressed in all black and walked past some apartment buildings until they came upon Shirley's apartment. They took Shirley's spare key from under one of her many flower pots and unlocked the door.

Promise checked the living room and kitchen, while Shad checked the two bedrooms and bathroom. Next thing she knew, she heard a loud *thump* and a groan. Running in the first room ,she found Shirley knocked out on the floor. "What did you do? I thought we said we were going to let her walk out between us, with a gun to her back," Promise said.

"Man, when I came in the room, she jumped on my back from behind the door. I had to knock her ass out. The bitch was trying to stab me!" Shad said.

"Shit! Now I gotta call Mark and have him pull up in front," Promise said, aggravated.

Mark picked up on the first ring.

"Yo, there's a change of plans. I need you to pull up in front of 5791 East Green Street," Promise said.

"And hurry up, nigga!" Shad yelled in the background before Promise could hang up the phone. "Come on. Let's get this snitchin' bitch to the front room," Shad said, ready to take care of her and get back to gettin' money. When he saw the headlights from the Toyota, he said, "Aye, find a sheet or something. We'll wrap her up and put her ass in the trunk."

"Use this," Promise said, handing Shad a blanket from the couch. She then went to the door and waved for Mark to come in. "Help Shad get her to the trunk and move fast." She told him once he came inside.

Their plan was to move faster than the ten minutes they actually spent there. It was supposed to be an in-and-out job, but shit happens.

* * *

On the other side of town, shit was just getting started. They tied Shirley's hands and legs to the chair. The bitch had a bewildered look on her face, like she was confused, scared, and shocked all at the same time. Little did she know, Promise was about to give it to her straight, no chaser.

"So it was you, huh? You snitched on my daddy, which led to his death, my mother getting locked up, and me being sent away to a bunch of fucked-up foster homes," Promise said, more as a statement than a question.

"I have no idea what you're talkin' 'bout," Shirley said.

"Look, Shirley, you're really pushing it. The only reason you're still alive and ain't got a whole magazine of bullets in your head, heart, and mouth is 'cause Shad wants answers," Promise replied in a menacing tone that she didn't even know she was capable of.

Shad came from a room in the back of the warehouse with a look of hate and disgust on his face. "All those fuckin' years I been comin' to you, considerin' you my favorite fuckin' aunt, and the whole time you was smilin' in my face, knowing you the reason my ol' man ain't been in my life?" Shad asked as chest rose up and down.

"Shad, I never meant for this to—" Shirley began to say.

"Shut the fuck up! I can't even think straight right now." Shad continued to pace back and forth, talking to himself and waving the gun around like a madman. Without any notice or warning, Shad caught Shirley with a bullet to each kneecap.

The gut-wrenching scream that escaped her mouth made her pain all the more real.

"Shad, I'm ready to finish this bitch off," Promise said, clutching tightly the chrome Beretta Shad had given her earlier that day.

"Naw, Promise, I got something special planned for her snitchin' ass. Ain't gon' be no snitches-gettin'-stiches-type deal here," Shad said. "Aye, Mark, bring me that stuff from out the back room," he ordered.

"What stuff?" Promise asked, with a puzzled look on her face.

Mark came into the big open space carrying two small kegs filled to the brim with clear liquid.

When Promise smelled the gasoline from across the room, a devilish smile crept across her face. "I like the way you think, Shad," Promise said.

Shirley sat there, helplessly grimacing in pain and saying nothing.

"All right, y'all. We're gonna drench this place in gas. This bitch gotta be gone for the old and the new," Shad said.

As Mark and Shad poured the gasoline all over the warehouse, Promise taunted her in her ear, "You couldn't take a couple years of lockup? You had to become a damn pussy-ass snitch? Well, guess what. Now yo' snitchin' ass is going to get cooked up real good." Promise noticed her begin to fall in and out of conscience, so she slapped her cheeks. "Un-uh! It's not time to sleep just yet.

I want you to be wide awake for your finale, and—"

Promise was interrupted from her taunts when Mark walked in and announced, "A'ight, it's all poured." He rolled an empty keg across the room, knocking it against Shirley's bloody left leg. It obviously sent another shot of pain through her body, 'cause there came a toe-curling scream.

"Did y'all leave a trail from the front door?" Promise asked, thinking about where they should light the fire.

"Yeah. There's a trail from there that hits every room but this one last," Shad answered.

At the front door, Shad and Promise both struck matches and threw them at the same time.

"Bum bitch! Burrrrrrrrn!!!" Promise yelled from the door.

They turned and headed to the car and never looked back.

"Shad, I know that was hard for you, considerin' she was blood and all and had you thinkin' she was a good auntie, but look at it this way, we just got revenge for both our fathers," Promise assured her partner in crime, looking back at the warehouse engulfed in flames as they rode off.

Chapter Twenty

After the Smoke Cleared

A month and a half had passed since Shad, Mark, and Promise had killed Shirley, but it was still the talk of Tampa.

Promise had been on about four different dates with clients who paid the big bucks. She treated herself to shopping sprees in Vegas, Chicago, Seattle, and Phoenix. Somewhere in there she found time to spend with Dezman, though he seemed to be acting kinda distant. Promise wrote it off, assuming he was just focusing on the game.

As she rested before work one day, her thoughts wondered to her mother. *I know by now she's probably heard about Shirley's murder. I better go visit her within the next couple of days and see what she thinks about it.*

* * *

Promise popped her pill 'cause she'd been quite on edge lately. She stood by the stage, waiting to do her set and go home. "Looks like a packed house tonight," she said to Mark.

"Yeah, this mu'fucka is packed, and it ain't even no special event going on," Mark responded.

"Do me a favor, Mark. After I do my set, I'm gonna leave. Can you escort me out? I'm not trying to be up in here all night dodging these rich snobs just to get out the door," Promise said.

"Fo' sho. I got you," Mark assured her.

With that, Promise started her way up the stairs to go onstage. She could feel Mark's eyes on her, his and everybody else's in the building.

Once her set was done, she headed to the dressing room. After counting her cash down to the dollar and taking out Tre's cut, She got dressed and prepared to leave. She expected to see Mark standing outside her dressing room door, waiting to escort her like he promised, but he wasn't there. *Damn! Can't depend on that fucka for nothing. He probably 'round here chasing some ass. Ugh! Guess I'll have to make it out by my damn self,* Promise thought.

She tried to go unnoticed, taking her time and not moving too fast, but going quick enough so nobody could stop her. She was dressed in a black Juicy Couture jogging suit with a hat to match and some all-black, low-top Forces; she'd thought the black ensemble would keep her low key, but that wasn't the case.

"Damn, girl! Let me get yo' number," a voice to the left of her said.

Promise tried to ignore him and keep it movin'. Shit, she was almost to the door.

Then she heard the same voice again, only this time it sounded more familiar. "Damn, ma. That's how you gon' do a nigga? Shit, I was just trying to ask you if you wanted to accompany me to the Bahamas, to Paradise Island to be exact!"

Promise stopped in her tracks and turned around. "Dezman?" she yelled. "Wh-what are you doing here?"

"Well, I came to surprise my baby with a trip, but seems to me you got other plans," Dezman said.

"I'm sorry, baby. I'm just tired of this club. I don't know how you knew I need a vacation, but I do."

"I told you a long time ago that you don't have to work in this place. Let me take care of you, Promise. I promise I'll never leave you or hurt you," Dezman said.

"I hear you, Dez, but my daddy promised me the same thing, and look where he's at," Promise said as a tear rolled down her cheek.

Dezman wiped it away right before it could drop. "That shit that happened with your daddy is awful, Promise, but he didn't mean to leave you like that. You have to trust me, Promise. Let me show you that I'm willing and able to take care of you, baby," Dezman said.

Promise wanted to believe Dezman, but she had been alone for so long that she'd grown used to it, and she wasn't ready to trust anybody's promises just yet. "Let's just get out of here," she said.

"No doubt," Dezman replied as he took her hand and led her out of the club.

* * *

Dezman popping up outta nowhere and surprising her with a trip was the highlight of Promise's week. Their trip wasn't scheduled till a couple weeks later, so she decided to go visit her mother's lawyer and see what progress had been made on her case.

"Hi, Promise," the front desk receptionist said pleasantly.

"Hey, Linda. Is William in today?" Promise asked, knowing he was a very busy man.

"Yes. He's actually finishing up a videoconference as we speak. Just have a seat. I'll let him know you're here."

Five minutes later, William came strolling out of his office. "Hey, Promise. I hope I didn't keep you waiting too long."

"It wasn't long at all. Besides, I didn't have an appointment or anything, so I gotta wait my turn."

"Okay. Well, follow me," he said, leading her back to his office. "I actually have your mother's file out already. Sorry I haven't been keeping you updated. I've been very busy. I want you to know I did go visit your mother. We talked about the case and what's to come in the future. Right now, I'm in the process of motioning the judge who sentenced your mother. I'm demanding a retrial on grounds that she didn't receive fair treatment in accordance with the law. Your mother's prior lawyer considered it an open—and-shut case and didn't do everything he could to help her," William said.

"How do you feel about my mother's chances of getting out?" Promise asked.

"The way I'm going about her case, I feel it's a strong possibility that she'll be released. When we take this back to trial, I'm going to focus on the fact that your mother was never read her Mirandas, not during the whole time she was in police custody. That, along with the fact that they didn't have a warrant to break into her property and take her like that, should get her off," William said. "There are protocols in place, and they ignored them. Promise, I wasn't going to tell you all this because I was afraid of getting your hopes up, but your mother told me she has always felt God would answer her prayer and bring the two of you back together outside those prison walls...and now I believe she may be right," William said.

"Oh my God! Thank you!" Promise jumped up ran around the desk and gave William a big hug. She could tell she'd startled him by the unprofessional reaction, but he received the hug in good spirits anyway. "You don't know how much this means to me, William!" Promise said as her eyes started to water, thinking back on the close-knit relationship she'd shared with her mother before that dreadful day. "Well, save those tears and make them tears of joy when Mrs. Brown is released," William said. "I believe that day is coming."

"This is the best news ever. I'm going to celebrate tonight. Thank you, William. Please keep me posted and let me know if there is anything you need," Promise yelled as she hightailed it out of his office, giddy as a kid on Christmas morning.

Chapter Twenty-One

Ready for the Bahamas!

All week, Promise kept busy, preparing for her romantic getaway with Dezman. She didn't spare any expense. She shopped at Dolce and Gabbana for a two-piece swimsuit, Ed Hardy for a multicolored one-piece with cut-out sides, and XOXO for a maxi-dress in all white, with gold accents. She also got some gold Giuseppe sandals, a Prada mini-skirt set that bitches would be breaking their necks to get a hold of, and some oversized Prada shades to set it off; the fly Prada sandals would have the chicks hating. She flopped down on her bed and smiled. In just one day, she'd be lying back on the sand in the Bahamas on Paradise Island, staring at the most beautiful crystal-clear blue water.

Promise wished Dezman could stay the night with her so they could go to the airport together, but for some reason, he couldn't get to Tampa International Airport until two hours before their flight was set to take off. She knew in his line of work, he'd never want to settle down. After all, he was a star athlete. When Dezman had first started bring up conversations about them becoming an exclusive couple and her quitting the business, Promise had thought it was the sex that had him talkin' like that, seeing as though she was putting it on him hard, but then the conversation started to come up more frequently, and she actually started considering it. *Maybe this trip will confirm whether or not we should be exclusive, she thought. We haven't spent more than two days at a time around each other, so this oughtta help clear some things up.*

Running late, as always (she was never a morning person), she continued to hit snooze on the alarm clock, only to wake up with an hour left to get to the airport, go through security, and meet up with Dezman. She sped through the city and made it to the airport in record time. Fortunately, airport security wasn't too much of a hassle, and with barely ten minutes to spare, she spotted Dezman with his back facing her at their departure gate.

He was dressed like he was going to the gym in a white V-neck t-shirt and the Celtics signature green and white basketball shorts with all-white Jordan slides and socks. Seeing his tall, well-defined structure moistened the place between her legs. "I hope it's not anyone special who has you standing up here waiting on them," Promise teased, breathing the words into his ear from behind.

"Yeah, the person is special—so damn special she can never be on time," Dezman teased back, smiling as he turned around to face his sexy traveling companion.

"Let's go get on this flight, smart-ass," Promise said.

* * *

Once their flight landed, they wasted no time checking into their very own private villa on Paradise Island.

Although they were exhausted with jetlag, Promise really wanted to do something; they could rest when they returned to the States. "Baby, since were kinda jetlagged, let's just do the boat ride," Promise pleaded, looking at the brochure. "It only takes a couple hours."

"If that's what you want, let's make it happen," Dezman said.

"Let's shower together so we don't have to waste any time. I don't wanna miss the boat. Says here that it leaves in two hours," Promise said.

"Hey, that's what I'm talkin' 'bout!" Dezman said with a sinister grin, rubbing his hands together.

"Un-uh, mister. Don't try nothing slick. Just a shower and were out of here. Don't get any slick ideas," Promise said already knowing what Dezman was thinking.

"Come on, Promise! I been missing you, girl," Dezman said in an almost begging tone.

The sound of his pleading made her pussy wake up. She had to control herself, 'cause she knew if she didn't, they'd be held up in the villa fuckin' each other mercifully all weekend. "I'm sticking to my guns. Just a shower, and then we out," Promise said as she stepped in the shower. She was glad for the luxury of a clear glass, wide shower with two showerheads and six sprinklers; if they'd have been confined to a smaller space, it would've been on, because they could barely keep their hands off each other. *Just don't pay him any attention, and we'll be in and out,* Promise thought. After showering and getting dressed in one of her many swimsuits that she'd packed, she was ready to head out.

"Damn, baby. All that for me? I feel like you're teasing me. You can't go puttin' something like that on and expect my hands to remain by sides. You'll just have to please excuse my hands," Dezman said.

The boat was a huge exclusive, reserved for the island's most exclusive visitors. With a glass of champagne in hand, Promise sat back to enjoy the long, peaceful ride. Lord knew she needed to clear her head and ease the stress she couldn't keep from building up.

She came to find out something unexpected about Dezman: The man loved to fish. He hooked up with a fellow basketball player, a New York Knick, and they fished for the whole duration of the boat ride. Then, Promise and the basketball player's wife, Nicole, spent the ride lying back and putting their pretty little manicured feet up.

"Dez, I'm hungry as hell," she announced as they made their way back to their villa.

"Shit. I thought fo' sho you could hear my stomach talkin' to my back," he replied with a chuckle. "How 'bout I set it up so we can eat the fish I didn't give away tonight?" Dezman said.

"Mmm. Sounds good. Let me hurry up and get ready to go," Promise said.

Once she was done freshening up and changing, she admired her overall look. The Emilio Pucci orange sparkly jumpsuit fit like it was tailor made just for her. The copper earrings and Brian Atwood copper sandals set the look on fire.

Dezman must have wanted to one-up her, 'cause he didn't disappoint with a white LRG button-down, crisp distressed jeans, butter pecan Timberland boots, and a platinum Presidential Role watch.

"Bay, the food was delicious. I've never had Bahamian food before, but I guess there're a lot of things I've never had that you're showing and giving me," Promise said with the widest smile.

"We've experienced something new together then, ma, 'cause I ain't never had no Bahamian food either. Dude on the boat told me we should try it. Anyway, that's what I been trying to tell you for the longest. I'm willing to show you things you've never experienced, Promise. You just gotta roll with me and me only," Dezman said.

Promise changed the subject. She really wasn't ready to go down that road and have that conversation right then. "If we weren't so tired, we could dance the night away under the clear, starlit sky but for now, just hold me, Dez," Promise said as she drifted off to sleep.

Dezman held her tight until he finally drifted off to sleep himself, dreaming of a future with Promise.

* * *

Promise woke up amped and rejuvenated ready for whatever the day's adventure would be. To her surprise, Dezman wasn't in bed. When she got out of the shower, she heard the door closing. "Dez, baby, is that you?" Promise asked, wondering where he'd been.

"Yeah, baby cakes. Who else?"

Promise smiled; she loved it when he called her that, and he knew it. "Where have you been?" Promise asked as she walked up to him and gave him a peck on his full, succulent lips.

"I went to check on the different exploring adventures Paradise Island offers. I think we should do Dolphin Cay," Dezman said.

"The dolphins are just going to be swimming around and we watch?" Promise asked

"Watch? Naw, baby. We're going to swim *with* the dolphins, watch them do tricks, and learn more about them. Now, just hush up and put on one of those sexy-ass bikinis so we can go," Dezman replied.

When they arrived at Dolphin Cay, Promise grew even more excited when they walked up and saw a trainer in the water, swimming alongside two beautiful dolphins. The creatures swam by her and flapped a fin up and down like they were waving hello, then swam away. *Oh, that's too cute,* Promise thought.

After they'd been in the water with the dolphins for well over an hour, hunger was starting to set in. "I'm hungry. Let's go grab something to eat," Dezman said.

"I'm down with that," Promise said.

"Rebecca, thank you for showing us a great time. I look at dolphins in a totally different light now," Dezman said to the trainer, who'd been shamelessly eyeing the pro ball player since they'd gotten into the water with her.

"Mr. Turner, would you like to go on a behind- the-scenes tour before you go get something to eat? I can take you and your *friend* to see where we feed the sea lions. You can see all of our dolphins and everything," she offered, flicking her wet lashes at him.

Promise wasn't a jealous woman, and she sure as hell could admit when another woman was beautiful; Rebecca was just that.

"Yeah. Shit, we can eat later. Fo' sho! I want every experience I can get while we're here. It's not every day I get to do things like this," Dezman said, smiling at the sexy trainer.

Promise stood there bewildered. *Oh, no this bitch didn't call me his "friend," like I'm just some pathetic groupie or jump-off.* Even though she wasn't usually the jealous type, it was starting to get to her, and she couldn't keep her mouth shut about it. "Hey, Rebecca, that's sweet of you and all, but next time you mention me, remember that I'm not just his friend. You gotta look at what position I'm in and remember your own," Promise said as she emerged from the water. "Now, show us the way," Promise said. She could feel Rebecca burning a hole in her back, but she didn't give a damn. She had to call the bitch out on that shit, and she was pissed as hell that Dezman hadn't even bothered to correct her himself. Still, she had to wonder why she cared so much. *Why the fuck am I so mad? Promise wondered. Is it because I really don't know my title with him? Am I a friend, girlfriend, jump-off? Is it because we're just friends but I want us to be more? But I know my job—and his—would hinder us from really being together.* Her thoughts consumed her the entire time they were on Rebecca's behind-the-scenes tour.

* * *

Yesterday had been an eventful day. After they'd finished the tour, they'd decided to try out the jet skis and banana boat, and it had been great fun. The night had been even better though, since they'd fucked each other's brains out and tried to suck every ounce of moisture from each other.

All Promise wanted to do now was to lie out and lounge by the pool, to be tranquilized by the waterfall, and maybe even get a full-body massage while she and Dezman really got to know each other. "Dez, let's just chill out by the pool today," Promise said.

"All right. That's fine, honey. Whatever you want," Dezman replied.

Promise smiled, knowing he meant it honestly.

* * *

On their fourth and last full day and night in the Bahamas, they decided to make it all about them. Promise got a mani/pedi, and then it was off to their romantic, candlelit boat ride.

It started off wonderful, and looking up at the moon and stars, she felt a peace come over her that told her everything would be okay. When the boat stopped and they began to float on the still water, Dez came over with a bottle of Moët and two flutes. Promise enjoyed the slow jams serenading her all the while, and they ended the night with a very intimate, romantic dinner at Nobu.

While she drifted off to sleep, she wholeheartedly thought about her relationship with Dezman. *He just has so much going, so many good things, and I don't want my lifestyle to mess up his reputation. There are already rumors circulating about us and whether we're a couple or not,* Promise thought. *I don't want to fuck up his career...or his life.*

Chapter Twenty-Two

A Bun in the Oven? Are You Sure?

Not again, Promise thought, sick of being nauseated, puking, and tired. She hadn't been able to sleep well since about two months after their trip to the Bahamas, and it was getting on her nerves. *What the hell is wrong with me?* she wondered; she hadn't even noticed that her eating habits had changed and she'd gained a few pounds. Although she couldn't remember her last period, she knew fo' sho she couldn't be pregnant. *I'm always careful,* she consoled herself.

She and Dezman had seen each other a couple times since their trip, but they hadn't talked much on the phone 'cause he was really busy. That sucked, 'cause Promise really wanted to let him know about how she'd been feeling.

Lord knew she hated doctors, but the way she'd been feeling lately, she knew she'd have to make an appointment—right after she stopped by Walgreens to pick up a pregnancy test. After she picked up the test, she called Tre to let him know she wouldn't going in to work that night. She knew he was getting pissed off at her; it wasn't her first time calling off or telling him what clients she would and wouldn't take. She decided if he did start any shit with her, she'd just cut ties and go into business for herself. Shit, she was already thinking about it. She shook the thoughts out of her head for the time being, though, because she had bigger fish to fry.

Promise followed the instructions on the test. She sat on the edge of the tub, letting time tick by while she waited as per the instructions on the pink box. She began to stress out as she waited. She really couldn't see herself being anyone's mother. When she sat and took the time to think about it, she realized she was nothing more than a high-priced whore. Just as that nasty thought went through her mind, the timer on her cell phone went off.

She instinctively looked down at the test; two dark pink lines stared back at her. "Shit! Fuck my life!" Promise said out loud. She then grabbed the instructions from the box read them over and over again, looking back and forth from the little diagram to the results of her test several times before it finally sank in. *Oh my God. I'm...pregnant? I'm fucking pregnant!*

Promise didn't really have too many people to share her news with, so her decision to not inform anyone until she went to the doctor to make sure she was indeed pregnant was an easy one.

She also wanted to make sure the baby was developing well and healthy. She'd been doing things that might endanger the baby's health, like drinking and popping her happy pills every night at the club.

Clueless as to what being a mother entailed—especially since she'd lost her own at such a young age—she made sure to make preparations for a parenting and birthing classes.

On the day of her doctor's appointment, she was nervous, scared, and aggravated, all at the same time. Promise hadn't spoken to Dezman in damn near a month, and she knew he'd been busy, but even still, he couldn't have been so busy that he hadn't gotten any of her voicemails or text messages, and it was starting to piss her off that he was ignoring her. Still, she wanted to believe his promises, and she had it in her mind that Dezman wouldn't do her like that. *Shit, he's probably laid up with some groupie ho,* but just as quickly as the thought entered her head, she dismissed it. *Naw. There's no way would he do that.*

Promise signed in and waited the few minutes until the nurse called her name. She filled out all the necessary paperwork, she requested a female doctor. The nurse then led her to a room in the back of the office.

Five minutes later, the doctor knocked on the door. "Hi, Ms. Brown," greeted a short, petite, dark chocolate, nice-looking woman in a white lab coat and small-framed glasses. "My name is Dr. Rebecca Cain." She smiled a sweet smile that took away some of the nervous energy that was rapidly growing inside Promise.

Promise smiled and replied nervously, "Nice to meet you, Dr. Cain."

"Well, let's go ahead and get started. I see here on your chart that you took a home pregnancy test, and it came up positive?"

"Yes. Two pink lines."

"Okay. Just to be sure, we'll give you another test here today. If you are pregnant, we will need to do some blood work and a sonogram to make sure that little bun in your oven is cooking up just right, with no complications," Dr. Cain said with a light chuckle, laughing at her own joke.

"That's fine. I'm sorry. I'm just...well, I'm very nervous. I wasn't really expecting this," Promise admitted in a shaky voice.

"It's okay, sweetie. You've to nothing to be afraid of, and we're here to help," Dr. Cain said, touching her hand gently to make her feel more comfortable. "We're going to make sure everything is just fine. I see my nurse already has the test set up. Just urinate in this cup. I'll give you some privacy, and I'll be back in a couple of minutes."

After Promise's pregnancy test came back positive once again, they drew blood. Next, they asked her to lie on a table on her back, exposing her nearly flat stomach.

"This will be a little cold, but not for long," Dr. Cain said as she applied the gel substance.

When Promise looked at the screen and saw for the first time what was living inside her, all of the bad feelings she'd been harboring melted away. It was now all about that precious being growing inside her belly. As she lay there looking at it, she thought about the baby-daddy right away. *Dezman is gonna have to deal with this—with us—sooner or later. You don't just make me feel like you're in love with me, spend all this time and money on me—not that I ever needed his money—and write me off. You don't do that shit to nobody, especially not me,* Promise thought.

"Okay, Ms. Brown, you can go ahead and get redressed. I'll set up your next appointment for one month from today," Dr. Cain said.

"That'll be fine," Promise said.

As soon as Promise got in her car, she tried Dezman on his cell phone; again it rang four times and then went to voicemail. She really wanted to get in touch with him to let him know she was almost four months pregnant with his child, but it didn't seem right to tell him that on voicemail. "Ah!!" Promise screamed as she hit the steering wheel with the palm of her hand, frustrated as hell. *His time'll come. It's gonna be checkmate for him after I air his ass on this shit.*

Chapter Twenty-Three

Makeover

Tired of dwelling on what Dezman was doing and where he was, Promise decided to do something for herself. She ended up at GreenTree Full-Service Spa, a nice, upscale place. Promise went for the supreme package which included a full-body massage, mani/pedi, mud bath, full-body wrap, facial, and eyebrow wax. They even had different names for their massages, and of course she went for the pregnancy one, even though she wasn't sure what that meant she'd be getting.

Promise lay back in her mud bath, thinking about a makeover. Lately she'd been open to change in her life. *Maybe a cut and color would lift my spirits. I think that's just what I'll do tomorrow. I may not feel my sexiest, I can look my sexiest, even at five months pregnant.*

* * *

After the day of pampering, relaxing, and just propping her swollen feet and ankles up, they were back down to their regular size. Promise sported her Alexander McQueen booties into the 813 Sho' Stoppers Salon, about to get a makeover and a new outlook.

While she sat in the lobby, she looked through a couple celeb magazines, searching for a new hot look. The makeover took half the day, but she walked out looking like new money. Her hair was razor cut just above her shoulders, with a couple strands of honey-blonde highlights at the top.

Promise hated shopping for maternity clothes because the styles and patterns all seemed to be ugly and frumpy, but since she was already at the mall, she decided to go check out all the heels that had been released that week. She bought every single pair that she thought were stylish enough for her.

She stopped by her favorite fast food restaurant, Chick-Fil-A, and ordered a twelve-piece nuggets, large waffle fry, and an extra-large lemonade to wash it all down. Oh, and she couldn't forget the Polynesian and Chick-Fil-A sauce.

When Promise got done pigging out on the food, she got the "itis" and couldn't move, so she decided to catch some Z's before work.

* * *

Promise woke up from her nap feeling refreshed and pampered. She got up and got dressed to go to work. The first person she ran into there, at the front door, was Mark. "What's up, Mark? How's it looking in there?" Promise asked.

"It's packed, like always. Do you need an escort up to yo' office? I don't want anybody hassling you. By the way, I love the new look. It's tight," Mark replied.

"Thanks. I can handle my own, though, Mark," Promise said.

"I don' know. That stomach pretty big now. I just want you to be careful and take it easy," Mark said, genuinely concerned.

"I'll be fine. Lemme get on in here," Promise said and walked into the club toward the stairs that led to the dressing room which sat next to Tre's office. On her way down the hallway, she spotted Jelly exiting Tre's office. "Coming from Tre's office again, I see," Promise said accusingly.

"It ain't nothin' but a thang. I had something to discuss with him, not that it's any of your business anyway," Jelly said with much attitude in her tone.

I don' know what this bitch problem is, but she better get it together, Promise thought before speaking. "Bitch, you better be glad I'm pregnant," Promise said, rubbing her belly, "'cause I'da done whooped yo' ass for that slick-ass mouth of yours!" Promise yelled in Jelly's face.

"Yeah, whatever. Save all that. I gotta go get this money, you know, since I'm head bitch in charge and all."

"You do that, but remember this, Jelly. You won't have that spot for long, so enjoy it while you can," Promise replied and walked off. "You're dismissed!" Promise said over her shoulder, without even turning around. *Tre must be fuckin' that nasty bitch. I don't care about that shit, though, and I don't see what her beef is with me, but she got the right one,* Promise thought.

Chapter Twenty-Four

Seven Months Pregnant

Promise looked in the mirror, feeling fat. Although she was still beyond gorgeous, her skin was glowing and blemish free, but her belly was growing more and more every day. She'd finally found out she was going to have a girl, and she just couldn't wait to spoil her to no end. Promise dreamt about how their relationship would be. She knew she would shower her little girl with plenty of love and kisses.

She hadn't heard from Dezman in nearly three months, and she was well beyond pissed about that. She was all good, though, 'cause she had a plan to fix his ass. She'd booked a flight to Boston, and it was set to leave in a few days. Promise had read in a blog magazine that he'd been spotted a couple places with a mystery woman on his arm, and the press speculated it was his new bitch. Promise was going to be sure to nip that shit in the bud.

Promise and her mother's attorney had been back and forth on the phone. He was working hard on her mother's case to make sure the defense wouldn't find any loopholes in the case he'd be presenting. William had arranged a trial for two months later.

Her mother called her at least three times a week, and they were in the process of getting to know each other again. Sweet Pea told Promise she finally felt like she had a reason to live. Promise was glad her mother never brought up Shirley during their conversations, but she knew that talk was coming sooner or later.

Since Promise hadn't been able to go on any dates with her clients or dance at the club, she kept the books updated, serving as the Sweet Spot accountant and making sure all the bills got paid and liquor refills got ordered and shipped. She even changed the theme of the club every now and then and made sure there was a hot celebrity host at least twice a week. Although she had plenty of money in the bank, Promise thought it would be a good to keep a steady cash flow coming in. *I'm not getting paid nearly as much as I was dancing and going out on dates, but this office shit will keep me busy so I'm not obsessing about hunting*

Dezman's ass down and giving him the business, Promise thought as she put in a shipment order for a couple boxes of Ciroc.

Tre and Shad had been blown when she came to them with the news of her pregnancy. Tre was more pissed than anything; he was worried about his money being fucked up, "cut short," as he put it. There was nothing he could do about it, though, because Promise was going to have her baby, regardless of how he felt. Jelly had been overjoyed to hear it, thinking it would mean it was her time to be on top, if even only for a little while.

Promise had even kicked her little addiction to her happy pills. After all, her daughter's health was way more important than the feeling X gave her. She also started spending a little time with a nice girl named Monica, who'd she met in one of the parenting classes. They were around the same age, though Monica, at twenty, was further along in her pregnancy and was ready to have her baby any day. Unlike Promise, Monica had been devastated with the news that she was pregnant. She flat out didn't want her baby. Promise remembered one of their conversations one day after a parenting class, when they went to lunch and Monica told her, "A baby can't do nothing for me but slow me down or ruin my life. I only got one life to live, and I ain't tryin'a spend it with some cryin', shitty baby." Promise never understood that, because to her, pregnancy was beautiful thing. Because of the little silly things that came out of Monica's mouth, she kept their time chillin' and hanging out at a minimum.

Promise didn't tell Monica much about her situation. She did mention that the baby-daddy was a professional NBA basketball player, but she kept the small details to herself, like the daddy's name.

"Well, girl, my flight leaves in a little while, so I need to eat a little faster," Promise said while they sat and ate at a sandwich shop near the Tampa International Airport.

"I don' know why you won't let me go with you so I can snag me a ball player," Monica said.

Promise rolled her eyes discreetly. "Girl, you're big and pregnant. How you gonna get a baller lookin' like you got a damn basketball stuffed down your shirt yourself?" Promise couldn't deny the fact that Monica was a very pretty girl, but she looked like she might pop any minute. Monica had had a rough life, but her beauty was undeniable. Promise was sure in her pregnancy-free days, she coulda charmed the wallet right out of any man's pockets. But she couldn't take Monica with her, because Promise was on a mission, and she didn't have time for the extra baggage.

Promise's doctor had already advised her she shouldn't fly at that late stage in her pregnancy, but fuck it, she had waited long enough. It was time to go find the no-good mu'fucka. She didn't know if her mother would be out by the time the baby came, and she didn't want to go through the birthing process alone. That scared her more than anything.

Chapter Twenty-Five

On a Mission to Find Her Baby-Daddy

During her whole flight to Boston, she had nothing on her mind but finding Dezman and giving him a piece of her mind. He still didn't know she was pregnant, so she knew he'd be shocked fo' sho, feeling like an ass for not being with her or helping her through it. He hadn't even been there to help her pick out clothes, shoes, or anything else their little girl was going to need. There wasn't an explanation or an excuse for his absence; he had basically just cut her off without so much as a goodbye, and that pissed her off more than anything, especially after all those promises he'd made, begging her to trust him.

She arranged to rent a car so she could get around Boston. She hadn't been to Dezman's house in a while, but she still remembered the address, so she put it in the GPS and let it lead the way there.

When Promise made a left onto Dezman's street, she noticed a nice-ass, candy apple-red Seven Series BMW. Even though the windows were tinted, there was something familiar about the driver's side profile. As Promise passed by the car, the woman paid her no attention; she was too busy on her cell phone. Promise was glad about that, or the driver would have surely noticed her staring hard at her.

Promise looked in her rearview mirror as the car prepared to make a left and exit the private estate neighborhood. She noticed the license plate: *"SO ICY"* and that was when it clicked in her mind. *Black Ice?* It had been so long since she'd seen her, so she thought she might be mistaken. *Naw, that couldn't have been her. What are the chances I'd run into that thieving bitch in Boston, on Dezman's street?* Promise shook the thought out of her head and pulled into Dezman's driveway to park.

There was another car parked there, but Dezman had plenty of cars. She hadn't bothered to call him for nearly two months, and when she'd tried to call him before she left Tampa, she was met with an automated message, "The caller you are trying to reach has changed their number. Message 09578." Promise was fuming mad about that. The mu'fucka didn't even give a damn about hearing from her and even went so far as to change his number so he wouldn't have to. *It's really on now, bitch-ass nigga,* Promise seethed. Dezman had let the perks of the NBA go to his head, and she was sure the girls, glitz, and glam had his ass going nuts.

She got out of the car, took a deep breath, and rang the doorbell. She covered the peephole and waited, but there was only silence. So she started to knock on the door, softly at first, but then she found herself banging and kicking on it in a rage. She even yelled his name. When there was still no answer, she realized no one was home.

Promise turned toward the rental car and noticed one of his neighbor's staring at her like she was a mad woman; he had a phone in his hand like he might call the police. She had to check herself, 'cause she knew she looked crazy, pregnant and acting all ghetto in that nice neighborhood of fancy estates. She was dressed like she belonged there, though, in her white Jessica Simpson one-shoulder ruffle dress that really showcased her stomach, with orange, ruffled fringe pumps that were so comfortable that they didn't bother her slightly swollen ankles and feet.

She sat in Dezman's driveway contemplating what she should do next. "Fuck it," Promise said as she punched the steering wheel. In the end, she decided to stay the night in Boston, and she made a trip to the nearby five-star hotel.

* * *

The next day, Promise woke up with the same thing on her mind: *I gotta find this scum-ass bastard wjo calls himself a man.*

Back in front of Dezman's estate, she noticed the same car in the driveway. She got out of the rental car and rang the doorbell. She waited a few minutes nothing happened. This time, instead of showing her ass, she decided to shake off the anger that was slowly rising within her, but that wasn't an easy task for Promise. *This mu'fucka wants to play games? Well, two can play this game.*

Promise sat in Dezman's driveway for four hours. Every time a car turned on the roundabout, she hoped it would be his, but none of them were. Pissed and stressed beyond belief, the pregnant Promise decided to take her frustrations out by picking up a brick and hauling it right through the front bay window of his place. That wasn't enough though; she needed to feel like she'd come for a purpose and not just a waste of time, so she walked all around the front of the place, bashing all the windows with bricks.

Finally, after she felt like she had blown off some steam, she sucked it up and headed to the airport; it was time for her to head home. It wouldn't be her last trip to Boston, though, and she hoped Dezman's nosey neighbor would give him the message loud and clear. After all, she had a life growing inside of her, and she would deal with the maker of that life sooner or later.

Chapter Twenty-Six

Court's in Session!

Taniqua's trial had been set for the day after Promise's final doctor's appointment. Promise had been trying to control her anger and stress level, but it was becoming unbearable. The only hope she'd held onto that could relieve her stress was her mother being released from prison after being locked up for almost ten years.

The next day, Promise woke up like any other, only way ahead of schedule. She took a shower and got dressed, watching the time carefully. She needed her mother to know that even if there wasn't anyone else in her corner, she was there for her, so she hurried to the courthouse. There, she walked in the courtroom and noticed that it wasn't packed; that was a good thing, as far as she was concerned. She did notice a couple around-the-way chicks and a few corner boys sitting discreetly in the back of the courtroom. Promise took a seat right behind William Spenser, who turned and gave her a reassuring nod and a genuine smile. At that same time, she noticed her mother being escorted in from the holding cell.

Sweet Pea looked different from the last time Promise had seen her; this time, her hair was out, not in those cornrows. It was pulled straight back, stopping at the middle of her back. Her hair looked healthier, and her face looked calmer than before.

She smiled weakly at Promise, who mouthed, *"I love you."* Taniqua winked and mouthed the words back to her daughter.

"All rise! The honorable Judge Michelle Fuller presiding in the matter of Spenser William vs. the State of Florida!" the bailiff said.

Judge Fuller banged her gavel. "Defense, are you ready to submit your case? If so, you may begin."

On cue, Mr. Spenser began, "Back on April 16, 1994, my client, Taniqua Brown, had her door kicked in by federal agents. Her husband was shot and killed in the process of trying to protect their ten-year-old daughter from witnessing what was going on. The feds were initially there to arrest Dontae Brown, but they never presented an arrest warrant. After Mr. Brown was shot and killed and Promise Brown was removed by DCF, the agents took my client into custody and questioned her for hours. She asked for a warrant—or at least a reason why they had barged into her house—but she was given no answers. She then asked for a lawyer, telling them she was overwhelmed. That was understandable, considering she'd just witnessed her husband being shot to death and her daughter being taken away. The officers then waited some time before awarding her a phone call to her lawyer. Something transpired between her and her lawyer, and eventually, he did not see it fitting to provide her with any deserved defense, as per his duty, thus prompting the prosecution to have their way with her. The only crime my client committed was being in love and marrying a man who was involved in illegal activities, but she had no reclamations of them. As far as she was concerned, her husband was a construction worker. He even had the proper uniform. My opinion on this case is that they couldn't get to the man they originally wanted, so they went after his wife. In closing, the case against Taniqua Brown should be thrown out. The officers and agents did not have a warrant that gave them the right to enter my client's apartment, nor did they follow legal arrest protocol and read her the Miranda rights," William said in a self-assured, winning tone before he took his seat next to Taniqua.

The judge looked over some documents and shook her head, which made Promise nervous; she'd thought William argued a good case. With furrowed brows she raised her head and looked over the courtroom spectators and said, "Mrs. Brown has been in prison for almost ten years, and her original attorney failed to file an appeal. I find that quite unsettling. Mr. Spenser you just became her lawyer and found this out in less than six months. Mrs. Brown, you owe this man your life. Mr. Spenser, you've submitted the interrogation tapes, and what you said supports the evidence. Therefore, I have no other choice but to throw out Mrs. Brown's sentencing and request she be released from custody immediately. Although I was not the judge at the time of her original trial, I feel a civil duty to apologize on behalf of this court and the justice it attempts to serve." Then she banged her gavel to make it final.

Promise jumped out of her seat with lightning speed, jumping up and down screaming, "Thank you Lord! Oh God, thank you!" forgetting that she was very pregnant. A sharp pain ripped through her midsection. She doubled over in pain, clutching her stomach.

Her mother ran to her side seeing the pain displayed on her daughter's face.

"Ma, I think I…I think I peed on myself," Promise said, totally forgetting what the doctor and birthing classes had taught her.

"What, baby? Are you okay?" Taniqua looked down and examined the liquid running on the floor, "Oh no! She's in labor. Call 911! Somebody call 911! She's eight and a half months pregnant. It's going to be okay, Promise. Just hang in there."

And that was the last thing Promise heard before blacking out.

G STREET CHRONICLES
A NEW URBAN DYNASTY

WWW.GSTREETCHRONICLES.COM

Epilogue

Seven months passed. Promise had been keeping to herself, spending a lot of time in her new home with her mother and her healthy, beautiful daughter, Deziray Sweet Pea Brown.

A month into having her daughter home Promise started receiving anonymous letters in the mail. Someone knew what she and Shad had done to Shirley and they were threatening to expose it all. Things were really starting to get weird.

At the trial, she was so overwhelmed by her mother's verdict that her water broke. She fainted and was rushed to Tampa General Hospital. After being in labor for nine hours and finding out she was severely Anemic. Promise gave birth to a five-pound, eight-ounce healthy baby girl.

Once she got home, Promise rested for two months. She wanted to get back to work and her money—making mission. Although she was sitting on a good amount of money that wasn't enough for her she, wanted to be able to take care of her mother and daughter so they wouldn't have to want for anything ever. She used her mother and daughter as her excuse to get back to work, but in reality she'd become money hungry.Once she got home, Promise rested for two months. She wanted to get back to work and her money-making mission.

Promise got a gym membership and hired a personal trainer. Within five months, she lost all her baby weight and was back in tiptop shape. Trying to find out who this anonymous person sending her at least one letter a month would be harder than she thought. She sat down and thought it over time and time again about who it could possibly be. Who would actually take the time out to worry about her life? This issue wasn't at the top of her list though.

Her first order of business would be going down to the club to take her spot back as head bitch in charge. She'd heard through Mark that Jelly was now head bitch and Tre's main mistress. *That won't last long, 'cause the queen is back! Maybe leaving Tampa for a while won't be such a bad idea. Hopefully the letter stop,* Promise thought as she got onto the next order of business heading to Boston for a couple months, maybe even hiring a private investigator. Since her baby-daddy wouldn't come to her willingly, she would go to him forcefully… and this time she would get answers.

The Saga Continues in the Sequel
Black Ice: So We Meet Again!

BLACK ICE...
SO WE MEET AGAIN

G
STREET CHRONICLES

I would like to dedicate this book to all of my supporters..

I appreciate y'all I do!!

Prologue

Seven months had passed and Promise had been keeping to herself, spending a lot of time in her new home with her mother and her beautiful, healthy daughter, Deziray Sweet Pea Brown.

At the trial, she'd been so overwhelmed by her mother's verdict that her water had broken right then and there. She'd fainted and had been rushed to Tampa General Hospital. After being in labor for nine hours and finding out she was severely anemic, Promise had finally given birth to a five-pound, eight-ounce healthy baby girl.

Once she got home, Promise took a couple of months to get herself back to normal, feeling eager to get back to work and her money-making mission. Although she was sitting on a good amount of money, that wasn't enough for her. She wanted to be able to take care of her mother and daughter so they wouldn't ever have to want for anything. She used her mother and daughter as her excuse to get back to work, but in reality, Promise had become money hungry.

A month into having her daughter home, Promise started receiving anonymous letters in the mail. Someone knew what she, Shad and Mark had done to Shirley, and they were threatening to expose it all—things were really starting to get weird. Trying to find out who was behind the anonymous letters was proving to be more difficult than she'd thought. Time and time again, she'd sat down to think it over. *Who it could possibly be? Who would actually take the time out to worry about my life?* Still, this issue wasn't at the top of her list. Promise had other things on her mind.

She realized that her pregnancy definitely had an impact on her body so to get her shape back, Promise purchased a gym membership and hired a personal trainer. Within five months, she'd lost all her baby weight and was back in tiptop shape.

Her first order of business would be to go down to the club and shake some shit up. She'd heard through Mark that Jelly had stepped up into the head-bitch-in-charge. *That won't last long, 'cause the queen is going to be officially back real soon!*

Her thoughts drifted to her plans of heading to Boston for a couple of months. Hiring a private investigator may not be a bad idea since her baby-daddy wouldn't come to her willingly. She'll just go to him forcefully…and this time she'll get her answers. *Maybe after I leave Tampa for a while, the letters will stop,* Promise thought as she began to again think about hiring that investigator.

Chapter One

Welcome to Boston!

"Ma, I'll be calling twenty times a day, and remember there's always LooVoo and Skype. We can do that once every other day. Money isn't an issue, so whatever you or Deziray need, just get it. I don't know how long I'll be gone, but I'll send for you guys at least twice a month. I have to have my two favorite girls around!" Promise said as she exited the car at Tampa International Airport.

"Love you, ma. Keep my baby safe," Promise said, leaning down to kiss Deziray on the cheek. "Mommy loves her little princess. Be good for Granny."

"What have I told you about calling me that? I'm too young to be called Granny. Deziray will be fine. My concern right now is you. Be safe up there. Don't get yourself in any trouble searching for that damn man."

"Monica, you watch out for my baby," Sweet Pea demanded, looking serious as a heart attack.

"Don't worry. I got her. We're good," Monica assured.

"Monica, grab ya luggage. We're about to do the damn thing," she said, strutting to the trunk of the car, dressed to impress in her True Religion fitted jeans and high-low tunic top with red-bottom heels.

Since she'd had her daughter, she and Monica had grown kind of close. Even though Monica had given up her adorable son at birth, it didn't seem to bother her to be around Deziray.

* * *

After touching down in Boston, Promise felt refreshed and didn't want to waste any time. She was ready to hit the town for the night. "Girl, I have an investigator helping me on this search for Dezman. Why don't we just take a week to ourselves, let loose and party?" Promise suggested.

"You don't know how happy I am to hear you say that. I could use a week to just party and bullshit with some sexy men with long pockets," Monica said.

"Bitch, I thought I was a money-lover! Damn, you beat me. I think a new environment would definitely bring new clients and more money. You down? I'm only asking 'cause I'm all about my coins," Promise said.

"Of course I'm down! I'm about mine too," Monica replied.

"Well let's drop these bags off at the hotel, go shopping, and find out what's popping for tonight," Promise said.

* * *

"Okay, so what did you decide our plans are for tonight?" Monica asked, watching Promise peel off her clothes, leaving a trail through their suite.

"I heard that hot new rapper Rare Breed is supposed to be at a club called The Estate tonight," Promise responded as she stepped into a hot, steamy shower.

"Is that the one who just signed with Young Gunnas record label?" Monica asked as she walked into the bathroom and took notice of Promise's silhouette through the fogged-up glass shower door. *Damn! Look at that body of hers. Promise is...amazing. Since I started hanging with this girl on a regular basis, I've been having these feelings—sometimes these urges to touch or even kiss her. What's going on with me?* Monica thought.

"Yeah, that's him, chile. And that means we need to step out dressed to impress. So what are you gonna wear? The bebe bandage red dress or that violet Louis Vuitton one-shoulder fitted number that I love?" Promise asked.

"You'll see," Monica teased, leaving Promise to finish her shower.

* * *

"Girl, this line is hella long. I knew we should've gotten here earlier," Monica whined.

"Oh, shut the fuck up and quit your whining. I swear, sometimes you act younger than me. If you weren't so cute, I wouldn't hang with yo' ass. Now come on and watch me work," Promise said, twisting to the front of the line.

She really thinks her shit don't stank, Monica thought, *with her sexy ass.*

"Hey, baby. Don't you wanna take those strong arms of yours and move this rope so my girl and me can come in and liven up this party?" Promise said with a smirk and a wink at Monica.

"Actually, I don't want to do anything but my job. Just 'cause you're fine doesn't mean I'm going to give you any special privileges, unless there's something in it for me. By the look on your face, there isn't, so allow me to show you the end of the line," the doorman said.

"What, nigga? I'm not—" But that was all Promise could blurt out before being interrupted by a deep voice.

"These two ladies are with me," the mystery man told the doorman. "Eh, Truth, have the hostess deliver a couple bottles of Cîroc and whatever they're drinking to the VIP area," he said before he disappeared inside the club.

"Next time, do as I say like a good boy," Promise said, belittling the doorman as she entered the club.

"What will y'all be drinking tonight?" the mystery man asked.

"A bottle of Rémy Martin will be fine. We'll be on the dance floor. You can have the hostess send it to our reserved table. Thank you, hon,'" Promise said, walking off.

"What are you doing? I'm ready to party with whoever that was. Shit, I wish he didn't have his brim pulled down low…I wanted to see his eyes," Monica said.

"There you go again. You've gotta stop with the desperate act. Running behind some man just because he got us in the club is not how I roll," Promise replied.

"Well excuse me, Miss Too Good for Everything," Monica said, aggravated. *First night here, and I've already had it with her better-than-thou attitude. Damn! She never used to act like this,* Monica thought.

The night went on with drinks flowing continuously, and the girls occupying space on the dance floor for the majority of the night, catching the attention of every man in the building with their vivacious movements and gyrations.

"Here comes the waitress with another order of drinks. I wonder what nigga these are from," Monica said, louder than needed.

"Probably from some desperate dude with dirty thoughts running through his mind," Promise retorted.

"I don't give a damn who they're from. I haven't had to pay for a drink all night, so he and all the other niggas up in this bitch can continue having all the dirty thoughts they want," Monica replied, laughing.

"Here's a glass of Moët for you and a blue Long Island Ice Tea for you, courtesy of the man in the red sweater, sitting at the bar," the waitress said.

"Bitch, my trip is going to be shorter than I expected. That looks like my no-good-ass baby-daddy sitting next to the nigga who sent us these drinks," Promise said, motioning toward the bar.

"Eh-yo, li'l mama. My dude said he been checking for you all night. He at least thought you would have the courtesy to thank him for the kind gesture at the door, the bottle of Remy Martin, or something. Shit…anything," Truth said.

"Listen, right now isn't the best time. I'm trying to catch up to someone real quick," Promise said, trying to move past him and look around his six-four frame.

"You must be one of those ol' sadity-ass bitches!" Truth said, looking at Promise with a glimpse of disgust. *Why this nigga always going after these pretty boogie hoes?* he wondered.

"Listen, Truth, I don't know you, but don't come over here disrespecting my homegirl like that. Tell your homie thanks for the bottle and for getting us in the club," Monica said quickly, trying to defuse the heated situation.

Promise looked back over to the end of the bar and saw two empty seats. *Dang it. I know that was his ass. Where the fuck did he go?* She scanned the club but came up empty and didn't see Dezman anywhere in the sea of partiers. She glanced over at her friend and saw that she still had company. *Why the hell is he still standing there talking to Monica?*

"See, sweetie? That's all a nigga was asking for—a simple 'thank you.' Yo' homegirl acts like she's too good to do that. Oh, and I see you caught my name at the front door. What's yours?" Truth asked.

"Oh, how rude of me. My name is Monica," she replied, smiling.

Promise had about enough of the exchange between Monica and the stranger from the door. *I know these mu'fuckas ain't flirting.*

"Hey sexy. What's got your mind so occupied?" asked the deep-voiced man who'd gotten them in the club, catching her a little off guard.

"Look, I really don't have the time or the energy to deal with anyone right now," Promise all but screamed.

"Dang, ma! I don't know what nigga fucked ya night up, but you're too fine to be acting like that. Seriously."

Before Promise could respond, she noticed just how fine this man standing in front of her really was. As she stared at him, she realized he looked a little familiar. *Wait a minute. Could this be that hot new rapper Rare Breed? His hair is cut a little shorter, and he looks way taller than he does on the videos. Hmm...* Promise contemplated. "I've just been going through a lot lately and don't have time to chat it up with some no-good man who's only out to get between my legs," Promise replied, trying to take the easy route.

Whoa. This chick must not know who I am. Shit! I'm the hottest rapper in the game, Rare Breed thought. "How about you let me and my boy Truth take you and your girl out for a bite to eat? I mean, this club is cool and all, but I can't get to know you under this loud music. Y'all look like y'all have had enough to drink anyway," he said.

"I don't even know your name. I don't care how much we've had to drink, me and my girl ain't about to leave with niggas we don't know." Promise replied, knowing damn well she wouldn't mind leaving with him.

"You don't seem like just some around-the-way girl, although your attitude is showing me something different. I like that. My name is Mike, but err'body calls me Rare Breed."

So it is him. Oh yeah, I'm about to play this nigga. He only wants one thing anyway. What he don't know is that this pussy has a price, and it's very hefty, Promise thought. "Rare Breed, huh? Well, that's a unique name. I guess I wouldn't mind going to breakfast with you, since you don't look like a killer or anything. Let me see what my homegirl wants to do."

Monica and her stranger friend had made their way over to the bar and were immersed in deep conversation.

This bitch better not start no shit, 'cause Rare Breed wants to take me to breakfast, and I'm going...bottom line. He's so damn fine, a sexy thug. He looks like he's from the streets, but he's not the streets, Promise thought as she walked up on a very sexual conversation that she could hear going on between Monica and her new friend.

"I'm that dude. The way I lay this pipe in the bedroom will have you coming back for more and more," her male companion bragged.

"Nigga, this pussy is just like pure coke. It'll have you addicted," Monica flirted.

"Hey! I've heard enough. Before you two fuck each other unconscious on top of this bar, ya boy said he wants to go get something to eat. Are y'all down? 'Cause a sista girl is hungry," Promise announced, rubbing her flat stomach.

"Fo sho. I was just telling Monica that I'm so hungry I could eat her all the way up," he answered, winking at Monica.

"Truth, your ass is so crazy. I told you what this pussy will do to you. You really want that to happen?" Monica said, laughing uncontrollably, clearly drunk.

"I don't wanna hear all that from you freaks. Monica, bring yo' ass on. Truth, is it?"

"Yup."

"All right. We'll follow y'all in our car," Promise said, trying to hold Monica up.

"Aight, that's cool, ma."

Promise and Monica headed toward their car. "No more drinking for your ass. When we get to the restaurant, it'll be nothing but water and Sprite for you. Now let's go," Promise said, growing more and more aggravated by the minute.

"I'm good. Dang, girl! Stop tryin' to be my mother," Monica said, nearly fuming.

"I'm just looking out for you like always, that's all. Do you have your seatbelt on?"

"Yeah, my seatbelt is on. Shut up!"

"Damn. We should've gotten a limo for tonight. I'm really not up to driving. Where the hell are they anyway? It sure as hell don't take this long to pick up a car from valet parking," Promise stated, agitated. As soon as she finished complaining, he pulled along side of them in a convertible Lexus and beeped the horn so she could follow.

"You must like ol' boy, 'cause you're acting all different. What happened to the Promise from earlier? The one who wasn't even willing to thank that same dude for getting us in the club?" Monica said, checking her cell phone.

"Not that it's any of your business, but his name is Mike. And I never said I like him, so don't go assuming shit. I'm just hungry, and he offered to take me to breakfast, so it all works out," Promise replied, short and sweet. *She doesn't need to know that Mike's actually Rare Breed, and she damn sho don't need to know that I like him. I've been getting all types of weird vibes from her anyway. I wonder what she's going through. I don't know what it is, but I'll get to the bottom of it*, Promise thought as they rode the streets of the city.

"Yeah, right. Tell me anything," Monica replied, not believing a word of Promise's declaration. *That Mike sure is fine though—tall, with a brown sugar complexion, smooth skin, perfect straight, white teeth, a low fade, and just the right amount of muscles. Damn. He could be kin to that sexy-ass R&B singer Trey Songz. Truth is fine as well though, with his light skin, pearly whites, bald head, and that very muscular build. He could be twins with LL Cool J with those lips of his. Mmm...I'm sure he can eat a mean pussy*, Monica thought in bliss.

"Monica! What are you over there thinking about...all up in No Man's Land? I'm just talking and talking, and you haven't responded to anything I've said."

"My bad, girl. I'm just thinking 'bout that fine-ass Truth. Mmm, mmm, mmm...what I would do to him," Monica replied.

"Don't give that nigga too much attention. Unless he's breaking you off right, ain't no fucking going on tonight. Ain't shit free in this world, girl. You know that," Promise scolded.

"Damn, Mama. I thought you were dead, but yet you just keep reappearing," Monica said sarcastically.

"Whatever. I'm just trying to put you up on game. Don't be letting niggas get the pussy just 'cause they take you out to eat." She pulled into the parking lot. "Thank God we're finally here." Then she had a good look around. "What!? Those fools had us follow them all the way across town just to eat at Perkins? Let me see what time it is, 'cause I don't plan on staying out all night," Promise said as she applied a fresh coat of her favorite Mac lip gloss.

"Before we go inside, I want you to listen to me, Promise. You might not think it, but I am a smart woman. I can handle and take care of myself. I've been on my own in this crazy world, fending for myself for just as many years as you have," Monica stated.

"I'm just trying to look out for you, that's all," Promise replied.

"It's cool. No hard feelings. That pearl-white, drop-top with the mirror tint is nice. These mu'fuckas have to be working with some stacks. Their asses are probably drug dealers. But then again, when was the last time you saw a drug dealer with a Black Card? Aren't they hard to get? That nigga Truth paid for my drinks with one of those," Monica said as they exited the car.

"Yeah, I peeped the car out. It's hot. American Express Black Cards are kind of hard to come by. They don't just give them to anyone," Promise confirmed nonchalantly. The two friends looked at each other and smiled, then got out the car to meet the men who were walking toward their car.

"Sexy, are you ready to eat? I hope you're not one of those pick-at-ya-food types. I like a chick who don't mind grubbing. Although it may not look like it, I love to eat," Rare Breed said.

"Shit, *I* love to eat. Breakfast is my favorite, but seafood is my heart. There! Now you know something about me," Promise joked.

"Good to know, ma," Rare Breed replied with a grin. "I won't forget it." He took her hand and led her to the door of the restaurant.

Once inside they were seated and the waitress immediately took their orders. Everyone enjoyed their time together while they waited for their food. The good conversation flowed, but then the questions started.

"So where are y'all from? I only ask 'cause, judging from ya swag, it seems like y'all aren't from Boston," Monica said.

"You're right. We're from Atlanta, but we live in Miami, Florida right now," Rare Breed, replied, staring at Promise as he spoke. *Damn! This girl's beauty is truly undeniable. What I saw at the door of the club was real,* Rare Breed thought.

"Y'all live in Miami? What a coincidence! We live in Tampa, Florida," Monica all but screamed, far too excited.

"Is that so? Hmm. Sounds like this is the start of a long relationship," Truth said, smiling hungrily at Monica.

"I sure hope so," Rare Breed said, nodding his head up and down as he continued to look at Promise.

Breaking the flow of the conversation, the waitress showed up with the food.

"Now that's what I call quick," Rare Breed commented.

"I have to agree with you on that," Promise said, throwing him a little smile.

As soon as they began eating, Monica started up again, "So, Truth, what do you do in Miami?" Monica peeped the flustered expression on Promise's face.

Dang! Here she goes again. Why is she asking all these damn questions? Her ass is never this interested in knowing so much about a dude. All she usually wants to know is how long his pockets are, Promise thought, tired of the Twenty One Questions game.

"Me? Well, I'm a—" But Truth didn't get to finish his response.

Promise jumped up and screamed, "Hey! See that little thin, short, white guy with the wire-rimmed glasses? That mu'fucka has been taking pictures of us! " she seethed.

He pulled her in close to try to calm her so she wouldn't draw more attention to them. "They never quit, do they? I know it's their job, but damn! Can't I live my life?" Rare Breed said out of the blue. "My bad baby. Every since I signed that contract, people've been following me, taking pictures of me, coming up to me and asking questions. I don't want this shit. I just want to do me. I don't mind the fame but I hate not being able to do the normal things any more…there's always somebody pointing, staring or doing something," Rare Breed whispered in her ear, frustrated with the entire situation.

"Ra…er, Mike, let's just go. I've lost my appetite anyway," Promise said, almost letting the cat out of the bag by revealing his rap name in front of Monica.

"Are you sure, ma? I know you were hungry,"

"I'm sure," Promise said, grabbing her limited edition Michael Kors bag.

"Come back to my presidential suite with me. I can have breakfast delivered," Rare Breed offered.

"Nah. I think I'll just head back to my room and get some rest. I have a couple of things I need to take care of tomorrow," Promise said, though she wasn't planning on doing anything but shopping and for some reason, there was a part of her that wanted to go with him.

"What about tomorrow night then? Let me come through, scoop you up, and treat you like a queen," Rare Breed said not wanting to give up.

"I'll let you know by tomorrow afternoon if we can link up. Let me see your phone, and I'll give you my number. You can hit me up around 5:30, okay?" Promise said.

"Okay, that's cool. This is *your* number, right? I don't need you to be playin' a nigga. Like I told you, I'm not just any nigga. I'm *that* nigga!" Rare Breed said, wiping his mouth with a napkin.

"Just do what I said. It's my number, *that* nigga," Promise said mockingly.

"I'm going to have to put your ass in your place, 'cause that mouth of yours is something else. Truth, let's go," Rare Breed said as he walked out the door.

"Why is Mike always ordering you around, baby? Y'all are two totally different people," Monica said to Truth. Hell, you don't have to leave with him. You can come back to my suite with me," Monica tempted, oblivious to the fact that her invitation might have insulted the man.

Promise shook her head as she stood there listening to her girl dissolve into a chump.

"Fuck you mean he doesn't order me around? I'm my own person. I'll fuck with you later, ma. You just blew the fuck out of me," Truth said, heading toward the door.

"Wait! I didn't mean it that way. Truth? Truth! I know you hear me talking to you," Monica yelled after him but never got an answer.

"Girl, you've gotta do better. That's all I'm going to say," Promise replied, disgusted.

Chapter Two

It's Not My Fault Your Career Is Going Down the Drain

"Hey, baby, the wedding planner is meeting me downtown today. I'm gonna take your credit card and go shopping for my...I mean *our* wedding, okay?" Black Ice asked, removing the card from Dezman's wallet.

"Wedding? What fuckin' wedding? I'm losing endorsement deals left and right, and you think I'm worried about some million-dollar wedding? Girl, leave me be. I'm going back to sleep," Dezman snapped, flipping over in their California king bed.

"Your career is fine. I'm sure the testing center results were just a mistake. There weren't any enhancement drugs in your system, baby. Now I'll be back later," Black Ice assured him.

"Bitch, haven't you been listening to anything I've said in the last month and a half?" Dezman yelled.

"Of course I have. I've heard every word. All I'm saying is that you've gotta keep the faith. Later, babe," Black Ice said, sashaying out the front door, ready to shop till she dropped. *I'm sick and tired of being sick and tired of this nigga's shit,* she thought. *His whining is getting on my fuckin' nerves!*

* * *

"Jelly! Girl, have you landed yet?" Black Ice asked as soon as Jelly picked up the phone.

"Yeah. I'm just settling into my room. What's wrong with you? You sound pissed," Jelly asked, hearing the frustration in her voice.

"Girl, it's Dezman again. His attitude is getting worse, and on top of that, he has the nerve to act like I have to accept it or leave. All he does is eat, sleep, and shit all day. He went out with his former teammate the other night, but *we* haven't been out in two months."

"B.I., you can't leave. We have to stick to the plan. If you leave him now, all the hard undercover work we've put in will have been in vain. I don't know about you, but bitch, I'm tired of stripping and fucking all these niggas for a couple of stacks."

"I know girl but how does a big, strong man like that just lay around crying like a baby. He needs to be figuring shit out!"

" I heard that but still, you have to hang in there. Shit! I'm trying to be set for life. Tre's mad at me 'cause I told him I need some time off to get some important affairs in order. He almost had a damn heart attack. You know that ho Promise took extended time off. You'd think after the nine months she took off to squeeze out that bastard child that she'd be broke by now. We both know that little money Tre was paying her to be his personal accountant wasn't nearly as much as she was making dancing and escorting. Somehow, though, this bitch got enough money to take more time off," Jelly ranted.

"Hey, now, I called yo' ass to vent, and here you are venting to me. Did you ever find out what she was taking the extra time off for or where she went?" Black Ice asked.

"Nope, but I know she left her mother in charge of keeping her daughter."

"Did you at least find out where she went?"

"No, but I've already devised a plan to shake shit up at that household. You'd be surprised what a good pussy can make somebody do and say," Jelly said, laughing at the blueprint she'd mapped out to destroy Promise's life.

"I'm so glad we kept in contact after I left Sweet Spot. If we hadn't, I wouldn't have found out about my man of four years. That nigga swore up and down that he loved me and that I was the one he wanted to be with. He went as far as to say he wanted us to have kids but he wasn't ready for them just yet. Then he went and got that ho pregnant. On top of that, she had a girl—the fuckin' baby girl *I've* always dreamt of having. I had to fake a miscarriage just to get him to feel sorry enough for me to cut all ties with her ass. Whether she knew or didn't know isn't my concern. My concern is making sure she never has a good night's sleep again in her life," Black Ice raged.

"Well, damn, girl! Tell me how you really feel," Jelly joked.

"I'm glad you think this is a joke. Now go on and bring your ass down here so we can go shopping for tonight. We're hitting a club up somewhere. You got about three minutes. Oh yeah…call our source before we get started and find out where that little man-borrowing whore is," Black Ice yelled as she hung up and pulled up in front of Jelly's hotel.

Chapter Three

Who Could've Sent This?

"Promise, I told you everything has been fine. Deziray is still a happy baby, although I'm sure she misses her mommy," Sweet Pea said.

"Aw, I miss my love too. Were you able to set up the ooVoo and Skype so that we can chat live on video?" Promise asked, ready to see her baby girl.

"Yes, Mother. Is that what you want me to say? Remember I'm your mother—not the other way around, Promise. I'm handling your business and holding down your fort. Quit worrying so much, baby. It's not good for you," Sweet Pea replied.

"I know, Mom, and I trust you. It's just that, you know, Deziray is my first and only child so I want to make sure everything is right with her. And, hey, Ma, when you get the mail, please don't open anything other than the bills," Promise said sweetly.

"I don't want to be all up in your mail, chile. If it don't have my name on it, I'm not opening it," Sweet Pea said, clearly irritated.

"Okay, kiss Deziray for me and tell her I love her. I'll see y'all on ooVoo or Skype tomorrow," Promise replied, sensing her mother's irritation.

"Will do, baby. See you tomorrow. I love you," Sweet pea replied.

"I love you too."

* * *

"You want to go check the mailbox with Nana? I can't wait for you to really start moving those legs, getting around and talking to me in that sweet little angel voice of yours," Sweet Pea said, laughing as she picked Deziray up.

The baby cooed at her as they made their way down the driveway.

"I just checked this mailbox the other day, and now it's filled up again. Look at all these damn catalogs—D&G, Gucci, Louis Vuitton. I think my child, your mama, may be addicted to shopping. Hey, look! There's an envelope marked for

me! I wonder who it could be from. There's not even a return address. Hmm..."
She struggled to carry the mail and the baby. "Let's get you back inside. You're
getting heavy, Dez," Sweet Pea said, still carrying on a one-sided conversation
with her granddaughter and failing to notice the dark, unmarked car.

Whoever the driver was, he or she was watching her every move while the
woman thumbed through the mail with her one and only grandchild on her hip.

"Don't you start that crying, Deziray. Nana just changed you. You didn't
want your bottle, so you must be sleepy. What time is it anyway? Oh! It's 1:48,
definitely past your naptime. Let's go get some rest, and I'll tend to this mail
tomorrow," Sweet Pea said.

Chapter Four

Getting To Know the New Fella in Her Life

"You're finally up, huh? I tried to wake you up so you could go shopping with me, but you were out cold. Mike called. He wants to make up for our botched-up little date the other night, so we're hitting the town tonight," Promise said as she set her bags down on the couch in the living room of their suite. *Damn. I shouldn't lie to her. I'm glad the bitch was asleep, My day of shopping was much more enjoyable without her ass.*

"You know how I am after we stay out all night drinking. I can barely lift my head the next morning, but you always wake up with a burst of energy," Monica said. "Hey, that reminds me. Why would that man have been taking pictures of Mike anyway? And he called you? That's what's up! Where are y'all going tonight?" Monica asked. *Lucky bitch! Why the fuck hasn't Truth called me yet? Damn!*

"You're right in saying yo' ass can't handle your liquor. I don't know why that man was taking pictures of Mike or any of us. If you ask me, he seemed like he may have been some type of weirdo. I'm not sure where we're going tonight...he said he wants to surprise me. You haven't heard from Truth yet?" Promise asked, knowing she hadn't because Rare Breed told her Truth had no intentions of ever calling her.

"For your information, I *can* handle my liquor. I always just have to sleep it off. I guess you're right. It did look like ol' boy was taking pictures of all of us. As far as Truth, we've talked, but we ain't set up a second date yet. I guess he's still kinda pissed about my suggesting that Mike runs him," Monica lied through her teeth.

"Well, in that case, what are you going to do while I'm out tonight? I have no idea when I'll be getting back in," Promise said, going through her new purchases.

"I'm a grown woman, Promise, capable of entertaining myself. Maybe I'll find a little lounge to go to. I'll have a couple drinks and possibly find me a little friend until Truth steps his game up," Monica replied curtly.

"You should try calling Truth and apologizing. I'd rather know you're with him than some stranger in a place you know absolutely nothing about." Promise noticed Monica's scowl and assumed she had gone too far. "Just be safe please," Promise said as she headed to her room to prepare for her date.

Yeah, I'll be safe, but one of these Boston niggas with money will definitely be fucking my brains out tonight. I want this nigga, whoever he may be, to knock all my lights out, Monica thought as a wide smile spread across her face. *She may try to be little miss proper but the bitch in me is gonna get paid tonight!*

* * *

Promise ran to grab her ringing cell phone that she left lying on the bed. "Hello?"

"I'm here, gorgeous. You ready?" Rare Breed asked when he pulled up in front of the Boston Harbor Hotel.

"Yes, I'm ready, but I'm not sure I'm dressed properly for the occasion since I don't know where we're going," Promise replied, looking herself over in the ceiling-to-floor mirror.

"Whatever you have on will be perfect for this occasion. Now come on down. I have a surprise for you," Rare Breed said.

"Okay. I'm heading down right now," Promise answered, excited to see what he had in store for her. "All right, Monica. I'm goin'!" Promise yelled as she shut the door of their suite.

Rare Breed had the valet park his car and he entered the hotel lobby to wait for Promise. "Damn, girl! You sho know how to make a nigga weak in the knees," were the first words that escaped Rare Breed's lips when he saw her step out of the elevator.

"Well, you know, I do a li'l something," Promise said, striking a pose like she'd reached the end of a runway.

"Get yo' sexy ass on over here. Here. I picked it out myself," Rare Breed said, handing her the signature blue box straight from Tiffany & Company.

"Jewelry, huh? A girl's best friend!" Promise said as she began to open the box to look at its sparkling contents. "Wait…is this…? No! It can't be!" *Oh my God! This is from the new Tiffany collection! This thing must have cost more than $20,000.*

"I hope you like it, ma. I wanted to get you something special, but then again, I'm a man. I just stuck to what I know and got that for you. Here. Let me help you put it on. The saleswoman at the store told me it's one of the newly released Victoria bracelets or something like that," he said, trying to recall the details.

So it's true, Promise thought. "Thank you! It is a Victoria—an alternating bracelet in platinum, with marquise and round diamonds. This thing must be more than six carats!" Promise said, sounding a little overexcited.

"Yep…and it looks perfect on you," Rare Breed said proudly, then led the way to the hotel fine-dining Meritage Restaurant.

"Wait a minute," Promise said. "Where are we going? The front door is the other way." Promise asked, confused.

"Shh. Just go with the flow, okay?" Rare Breed responded. "Follow me."

"Right this way, Mr. Robertson. Everything is set up for you and your guest, and your food will be out shortly. Would you like me to open your bottle of Moët?" the waitress asked ever so sweetly.

"Yes, and please go ahead and pour two glasses. Also, can you make sure our dessert gets to our second location?" Rare Breed asked as he pulled out Promise's chair.

"Okay. I'll be sure to put your request in," the waitress said.

There's no one in the restaurant but us. This man is unbelievable.

"You're really going all out for the first date, aren't you? I mean, you're doing all this for me? You shut the whole restaurant down! I don't know how you pulled that off, but I'm happy you did. It really gets you a lot of points in my book," *This man shut down this restaurant, bought me a $20,000 bracelet and he doesn't even seem like he's the least bit worried about getting in my panties. He's definitely setting the bar high. I didn't plan on giving up this sweet, juicy peach tonight, but that just might change…*

"You're quiet all of a sudden. What are you thinking about over there?" Rare Breed asked as he caressed Promise's hand.

"I'm sorry. Did you say something? I'm just…trying to take all this in. No one has ever done anything like this for me before, at least not without wanting or expecting something in return," Promise admitted, snapping out of her daze.

"Well then it looks like I'll be doing a lot of things that you're not use to having done. I don't want anything except for truthfulness, honesty, time and if sex comes then I'll definitely take that too, but I'm not looking for it. I'm not like any of these other niggas, shit, they don't call me Rare Breed for nothing," he said.

"Your food is served, and dessert has been taken care of," the waitress said.

"What's under all these different lids? It's just the two of us, so why so many plates?" Promise asked.

"Seeing that we're still getting to know each other, and I only know that you like breakfast and seafood, I didn't know exactly what else you might want, so I ordered seafood, soul food, Italian, and last but not least, Asian," Rare Breed replied, taking the lids off the platters.

"Ooh! I love variety. I'll have something off of each plate. I know I told you seafood is my favorite, but Italian is a close runner-up," Promise said with a bright smile.

This has to be the perfect night. This man is amazing, he gave me a beautiful gift, we shared a private and intimate dinner alone in a top-notch restaurant, the meal which he ordered was delicious, dessert is waiting somewhere and to top it off, he made it very clear that sex is not what he's after. Damn, I must be dreaming!

After they ate and enjoyed some more champagne, Rare Breed stood. "I hope you saved some room for dessert," he said.

"Hmm. Well, my eyes always seem to be bigger than my stomach, but where are we heading now?" Promise asked as he led her deeper into the hotel. *I thought my outfit would be wasted, since we technically stayed in, but now it doesn't seem that way at all. Shoot! I'm glad I sexed it up for him. I'm having a great time, and clearly, there's more to come. I can't wait!*

"Yeah, I feel that way sometimes too. I have hungry eyes but an average stomach. Now stop being so nosy. You'll see where we're going in a minute," Rare Breed replied with a crooked smile.

"We're going to take a turn here and head to our final destination of the evening," the hostess said. "I'll let you take it from here, Mr. Robertson. Let me know if you need anything else," she mentioned before she disappeared around the corner.

"Now for this surprise, I'm going to have to blindfold you," Rare Breed said, pulling a bandana from his pocket.

"Hmm. Okay, but remember that we're still getting to know each other. No freaky shit, mister—or not yet anyway," Promise said with a slick smile.

"I'm not trying to take advantage of you, if that's what you're thinkin'. I'm just trying to show you that all niggas ain't the same." Rare Breed opened the door and guided Promise through it.

When he removed the blindfold, Promise's eyes adjusted quickly and focused in on a beautiful indoor pool with red rose petals floating in it, surrounded by what seemed like thousands of candles.

"That cabana over there is just for you. I want you to go in there and pick out whatever bikini you like. Put it on and join me in the Jacuzzi," Rare Breed instructed.

Promise was happier than a fat kid with a whole plate of ice cream and cake.

Oh my God! This man is truly amazing. Hell, he's outdone every nigga who's ever taken me out! Look at this! A bathing suit in every color, style, and designer. Shit! I wish I could keep them all, but I guess this one will do. Mmm...once this nigga sees me in this number, he might bust on himself right then and there. All my finesse is going to be showing, Promise thought, changing as fast as she could. After she'd squeezed her curves into the slinky bikini, she walked up behind him. "So? What do you think?"

Rare Breed was busy pouring two fresh glasses of Moët, but he turned around quick to have a look at her. "Damn, girl! You're drop-dead gorgeous, like you oughtta be on the cover of the *Sports Illustrated* Swimsuit Edition. That thing looks like it was painted on," he complimented, trying to ignore his manhood that was slowly rising in his shorts.

"You know, you're really impressing me tonight. Did you think of all this on your own, or did you just hire someone to plan this? Half the bikini fashions in there aren't even set to come out until summer, but you somehow managed to get them a whole season early. I mean, seriously, you've got me wearing an Oscar De La Renta straight from Italy. Look at me in this Watercolor Grid Bandeau Halter Bikini! Since I live in the South, I wear bathing suits a lot, so I know to have this one a season early is almost impossible, like some kind of fashionista's dream!"

"So, I take it you like it?"

"I do okay taking care of and treating myself, Mike, but it means a lot more when someone else does something nice for me. Really, this is so sweet. You truly are a Rare Breed," she teased with a smile. "You've helped make the last year of my life a distant memory. Thanks for helping me forget some of the shit I've been through," Promise said. "I apologize for going on and on but I wanted you to know how much all of this has meant to me."

"Not a problem, ma. Yes, I thought of all this myself, but I did have help executing it all. I've never done anything like this for a woman. I know you probably think this is weird, coming from a man who took you to Perkins at 3:00 in the morning, but there's just...well, there's something about you. I know we just met, Promise, but as long as you stay true to me, never lie to me, and always keep it real—like your name—I'll be down for you to ride with me all the way. The industry has so many sharks in it, so many people only out for themselves, but I don't think you're one of them. I can already tell you've been through a lot. I know the look, 'cause I've been through a lot of shit myself. I got a feeling this might be the beginning of an everlasting journey, if you're willing to help me make it that way," the rapper said, meaning every word.

Promise was speechless, just staring at him with utter amazement and admiration as she sipped her champagne.

"Okay. Enough of all this touchy shit. Let's get in the Jacuzzi, drink a little, enjoy each other's conversation, and maybe get a little closer. I'm not trying to go too fast or anything or push you. I'm just saying that if it goes there, I'm not going to fight it," Rare Breed explained, his award-winning smile melting Promise's heart.

"I second that," she said. "The soaking, sipping, and enjoying each other's conversation and company sounds good to me, but the jury's still out on the rest, okay?" she said coyly, slipping off her pumps and easing down into the warm, churning water. *I'm so enjoying this cat-and-mouse game. I might just be willing to see where this goes after all,* Promise thought.

* * *

This little lounge is jumping! I bet any amount of money Promise isn't having nearly as much fun as I am. That fine tenderoni been staring at me all night. He just don't know his ass is on the verge of getting all this, especially considering my six cups of Crown Royal and Pepsi. On top of that, those two groupie bitches in the corner been eyeballing me all night. Damn! Can't a single woman come out and enjoy herself by herself? The one with the blonde weave and pretty eyes is sexy. Shit! Look at them legs...they go on for days but nah, I want some dick tonight. Maybe I'll see her again. Aw, fuck. Let me quit procrastinating and go see what's really good with this sexy ass dude. I'm ready to blow this joint anyway. I been here like three hours, and ain't nobody else caught my interest, Monica thought.

"Hey, baby," she said, approaching him, "you've been checking me out just as long as I've been checking you out. I think that means something," Monica said, sliding her hand under his shirt and gliding her middle finger up and down his torso.

"Yeah, I've been checking for you. You're working the hell out of that dress. Why don't we get on out of here so I can see if you look as good naked as you do in that mu'fucka?" he suggested, running his hand damn near all the way up her inner thigh.

"Hmm. Well, I think that can be arranged. What's your name? I had a car service bring me here, so if I'm leaving with you, I need to let my driver know," Monica said, remembering Promise's advice to exercise some type of common sense.

"Check the chain, Name's Q. Go ahead and wrap everything up on your end, and I'll pick you up out front," Q said. He grabbed Monica's ass one more time before he walked off, leaving her nostrils filled with Dolce & Gabbana cologne. *This bitch got a car service to bring her here? Damn. She must have some cash on her. Sounds like she's right up my alley. I'll take her to the spot across town, spike her drink, fuck her triflin' dumb ass, pretend to be asleep, and when she wakes up, I'll be long gone, with a pocketful of money. Yeah, that's what's up!* Q thought as he popped his collar feeling himself.

I'm about to take this nigga on a rollercoaster ride, Monica thought as she stumbled up to her driver. "Mark, uh…John? No…Jacob or whatever your name is, I got a ride, so you can go on and occupy yourself elsewhere. I'll check ya later," Monica slurred.

"Are you sure about that, ma'am? I personally don't think it's a good idea. No offense, but you don't look like you're in any shape to be leaving with a stranger," the driver said.

"I'm good! I'm a grown-ass woman. Damn! Why doesn't anyone get that?" Monica screamed.

"Maybe because you're not acting like a grown woman," the driver said under his breath. "Anyway, you're the boss. Just be safe," he said, walking toward the driver side of the car.

Beep! Beep!

"Hop in, ma," Q said as he pulled up in front, just like he'd promised.

I know this nigga ain't honking at me! What the fuck kind of car is this? A fuckin' old-ass Honda Civic? Really? Shit, what have I gotten myself into? Oh well. At least the paint isn't all cracked up and rusting, Monica thought as they rode for what seemed like forever.

"You want some more to drink, ma? I got some Henn and Coke already mixed in a bottle behind your seat," Q said as he pulled up to a Motel 6 that looked too dilapidated to leave a light on for anybody.

He drank some of his pre-mixed drink. *I really didn't want anything, nor did I need anything more to drink but with the way this motel looked, I needed to make sure my high didn't wear off too soon.* I thought to myself. *Shit! This li'l ol' cheap-ass nigga got me riding in some old-ass car, drinking a premixed hot drink out the bottle, and then he's got the nerve to take me to a Motel 6? Next thing I know, this mu'fucka gon' expect me to pay for the damn room too. Shit! I hate to admit it, but Promise was right…I shouldn't go in this dump. I need to go on back to our suite. Oh well, I'm here now.* Monica gave up on the fight she was having with herself as she slid out of the car and joined Q as he stood waiting at the front of the car.

"I already got a key, so we can go right in," Q said, ready to fuck the shit out of the wealthy piece of ass he'd lucked up on.

Yeah, let's go ahead and get this shit over with. Maybe the dick will be good, at least, Monica hoped. But when she walked out of the tiny bathroom, she couldn't believe what she saw: There was Q, sprawled out on the bed, buck naked with his legs spread eagle. *Is this nigga serious? No foreplay or nothing? Just get right to the point? Damn it! I'm close to saying fuck this, 'cause fine as he is, he ain't worth all this,* Monica thought.

"Bring yo' li'l fine ass on over here so I can give you some of this *Mandingo* dick," Q said, sliding a condom on.

Oh, what the hell? I'm here. Why let the dick go to waste? Monica thought. "Did you taste that Hennessy and Coke? That shit was strong as hell. Got me felling all warm inside," Monica said, climbing on top of him.

"Really? It didn't seem strong to me. It's exactly how I like my women—smooth and easy to swallow," Q said, guiding his dick inside and thrusting deep. "Shit! This some good-ass pussy. It feels like yo' shit gripping my dick! The deeper I go, the tighter you squeeze. C'mon and turn over and back that fine ass up," Q said, grunting.

"Shit, Daddy! That's my spot. Mmm…ah…fuck my pussy. Come on! Don't slow down now! Fuck it. Lie on your back. I'm about to ride this dick," Monica said, biting her lip. With sweat pouring down her back, she went to work. She loved to be on top because she felt more in control that way, and her tryst with Q was the most exciting sex she'd had in a long time.

"Tell Q whose pussy this is. Whose is it?" Q asked, feeling like he was getting the job done.

"Fuck, Q! I'm about to cum! I'm about to cum!" Monica yelled, on the verge of pulling her fusion hair out.

"Shiiiit! Me too. Let's bust together. I can't hold it no longer. Ahhhh!" Q yelled before he grunted and went stiff.

"I was just about to cum, Q. Damn! You coulda let me get mine first. You're gonna have to eat this pussy or something. I did too much for you to not catch at least one nut," Monica said, dead serious.

"Man, lie yo' ass down and let me just get a quick break, then I'll get right back in that pussy, a'ight?" Q said, pretending to doze off. *Damn! Why the fuck hasn't the drink kicked in yet? This bitch supposed to be knocked out cold. Instead, her ass tryin' a go another round. What the fuck?*

Chapter Five

Ain't That 'Bout a Bitch?

"Hey, baby. What new information do you have for me?" Jelly asked.
"Well, damn! I miss you too, woman. That's what we do now? Only talk when I have information for you?" asked Mark, the Sweet Spot security man.

"Baby, you know it's not even like that. I'm just really ready to stick it to that bitch. She walk around like her shit don't stink, but it does, and I'm going to make her smell it herself. I do miss you though, Mark," Jelly said.

"I hear you. But don't get up there and start acting brand new, 'cause when you was here, yo' ass couldn't stay away from me. You was always begging for the dick," Mark said, readjusting his manhood.

Nigga, you just don't know I was only around your ass because I was doing what I had to do. I don't want your ass! What can you do for me, being a security guard at a high-priced strip club? Nothing! Nigga can't even afford half of my expenses, Jelly thought.

"Listen, bay, it's not even like that. You know how me and B.I. get when we're around each other. Time just flies by. It's only been a few days since we've talked. It's not like it's been two weeks. I know you're missing this good-good, but damn! You don't have to act like this," she said.

"Well, you better tell a nigga something. I'll be taking a trip up there in about a week and a half. I need to tie some things up down here first though," Mark said.

"Aw, you're coming to see me? I can't wait," Jelly said, rolling her eyes.

"Just be ready for Daddy when I get there. Oh yeah. I found something out about Promise. Word is she's on the hunt to find her baby-daddy, using all means necessary," he said.

"Oh, I'll be ready for you, Daddy. But about Promise, does that mean she could possibly be in Boston right now, as we speak?" Jelly pried.

"She could be. I tell you one thing though. She damn sho ain't in Tampa right now. Look into it, and I'll do my part down here," Mark said.

"All right. Let me go ahead and get on that. Boy, B.I. is going to be hot, I tell ya. I'll hit you up later," Jelly said.

"Fo sho. Tell B.I. I said what up and hold that shit down," Mark said before he hung up.

* * *

Later that day, Jelly met up with Black Ice at the La Belle Nail Salon. "What's up, chick? How are things going at home?" she asked.

"Girl, it's the same shit, different day. He still doesn't wanna do shit with me, and it's gotten to the point where he barely wants to touch me. It's crazy, 'cause I know that nigga loves sex. I think he's missing that bitch Promise. I walked in on him while he was on the phone with one of his homies, and I heard him say her name. I don't know what he said before that, but I know the conversation was about her. I just keep thinking about last year, the day I saw her turning on his street. What if he hadn't left a day earlier for his game in Miami? He would've been there. I think I'm losing him, Jelly. So much has been going on, and he seems so…distant. It seems like he wants to right all his wrongs or something," Black Ice said, finally admitting what she'd been thinking for a while.

"I know it's hard, and I know you wanna find happiness with Dez, but we have a bigger mission right now. Our goal was never for you to catch any feelings. You were supposed to make him fall for you, get married, and stay with him for a couple years, just long enough so you could drain him for everything you can get. Don't tell me somewhere along the lines you've caught feelings for this nigga," Jelly said, not at all happy at how weak Black Ice seemed.

"Do you really have to ask that, Jelly? I've been with the man for four years of my life. I know in the beginning I was just after his money, but it's not like that now. No man has ever treated me the way he used to. I remember all those things he said to me. Hell, he loved me when I really didn't even love myself. Shit, Jelly, no offense, but Dez actually wanted more for me than just being a stripper for the rest of my life. I guess I fell for that fairytale world I was living in with him in the beginning," Black Ice said, feeling a great burden lifting off of her. She was glad to finally tell Jelly the truth.

Fairytale is right! I can't believe this bitch. I knew I should've been the one to fuck Dezman that night instead of meeting up with one of my regulars after my shift at the Sweet Spot. All this time wasted. Shit! Maybe I can alter his thought process and get him to focus on me instead of going after Promise. I'll get him out of this funk and take both of these dumb bitches out at the same time, Jelly schemed.

"I don't know what to say, B.I. You've got me speechless. I know you've come to care about him, but damn, girl! It sounds like you're head over heels in love with the nigga and that shit is making you soft. What are you going to do if Dez really is thinking about making things right with his baby-mama and child?" Jelly asked, knowing exactly what buttons to push. "Then what? He's going to just leave you sitting there looking crazy and they'll be off starting a happy little family?

"Honestly, I'm at the point of no return right now. If I have to kill her, him, or both of them just to keep them apart, that's what I have to do," Black Ice said, as serious as a Category 9 hurricane.

Hmm. I got no problem with you takin' that Promise bitch out, but you won't be killing Dez. Somebody has to finish this mission off the right way. If I have to step up to the plate I will, Jelly thought.

"What are you thinking about, Jelly? You just went silent on me," Black Ice said.

"Oh, girl, my bad. Just got a lot on my mind, I guess," Jelly replied, more than ready to go.

"Well, don't worry about anything. Once Dezman and I are married, it'll be a wrap. He's going to be all about me and getting me pregnant. Shit, the other night when he was drunk, I bit a hole in the condom before we fucked. If he won't give me a baby willingly, I'll force an accident. We'd stopped using condoms for a while, but then when he found out Promise was pregnant, he wanted to start using them again. Can you believe that shit? It infuriated me! If I don't get my wedding soon, at least I'll be having his baby. One way or another, Dezman will give me what I want," Black Ice said, her blue eyes turning red.

"Okay, girl, Do what you gotta do. Let me just inform you about something I learned today. Promise is not in Tampa right now. Word is that she left her mom in charge of her daughter, and she hired a private investigator because she's using all means necessary, according to Mark, to try and find her baby-daddy. As of right now, Mark is trying to find out if Promise is in Boston, right under our noses," Jelly said, letting the cat out of the bag and sending B.I. over the edge.

"What!? I know that bitch ain't back in Boston. Shit! What am I going to do? I got Dezman to move out of the mansion, but I know he ain't gonna move out of state—not right now anyway. I can't lose my man to that bitch. I won't! Shit, Jelly, I gotta go. Hit me up later and let me know what you find out," Black Ice said, gathering her things in a hurry.

"B.I. you can't leave like that! Girl, your nails aren't even dry, and you've only got lashes on one eye!" Jelly said, giggling on the inside at the frantic look on Black Ice's face. She'd never seen her like that before. She'd always known Black Ice as a strong-minded, take-no-shit woman, but the pitiful image before her was nothing more than a joke.

"Fuck all that. I'll come get this shit redone tomorrow. I gotta get home. Bye, girl," Black Ice said as she all but ran out the door.

Perfect! I got that bitch falling apart at the seams. Promise could possibly be here in Boston, and the ball is in my court. These hoes don't even know it, but they gon' learn today, Jelly thought, turning on the massage chair.

Chapter Six

Signed, Sealed, and Delivered

"All this mail, and you with all that energy, little girl. You're always pointing to something. What do want now—juice, treats, or you want to watch some cartoons on TV? Nana just loves her little girl," Sweet Pea said, smiling at her granddaughter before she looked through the pile of mail again. "Let's see…bill, bill, bill, bill…oh! Here it is, that envelope addressed to me. Let's see what we have here."

She opened the letter and began to read…

"Well hello there, Mrs. Taniqua Sweet Pea Brown, widow of Mr. Dontae Biggs Brown. I could play mind games with you and deliver this message in a riddle, leaving you to figure out what it means, but honestly, I don't have time for all that. I need to get the wheels on this mission spinning now. Your precious little daughter isn't the angel you think she is. She's a murderer, an escorting whore, and a wannabe man-thief, but that's been nipped in the bud. Let me break all this down to you. Your daughter is the reason Shirley is dead. That's right. Promise plotted and ultimately carried out the murder of the woman who had a part in your husband's death, the one who snitched on your husband, her father. I know your daughter calls herself a 'high-class entertainer,' but have you ever asked Promise what that entails? Probably not, so let me fill you in. On top of your daughter being a stripper who takes off her clothes for rich men, athletes, music moguls, and actors, she also goes the extra mile and puts in work when she's not at Sweet Spot. That's right. Your little girl flies to different states to sleep with men who pay her thousands of dollars for her time. Also, that baby, your grandchild, was supposed to be my baby, but no! Why? Because your man-borrowing daughter fucked my fiancé and ended up pregnant. I will do whatever I have to in order to make sure she and that bastard child stay the fuck away from my man. When it comes down to it, I don't think it's his baby anyway. Her mother is a whore and that baby could be any man's baby, because Promise has been lying down with men all over the United States like the whore she is...

Signed, Sealed and Delivered,

A Mad Black Woman!"

Oh my God! This can't be true. My daughter, a killer, escort, and man-stealer? I can't—no, I won't—believe these lies about my Promise. The police never did find Shirley's murderers and speculated that it seemed as though the job had to take more than one person. Surely my Promise isn't capable of killing anyone...or is she? I haven't been in her life for so long that I just don't know. And escorting? What in the world would push her to do that? I'm not saying being a dancer is any better, but damn! At least she was leaving the club with some morals and dignity. To sleep with a man who is already involved with another woman is just beyond me. I know my daughter is way better than that. Did she know he was engaged? Probably not. He's an athlete for Pete sake. I can't believe I'm sitting here questioning my own daughter's morals, Sweet Pea thought as she stared at her granddaughter.

"What has your mother gotten herself into?" Sweet Pea asked the baby.

Deziray only smiled at her and pointed at the cartoons on television.

I need to take a load off. I need a strong drink and someone to talk to. Hell, maybe I can get some of my old go-to, what I used to use in the past when I wanted to clear my mind. I wonder if Ron and them still live over on Chestnut, in the projects, Sweet Pea considered, unsure of what to do next.

"No. First, let me call this damn girl and find out what the fuck is going on, Sweet Pea said out loud as she dialed her daughter's cell phone.

There was no answer.

Hmm. Okay, Miss Lady! I wonder if she realizes all the trouble she's in. Is that why she really left? Maybe she thought it would be safer for Deziray and me without her here, Sweet Pea thought, her mind running rampant. Feeling the need to clear her head, she decided to get out of the house and take her granddaughter for a ride. Since she'd gotten out of prison she hadn't been to her old 'hood, but it was time for a trip down Memory Lane.

* * *

Sweet Pea breezed through her old 'hood in a her Limited Edition Toyota 4Runner, decked out with the hottest rims, mirror tint, and chrome in all the right places, thanks to Promise. Sweet Pea reminisced as they rode past the spot where she and Biggs had first met. "Dezi, this is where your nana used to hang. Your granddaddy and I ran these streets. Yep, these very same streets."

Deziray was buckled in her car seat, wide-eyed and staring out the window, as if she knew what her nana was saying.

When Sweet Pea turned down one very familiar street, old memories flooded her mind. She thought her mind was playing tricks on her when she saw T-mack up the block. *What!? That can't be him. They told me he was dead!* After a closer look, she realized it was indeed T-mack. Stunned and happy at the same time, she pulled over, got out with Deziray, and went after him. They turned the corner just in time to see T-mack going into his mom's apartment. She walked right up to the door and knocked, as giddy as a schoolgirl.

"Damn! Who dat? I just walked in the house and ain't even had time to take my shoes off," T-mack complained as he opened the door.

"T-mack? It really is you!" Sweet Pea said.

"Yes, and you are?" T-mack replied.

"They told me you were killed in prison, but here you are, alive and well and looking as smooth as the last time I saw you. What's it been? A little over twenty years?"

T-mack pulled the door all the way open and studied the woman's smiling face. "Sweet Pea? Girl, is that you?"

She nodded excitedly.

"Damn! You look good. I see prison ain't did you no wrong, huh? When I came home, the first thing I did was look you up. I heard about all the fucked-up shit that went on with Toni, Biggs, Shirley, and you and my daughter. Matter fact, where is she? I have twenty years of making up to do."

"You...remember? I told you before, when they locked you up, that I didn't know if Promise was yours or Biggs.

It didn't matter what Sweet Pea was saying. I know that little girl she had was mine. "You mean to tell me this is my baby's baby? My granddaughter? Let me hold her," T-mack said, taking the baby into his arms. "You're a cutie, ain't ya? Girl, you're gonna be a heartbreaker like your granny when you get older. Come on in, Sweet Pea."

Sweet Pea happily accepted his invitation and stepped inside his place. "I see everything is still about the same in here. That woman sure loves her some red and black. How is Ms. Jones anyway?"

"That's actually where I just came from," T-mack said, his eyes saddening. "A week before I was set to get out, she was admitted into the hospital. When I got home, I wondered why my favorite woman in the world wasn't here to greet her only son. I found out from my uncle that Mom's been battling cancer. He said her health's been deteriorating these past couple of years. She never bothered to tell me anything while I was locked up. When I went to the hospital for the first time, I asked her why she never told me anything. She said she didn't want to worry me." T-mack began to tear up.

"I'm sorry to hear that. I know how much you love your mother. I'm sure she was just trying to look out for your best interests. She did what she thought was best. She didn't want you sitting in that cell thinking and worrying about her all the time," Sweet Pea told him, feeling a little emotional herself.

"I know she had good intentions, but damn. Lung cancer, on top of diabetes and high blood pressure, is a lot for anybody to deal with. I should've known something was off when she answered the phone. She sounded different. Also, her visits went from twice a month to once every three months. I blame myself for not making her take better care of herself, for not paying closer attention. I was so busy counting down the days till my release that I never paid her close attention. I swear, in my eyes, my mom is a Superwoman. This shit hurts so bad 'cause I don't know what I would do without her. I'm praying she can keep fighting."

"Listen, T-mack. I sat in prison for years asking, pleading, and begging God to tell me why. Why did He let my family be ruined? What did I do to deserve that? One day I went to the chapel, sat down, and had a one-on-one talk with the Lord. He opened my eyes to a lot of things that day. When it comes down to it, everything happens for a reason. When and if it's time for Him to call us home, we can't say we're not ready or ask for an extra day or even an extra hour. Once He sends a call for his angel to come home, we can't be mad or upset. We can only rejoice, knowing she's on her way home," Sweet Pea said, repeating what someone had once told her.

"You're right, Sweet Pea. You have always known what to say to open my eyes or calm me down. Aw! Look here. The little one has fallen asleep on us. If you're gonna be here a while, I can put her in the bed."

"Sure, we'll stay a while longer. I needed to get out of the house and relieve some stress. Believe me, I didn't expect to run into you, but I'm glad I did," Sweet Pea said remembering the trouble their daughter was in.

"Hold that thought. I have something that will clear both our minds. You still smoke, don't you?" T-mack asked before he disappeared up the stairs.

"I haven't smoked in forever, but I wouldn't mind. Maybe a couple pulls will help ease my mind."

"I got that good shit from this young cat over in the cut. The dudes on the block say he got the best shit running. I'm kind of thirsty, so while I roll this, why don't you pour us something to drink? My moms should have some gin somewhere in the kitchen. While you're at it, find us some snacks. This joint is gone set us right. Is that what the young'ns calling it these days? A joint?"

Sweet Pea laughed. "T-mack, you're still the same old fool! From what I know the young'ns are calling them blunts, L's or gars. Don't try to make me feel old! Remember, I'm still a few years younger than you."

T-mack sat back and started to reminisce, thinking about everything that had gone down. He had not been happy to discover that Sweet Pea had been seeing Biggs the whole time they were together, but there wasn't anything he could do about it since he'd found out after he'd been locked up. A week after his sentencing, his mother had informed him that Sweet Pea was pregnant. A lot of time had passed since then, and he wondered if Sweet Pea still loved him or even wanted him. *If nothing else brings the truth out of her this shit will,* T-mack thought as he spread a white, powdery substance on top of the weed in the blunt while Sweet Pea was getting them something to snack on. *I guess this is what a nigga has to resort to just to get some piece of mind. I thought being free would set me right. I can't feel bad though. Weed just don't do it for me. Shit, at least I'm not a crack-head,* T-mack thought, trying to justify his cocaine use, something he was quickly becoming addicted to.

Chapter Seven

What a Night!

Promise woke up in her room alone. She knew she'd fallen asleep in Rare Breed's arms, but he was gone now, and she couldn't figure out when he'd left. She turned over and noticed a lime-green envelope on the dresser. She opened and pulled out a letter.

"Hey, sleeping beauty!
You like the envelope, don't you? I know it's a personal touch. I picked it up just for you. Yeah, I remembered your favorite color. I know you're wondering why I wasn't around to wake you up this morning. I had a couple of meetings with some promoters who want to book me for some events, shows, interviews, and appearances or whatever while I'm down here. Being the person I am, I can't have everybody handling my business for me. I want to know what's going on, so I have to be at every meeting. So I'm sorry I'm not there with you right now, but I hope you understand. Trust me, you'll be back in my presence soon. Last night was on point! I'm not even going to lie. I think that was the first night I've ever slept next to a female all night without fucking I respect you for that, 'cause it's too many bitches out here ready to drop them draws at a moment's notice. You're not like that, and that's another thing I adore about you. Let me go ahead and wrap this on up before I end up jumping back in the bed with yo' fine ass. You look so sweet and innocent when you're sleeping. I'll hit you up and we'll set something up for tomorrow. Today is going to be a real busy day, so it'll probably be late when you hear from me.
Signed, that nigga, Rare Breed."

"Damn! I haven't felt this happy or smiled this much because of a man since Dezman," Promise said. *Shit, I'm lovin' it, like McDonald's! Monica's gonna trip about this, especially since she wasn't able to chill with Truth,* Promise thought, and she hurried to go brag to her friend.

Promise knocked on Monica's door. "Hey, girl, I bet you didn't have as much fun as I did last night! Come on now. Don't be all salty. I know you hear me. Monica!" Promise said, standing outside of her door. She waited a minute for a response then entered her room and found that Monica's room was empty. *Now I know this bitch ain't wake up, leave early this morning, and make up her bed. Naw, that ain't possible. Look at this shit! The mint's still on top of her pillow from when the maid changed her sheets yesterday. I don't believe this shit. That ho didn't come home last night. I wonder what she got into...or who got into her,* Promise thought, laughing at her own little joke.

* * *

KNOCK! KNOCK!

"Hey! You need to make up your mind and pay for another day or check out. Our housekeeper needs to get in there and get the room ready for *paying* customers," the woman from the front desk of the Motel 6 said.

"Promise, get the damn door. You know I'm not a morning person," muttered a sleepy, half-hung over Monica. "Wait...what the fuck did she say about paying for another day? Where the hell am I?" Monica, confused, finally opened her eyes and came to the realization that she was not in her comfortable presidential, but in a run-down, smelly, outdated hotel.

"Fine. You want to play it that way? Then I'm going to call the police and have them haul your ass out of there. I've got a motel to run, and I don't have time for this shit!" the angry desk clerk yelled.

"Hold on a minute! Damn!" Monica said, struggling to regain her composure. She dragged herself to the door, still looking around the small, shabbily furnished room, trying to figure out where she was. "Ma'am, listen...I don't even know where I am. I don't remember coming here. I have a presidential suite at the Boston Harbor Hotel," Monica said, squinting her red eyes to try and shield them from the sunrays bursting through the thin curtains. Just as she opened the door for the hotel employee, she heard the familiar ringtone on her phone and knew she had an incoming call from Promise. "Hold on a second! Let me get this," she told the hotel employee. She then stumbled over to the side of the bed and found her phone, on the floor, in a scattered pile of her belongings. *What the fuck? Why the hell is all my shit thrown out of my purse?* Monica wondered, wrinkling her brow in confusion as she answered the phone. "Hello?"

"Um, excuse me," the desk clerk continued, "unlike you I'm on the clock, and I need to get back to work. Then again, from the looks of this room, you're a working girl yourself." She looked around at the place and at Monica as if she were disgusted. "Be out of this room with in the next fifteen minutes. If not, I'll be back with the police," she threatened before she huffed and sighed and walked away. "Those damn prostitutes always come here, get drugged up, and then act crazy when they're told to pay up or leave. I can't stand this! I've gotta find a new job," she fussed as she stomped down the gaudy carpeted hallway.

"Who was that?" Promise asked, having heard the irritated woman in the background.

"Girl, I got no idea. I woke up in some strange hotel room with a hell of a case of cotton-mouth. Shit, I can't remember what happened last night."

"Is anybody there with you?"

"No, but I left the lounge with a dude named Q. I don't remember a damn thing after that. Promise, can you just come get me or send a car for me?"

"How am I supposed to do that if I don't know where you are? I really can't believe you, leaving some lounge in a strange city with a man you don't even know. Who the hell is this Q anyway? Monica, I know you get sick of me lecturing you, but that was stupid and immature. He coulda been a killer or something! This is the shit I be talking about when I'm always tellin' you to be careful. Damn!" Promise said, heated.

"I really don't want to hear your mouth. Don't you think I've been through enough? Just let me gather up my purse and shit so I can find out what raggedy-ass hotel this is," Monica said, regretting that she'd told Promise a damn thing.

"You've got some nerve. You really do. After this, how about you keep your ass here from now on. We're not in Tampa, Monica. Neither of us knows this place. I'm not trying to control you, but I asked you to come with me because you know I don't have many friends. You're the closest person to me. I want you to have fun while you're here, but I can't have anything happening to you. You're supposed to be helping me take care of business."

"I feel what you're saying, but if anything happens to me, it'll be on me, not you. Look this notepad here on the cheap-ass plywood dresser says I'm at the Motel 6 on Worcester Road, Exit 12," Monica said, frustrated. *This bitch is getting on my damn nerves. Since when did she become so caring? I'm about ready to just get my own suite and do my own thing.* "Can you come find me or send a driver or what?" She dug around through her purse to make sure everything was there, but it wasn't. *Hold up. Where the fuck is my money? Damn it! It was right here in the back zipper!* she thought as she frantically rummaged through her Nero Intrecciato Nappa Duo Bag. *I know it was in here!* After a moment of searching and no luck, she realized she'd been bamboozled. "That mu'fucka robbed me! Un-fuckin'-believable!" she screamed.

"What? Who robbed you? How do you know?" Promise asked, bewildered.

"That bitch nigga Q! He stole every last dollar I brought with me on this trip. I had it in the zipper part of my purse, and now it's gone. When I woke up, my purse was lying beside the bed, with everything dumped out. I can't believe this shit."

"Don't worry. I'm on my way, girl. From the sound of that pissed-off hotel lady, you best get on out of the room. Gather up your shit and get out of there. I'll be there shortly."

Damn it! This bitch wants to keep hollering about how grown she is, and she goes and gets her ass robbed. A fuckin' Motel 6? That asshole obviously fucked her to sleep, robbed her, and took the hell off. When's her dumb ass ever gonna learn? But whatever. I'm not going to say shit else, Promise thought as she put her keys in the ignition. "She never listens to a word I say anyway," she said out loud, shaking her head as she made her way to the hotel.

Chapter Eight

Important Information

The next morning, after Black Ice's and Jelly's chill night at the lounge, they decided to head to Sorellina Italian Restaurant for lunch.

"Thanks for last night, Jelly. I tell you, I needed that. I thought I was going to go crazy sitting in that house, trying to stay on top of every move Dezman makes. He was getting sick of me talking about, 'Ain't your girl in town? Why don't you show her the town, take her shopping, shit, out to eat or something?' I felt like he was just fed up with my presence. You know he's not used to me being around all day," Black Ice said.

"I'm glad I got your ass out the damn house too. I done came all the way up here. You think I'm about to have yo' ass playing detective/investigator all day every day? No! We had fun laughing at that drunk bitch who left with the broke-down wanna be Morris Chestnut-looking brother. She really thought she was hot shit," Jelly said, laughing.

"I was not playing detective/investigator, asshole. I was playing keep-my-man-by-all-means-necessary, even if that meant staying stuck up in his ass every move he made. Let's be real, a'ight? And ol' girl from last night was cute, looking like a bag of money. A bad bitch know a bad bitch, and she was a bad bitch. I gotta give props when they're due. You wrong about that brotha. He was fine, though he did look kinda broke."

Jelly's phone began to ring before she could argue. "Girl, it's Mark. I'm so sick of him calling just to check up on me. Nigga doesn't even bother giving me information anymore. Now he always wants to know what I'm doing, where I'm at, who I'm with, and every other fucking thing I'm up to."

"Jelly, just answer the phone. Shit, I told you you shouldn't have never put it on that man. We coulda found our information another way. Now you got that man hooked on the ow-nana, and you gotta take the call."

"Whatever, trick. I am. Damn!" Jelly said, smiling. "Hello?"

"Yo, I don't have much time to talk," Mark said. "I'm just callin' to let you know Promise *is* in Boston. I don't know how long she's been there, but I know she's there. My boy Truth is there right now too, so I'ma link you up with him. Maybe together, y'all can figure out exactly where she's located and what she's up to."

"Thanks, Mark. I'm—" Jelly started, but Mark was obviously in a hurry and cut her off.

"Look, girl, I'm out. Gotta handle some business for the club. I'll text you Truth's number later. He'll be expecting your call. And next time, answer your phone on the first ring, would ya? You got me chasin' down info on this bitch, the least you can do is answer your damn phone!"

Click!

"Why are you looking at the phone like that? You went from happy to surprised to mad. What did Mark say?" Black Ice asked.

"That mu'fucka got one more time to come at me like that. He keeps talking sideways, and I'm gon' convince Tre to fire his broke rent-a-cop ass! Shit! Anyway, I got some bad news. The bitch is here," Jelly said bluntly, not taking B.I.'s feelings into consideration.

Black Ice slammed on her brakes out of nowhere, bringing the car to a screeching halt. "What do you mean she's here? She can't be here! We're not even married yet. What am I going to do?" B.I. asked, sounding defeated.

"What the fuck do you mean, what are you going to do? You're gonna suck that shit up and find that bitch before she finds Dezman." *I can't believe I'm sitting here being the backbone. Shit's gotta change...and quick. What the fuck happened to her?* Jelly thought.

"Fuck it. Let's do it, 'cause that ho ain't takin' my man," B.I. said, revealing a glimpse of her old, strong self.

It's about fuckin' time she manned up! She was starting to really get on my fuckin' nerves!

"That's what I'm talkin' about! There she is. Where has the real you been all this time? That weak lover-girl shit was really beginning to irk my nerves."

"Shut up! When you find somebody you truly love, you'll understand what I'm going through. Anyway, let's get in here and eat, have a strong drink or two, and plan a foolproof murder," Black Ice said. She was absolutely sure of one thing: She wanted Promise dead. She just wasn't sure she wanted to be the one getting her hands dirty.

Chapter Nine

Feels So Right

"Sweet Pea, she's really my daughter isn't she?"

"Look T-mack, I was with both of y'all, though Biggs didn't know that. He raised her as his own. I couldn't tell him anything different 'cause he was crazy about that girl, right up till the day he died. He got himself killed trying to protect her from being in a situation she wasn't supposed to be a part of. She helped me get out. Since then, I've been living with her and helping her take care of my beautiful granddaughter here. Promise is in Boston right now, handling some business."

"What kind of business that she had to leave you and her daughter here alone."

Sweet Pea explained everything to T-mack. She told him about the letter she received and exactly what it said. Then Sweet Pea just stared into T-mack's hazel eyes and caught the little specks of green that still lingered there; they'd always stuck in the back of her mind, because whenever she looked at Promise, she knew where the girl had gotten her eyes.

T-mack smiled.

Sweet Pea leaned back and felt herself drifting off as she stared into those beautiful eyes.

* * *

"T-mack, oh my God! How long was I knocked out? Is Deziray okay?" Sweet Pea asked, slowly coming to from her drug-induced sleep.

"The baby's fine. She woke up wet, so I changed her with a diaper from your bag. It was tough figuring out which way to put those Pampers on her, but I eventually got it. I made her a little something to eat too, and then she watched cartoons, which knocked her back out," T-mack replied, sounding proud of himself.

"Okay. Thanks. Has my cell phone rang yet? Promise should've called by now. Damn girl done got to Boston and is probably living it up," Sweet Pea said, shaking her head at the thought.

"No, your cell phone hasn't made a peep. But hey, instead of you jumping down her throat with all those accusations, why don't you sit her down and simply ask her face to face? That letter could be from anyone. Maybe it's just some scorned woman, mad because her dude is taking their money and spending it on her," T-mack said.

"I hear what you're saying, I guess. Anyway, Deziray and I have to get going. It's late, and she needs a bath," Sweet Pea replied, trying to gather herself, but she felt as though something wasn't right. In her mind she wanted to move, but her body wouldn't let her.

"That had to be some hella-fyed weed. That shit took away my stress, warmed up my body, and put me to sleep. I never felt this way before after smoking a joint. Whatever that was, I'm going to need you to get more of it, because the way things are going right now, I'll need some on a regular."

"Yeah, that shit was on point, huh? I'll get you some more. Shoot, Sweet Pea, I'll supply you with as much as you need. Now come on and let me help you up," T-mack replied.

Once she was to her feet, he said, "You all set?"

"Yeah, I think I'm fine now…ready to get home and get this little one ready for bed."

"It's kind of late, so I'll walk y'all to the car. Oh yeah. I'm gonna see my mother tomorrow, so if you want, I'll come by after I leave there," he said as they made their way down the side walk.

"Do you want me to go to the hospital with you? If so, I could take you."

"Naw. I got something I need to handle before I go see her. I'll be all right. Thanks though."

"All right, T-mack. Don't get yourself in trouble, talking about handling some things. I just finally found you, and I'm not trying to lose you to the justice system again," she said sincerely.

"Man, I'm not going back to that life and damn sho not that hellhole. You shouldn't even throw that out there anyway. You know I was wrongly accused for that armed bank robbery," he said matter-of-factly.

"Yeah, but that wouldn't have happened if you wouldn't have been hanging with Debo and them," Sweet Pea said.

"I see ain't nothing changed. No matter what I do right, I'm still gonna be wrong in your eyes. You're still talking that shit. Them was my boys. You know that," T-mack said, growing frustrated.

"What!? You know I ain't never tried to control yo' ass. I'm just looking out for your best interests. Those were your boys, huh? Then where were they when you got locked up? Tell me that, T.," Sweet Pea snapped.

"Whoa! Hold up, ma. You was my girl back then, so where were you?" was T-mack's comeback.

"You know what was going on with that T-mack," she said, struggling to strap Deziray in her seat. "Anyway, we haven't seen each other for over twenty years, and I don't wanna end this on a bad note, so I'ma go ahead and leave. Call me tomorrow for the address to the house. Tell Ms. Jones I said hello and that I hope she gets well soon," Sweet Pea said as she cranked up the car.

"I hear you. I'll tell her." He looked down at Deziray. "Bye, baby girl. Granddaddy loves you," he said, ignoring Sweet Pea's hard stare.

"You don't feel old calling yourself granddaddy?" she asked.

"Naw. It's a part of growing up and maturing. You shouldn't mind if she calls you her grandma either," he replied.

"Yeah, whatever. Later, T-mack. I gotta go get in contact with your daughter somehow."

"Okay. Just remember what I said about that. Ask before you accuse."

Chapter Ten

A Damn Fool

"This whole ride, you haven't had shit to say. I just picked yo' ass up from a run-down motel, and you get in the car like you just waltzed out of a five-star resort. What the fuck is up?" Promise asked, unable to continue to keep her cool.

"What the fuck is there for me to say? What do you want to hear, that you were right? Fine. You were right, Promise, but not everybody can be as perfect as you. You always get the best men, make the most money, and dress the hottest. Shit, Promise, the rest of us gotta do what we can," Monica said, laying down a guilt trip. *I wish this bitch would get off my damn back,* she thought.

"Perfect? Is that what you think I am? I'm far from perfect. Life has dealt me an ugly hand, but I get up every day and never blame anybody. I learned that when you don't have nobody else to depend on, you have to depend on yourself. You think I'm happy? You think things are easy for me? Damn, Monica. In the real world, some people don't think I'm nothin' but a high-paid prostitute or just a plain old whore. But I'll tell you this. I'm only doing this now so my daughter never has to stoop to this level when she gets older. Deziray will be set. I don't ever want her to go through what I've been through. If you think I act like I'm too good, that's your opinion, but I will continue to hold myself to a higher level. I've always felt like I'm worth more than what I'm doing, and I know others will see that too, in time. You know who opened my eyes and showed me that?"

"Let me guess. Him?" Monica asked sarcastically.

"Yes, Dezman…and I'm grateful for that. Not only has he given me knowledge, but he also gave me my little girl, who I'd gladly travel to hell and back for. All I'm saying is that you need to open your eyes, girl. This world doesn't revolve around you and your problems," Promise said, putting every bit of herself out there, which was something she rarely did.

Damn, this woman is sexy as hell even when she's putting me in my place!

"Wow. I never really realized your struggle. I mean, I knew what happened with your parents when you were younger, but that's it. Shoot, Promise. I never knew you felt that way. I guess I always assumed you acted like your life was so together. That's how you make it seem anyway. When it comes to your job, regardless of what it is, you're makin' plenty of money to provide for your mother and daughter. I want to get better. I really do. I'm tired of settling for less or ending up with men who seem like they have money. Even the ones who do have cash flow are stingy as hell or are only out to take what they want from me. I've become accustomed to jumping from man to man so I don't end up being hurt in the end. At least that's how I used to look at it," Monica replied, not even realizing she'd released some of her own true feelings.

"You're worth so much more than just a man's temporary attention. You gotta love yourself first, girl. 'Cause if you don't love yourself, how the hell you gon' love somebody else or expect someone else to love you? It took me a while to get to this point, but now that I'm here, I'm never going to let anyone take that away from me. Now I want to get *you* to this point."

"I totally feel what you're sayin'. I also want that feeling in my life. I feel like that's what I've been searching for," Monica said truthfully, though she was really over the conversation.

"Well, if you want that in your life, I don't mind helping you get it," Promise looked at her ringing phone. "Now who's this calling me? I hope it's Mike," she said with a smile and a twinkle in her eye. When she looked at the caller ID and saw a picture of her daughter pop up, that put an even bigger smile on her face. "Girl, it's my mama. I hope everything is okay with my baby," Promise said to Monica while fumbling to put her earpiece in before answering.

"Hey, Ma. How's my baby doing?"

"She's fine—just hanging around with her grandma, that's all," Sweet Pea replied.

"Did I just hear you call yourself a grandma? What prompt that change?" Promise asked.

"Um, someone told me that it doesn't mean I'm old, just that I'm grown and mature enough to accept it. So now I'm embracing it," Sweet Pea said very matter-of-factly.

"Hmm. Someone, huh? Someone who?"

"Just an old friend. Hey, but I do need to talk to you about a couple things. The sooner you're back, the better. So how are things going up there? Are you getting any closer to what you were trying to achieve?" Sweet Pea asked, getting down to the nitty-gritty of why she'd called.

"Things are going okay here, Ma. They aren't moving as fast as I'd hoped, but we're getting there." *Who am I kidding? I haven't even checked in with the investigator yet,* Promise thought.

"Okay. Well, when you hear from the investigator, can you find out how long you might be up there? Like I said, I need to talk to you, and it's something we should discuss face to face. Besides, I know your baby is missing you. It's been a couple weeks, and I still can't figure out how to work that damn computer. Something's gotta give, Promise," Sweet Pea said.

"I'm sorry about the computer, Mama, but what is it you have to talk to me about? You sound mad or something."

"Like I said, we need to talk in person."

"Well, if this lasts longer than a month and a half, I plan to come home for at least a week and spend every day of that week with my baby. I didn't miss her first word or her first wobbly steps, so I won't miss anything looking for a deadbeat man. You have my word on that. I think it's worth a try, though, and that's the only reason I'm trying. If he rejects or ignores my attempts to get in touch with him, I guess I'll wash my hands of him and just take his ass to court. If he don't wanna spend any time with her, he's damn sure gonna spend some money on his child," Promise said, having already made up her mind about that.

"Okay. I'll take your word on that. If it comes down to that, we'll talk about some of what I have to talk about and save the rest for when this is all over," Sweet Pea said.

"Okay, Ma. Sounds like a plan," Promise said stumped as to what it was that was so important but something she didn't want to discuss over the phone.

"Tell Monica I said hello. I hope she's keeping you safe. Love you. What's that thing you young'ns be saying? Oh yeah. TTYL," Sweet Pea said, laughing as she hung up, knowing damn well she didn't have no business talking like that.

"Did she really just say that? Girl, my mama just told me TTYL! Ain't that some shit?" Promise couldn't help but laugh.

"So Mom Duke's talking like she texting? Ha-ha! It surprised me you didn't tell her what's really been going on up here."

"Girl, she's my mother. As far as she knows, everything is fine and we're taking care of business. We both know that isn't the truth, but that's what we'll let her roll with," Promise said as they pulled up in front of their hotel. "Now I say we go shower, get dressed, and hit up the mall or some boutiques. I don't really know what the style is here, but I'm sure we can find something we like. I did the other day. After that, I'm staying in to get some rest for work tomorrow. Before we came up here, I did a little research and found some of the top strip clubs. Even if we don't dance, I've got a plan that'll help us find a man with fat pockets. Trust me, we'll get all their attention. Every man's interest will be piqued when they see two drop-dead gorgeous women walking into a strip club, as long as they know we ain't a couple. We'll have them following us around like dogs, eating out the palm of our hands. We can take care of business from there, if you know what I mean."

"Well, I respect you a lot more for not saying anything to your mom. And I'm always down to hit the mall and boutiques up, but in case you weren't paying attention, that nigga Q stole all my money. I can't do the shopping spree thing right now. I'll just wear something I brought with me. Money is always my motive, so I'm ready to get to work. I caught what you said at the end too. I'm down to go that route if the money is right," Monica replied, winking her eye.

"Don't worry about money. I got you. Now we're going shopping, so hurry up and wash ya ass so we can roll out. I'm about to do the same," Promise said.

"Thanks," Monica said in a whisper.

"No time for that. Let's just move our asses," Promise replied.

Monica smiled as she watched Promise walk away. *Move our asses? She sure as hell knows how to move hers!*

Chapter Eleven

Plans Moving Forward

Black Ice and Jelly had their plan laid out. As far as Black Ice was concerned, all that was left to do was to find Promise and execute their foolproof plan, but Jelly had something else in store.

"Hello, is this Truth?" Jelly asked.

"Yeah, this me. Who is this?" Truth asked, sounding a bit defensive.

"My name is Jelly. I don't know if Mark told you about me, but he seems to think you can help me."

"Yeah, he mentioned you and some of what you need help with, but I don't like to talk about shit like this over the phone. Can you meet me at the Copley Mall, at the Legal Seafood Restaurant, maybe late morning tomorrow?"

"Sounds like a plan."

"A'ight. Bet. See you at 11:30."

When Jelly got off the phone, she felt a twinge of excitement. Finally, she felt like the head bitch in charge, and she loved that feeling.

* * *

"You know what? I haven't danced in, like, forever. I bet it would be fun to just branch out and go to work. Maybe one day this week we can hit a strip club up and do what we do best, make lots of money, have plenty of bitches hating, and pop our pussies like that's what we were born to do," Black Ice suggested.

"I really didn't come down here to make money, but I'm not going to turn down a chance to bring in a couple stacks. I'm surprised you would even take that chance, knowing what's at stake. I mean, Promise is so close, but she can't be touched yet. She doesn't know what she has on her trail either."

"I'm not really takin' that much a chance. I'm really just lookin' for something to do. Anyway, Dezman has been hanging out with some of his old college buddies who are in town visiting. He hasn't been the least bit worried about me.

What's new though? I could stay out all night, and he probably wouldn't even notice."

"Then it's set! You choose the day, and we'll hop on the money train, girl," Jelly said, slappin' high-fives with Black Ice.

"You're so silly. I'm thinking this Saturday. I know it's a couple days away, but I think we'll be prepped and pampered in time."

"You got that right, girl!"

* * *

Jelly arrived at the mall a little after 11:00. She made her way to the restaurant to meet Truth. She noticed the seafood smell right away, even though the restaurant had just opened for the day. She wasn't much of a seafood eater other than a little shrimp and fried fish every now and then, and the smell of the fresh seafood began to make her stomach queasy. She stood outside the front of the restaurant. *This nigga better hurry up and get here. I'm not feeling too well. Why'd he choose this place anyway, when we coulda met at any of the fabulous stores in this mall?*

"Sup, ma? You must be Jelly. Hope I didn't leave you waiting too long. Some unexpected shit came up that I had to handle it."

"I haven't been here long, but you should never keep a lady waiting without a call or text."

"I feel you, boss. Enough of all this small talk. Let's get down to the nitty-gritty." *Damn! Mark didn't tell me how fine li'l mama was. I love redbones. After we handle this business, I need to find out if I can handle her other business,* Truth thought, looking her up and down.

"Okay. My friend and I are looking for this chick, and we got word that she's in Boston, but we don't know exactly where. We need you to help us find her."

"Hmm. He must not be some long-lost friend, or you woulda gone to the police. I'm no mind-reader, but I think I hear some vengeance behind those words. Do you wanna give me more details?"

"I guess you're paying attention then if you caught that. No, she's not a long-lost friend, but she'll really be a missing person after we find her. That's all I'm going to say. You won't be involved in that part, though, so you don't have to worry 'bout that."

"Well damn! If you don't mind my askin', what did the chick do to deserve all that?"

"She fucked with the wrong person, and now the person is out to get her. She just couldn't seem to leave well enough alone, so now it's on. Now she's here, and I want you to find out exactly where."

"Okay. I got you! I guess you ain't to be fucked with, huh?" Truth asked, wearing a devilish grin.

She said nothing and just stared at him.

"I'm just fuckin' with you. Lighten up some, ma! All I need is her name and a detailed description of what she looks like. Leave the rest up to me."

"Great. Her name is Promise. It's a unique name, so that should make it easier to find her. She's twenty-one or twenty-two, about five-seven or five-eight, with light skin and long hair that she usually wears in layers framing her face. She has unique eyes too."

"Unique how?"

"They're hazel, with specs of green throughout them. She loves labels, so she'll be walking around looking like new money."

"Wait…you said her name is Promise?" Truth asked in disbelief. *Hell naw! That's Rare Breed's new girl!*

"Yep. Why? Do you know her?"

"Naw, but like you said, Promise is a unique name." *What the hell am I s'pose to do now? I need to get to the bottom of this and see what's going on. What's her real reason for being in Boston?* Truth wondered.

"Yeah it is. How long do you think it'll take for you to find out exactly where she is?"

"It shouldn't take too long."

"Okay. You have my number. Just call me when you find something out." Jelly stood to leave, but Truth grabbed her arm.

"I do plan on calling you, but it'll be before I find ol' girl. We should chill sometime."

For the first time, Jelly checked Truth out from head to toe. Till then, she'd been so blinded by her mission that she hadn't realized how fine he was. *Damn! He looks good enough to lick, from the top of his smooth, bald head to his feet, hitting every spot in between. Look at this LL Cool J nigga! Mmm…Damn right we can definitely chill sometime,* Jelly thought. "Sure, we can hang out sometime. Hit me up when you're ready," she said, trying to sound casual. She bent over to pick up her purse, giving Truth clear view of her breast as her top fell away from her body. She could feel Truth checking her out.

"I'll do that, ma." *Damn! That girl might be the one to change a nigga ways,* Truth thought as she sashayed off without another word.

* * *

Dezman left yet another meeting with the commissioner of the NBA, and he'd finally got his answer to his question: Yes, they would drop him from the league due to use of enhancement substances. They'd also revoked his last MVP trophy and given it to the runner-up. When his phone rang, he just stared at it for a moment. *Who the fuck is calling me now? I'm not in the mood to be talking to nobody right now,* He thought. *Damn!* When he saw who was calling, he instantly got a headache, "What, Bria?"

"You know I hate when you call me that."

"You act like I'm calling you something other than your damn name. You're not Black Ice. Your name is Bria Stevenson, and I'm not using that whorin'-around name that everyone else calls you."

"I don't like that name though. You could call me your baby, boo, honey, or sweetie like you used too. I've explained to you plenty of times how that name makes me feel. It brings back all those horrible childhood memories. My mother called me a bitch and ho just to avoid saying my name because my father named me after his damn mistress. I'm named after the woman he cheated on my mother with for so many years and ended up leaving us for. I guess he loved her name that much."

"Yeah, yeah. I've heard all that before, but Bria is still your name, and we all gotta get over some shit in life. Anyway, what do you want? I'm going through a lot right now, and I don't feel like being bothered. I won't be coming home tonight, so you don't need to wait up."

"I know you're going through a lot, Dezman. Shit, I've been here with you every step of the way, going through it all with you. Don't do this to me. Don't shut me out. Just come home, baby. You know how emotional I've been lately. It hurts when you do stuff like this."

"There you go with that sentimental, emotional-ass shit. I'm not falling for it anymore, Bria. I know I've hurt you so much. I've heard it all before…my cheating, staying out late, forgetting to call, and fathering a baby with somebody else. If I'm so bad, fuckin' leave Bria!"

"No, Dezman! I'm not going to give you what you want. I know you want me to leave so you can be free to do and fuck whoever, but it's not happening. I've been here too long. I've put up with too much shit to walk away."

"Yeah, a'ight, ma. Keep singing that same song. But let me ask you something. What was today?"

"What do you mean? It's not your birthday or our anniversary, if that's what you're getting at. What are you talking about?"

"Been with me every step of the way, huh? Going through it all with me my ass! I bet if those too-high-ass heels were coming out today, you wouldn't forget that. My meeting with the NBA commissioner was today, dumb-ass. I'm done with you!"

Click!

Fed up with her lack of awareness and a conversation that was going nowhere, he hung up on her and felt good about it. He drove, trying to clear his mind and figure out where he should go from that point in his life—or what was left of a life anyway. In his eyes, his life had ended at the meeting. He couldn't imagine life without basketball. ""Fuck this, man! I know what needs to be done. I have to right all my wrongs one at a time, starting with finding Promise and Deziray. That's it. I want my family. I want Promise as my wife. It's time to finally stop running and face my family," Dezman said to himself. "I gotta do right by that woman and our child." And with that said, he made a U-turn and headed to the airport, ready to buy a one-way ticket to Tampa and to the future he'd finally made up his mind about.

"Who the fuck does he think he is hanging up on me like that?" Black Ice screamed as she dialed his number. Her call went straight to voicemail. She dialed again...same result.

"I can't believe this bastard! I stood by him through all this shit and now because I forgot one meeting, yeah it was an important meeting and I'm sorry, but I forgot one meeting and he says he's done with me! I don't think so, man. I'm real tired of this treatment and I'm gonna tell your ass as soon as you walk through that door!"

Black Ice was pissed and was sounding off to no one as if Dezman was standing right there. She thought about calling Jelly and telling her what had just happened but she decided against that. Instead, she poured herself a glass of wine and sat in the living room waiting for him to arrive home. She woke the next morning, slumped over on the arm of the couch...alone. Dezman never came home.

* * *

"Hello," Jelly answered, sounding as if she really didn't want to be awake yet.

"It's me. Get up, we're going to get some shit together so we can hit a spot and make some cash on Saturday. I gotta get out of this house."

"What's going on now?"

"Same old shit! I don't even want to talk about it. Just be ready."

"Okay, bye."

Black Ice showered, got dressed and headed out but not before trying Dezman one more time. Again, his voicemail.

Chapter Twelve

A New Addiction

Sweet Pea woke up later than usual the next day. She'd been awake damn near the whole night, unable to fall asleep. For some strange reason, her skin itched and felt as though something was crawling on it. It was almost as if she was going through withdrawal but from what? A little weed?

T-mack would be stopping by in a few. He hadn't called like he'd promised to during their phone call the night before, but she was sure he would soon.

"Hey, sleepyhead. You shoulda stayed up to keep Nana company last night, but you slept like a princess!"

Deziray sat there smiling at her grandmother. To the baby, Sweet Pea was just another funny character, like the ones in the cartoon shows she loved to watch, always very animated. "Nana!" Deziray said.

"Yes, that right, baby. I'm Nana." Sweet Pea smiled. It made her so happy to hear her grandbaby call her.

In the middle of the afternoon, after Sweet Pea had just put Deziray down for her nap, the doorbell rang, and she already knew it was. Before she answered the door she checked herself out in the ceiling-to-floor mirror in the foyer. *Damn, I clean up good,* she thought. Sweet Pea swung the door open with the biggest smile on her face, but when she saw the look on T-mack's face and the tears in his eyes, her smile disappeared just as quickly as it had appeared. "Oh my God! Come in. What's wrong?"

T-mack just stood there at the door, staring past Sweet Pea, with tears running down his face. He looked like a broken man and finally managed to utter, "She's…gone!"

"Who's go…" But before she could finish her question, she'd figured out the answer. He'd just come from seeing his mother at the hospital, and that had to be who he was talking about. Sweet Pea knew T-mack was a strong man and wouldn't have been so broken up over any other female but his mama. Sweet

Pea's mind ran rampant, and she wasn't sure what to say.

"No warning or anything! I swear, yesterday when I was there, they told me she was getting better, that she was coming full circle." He sobbed, and more tears wet his cheeks. "When the nurse called me this morning, I thought she was calling just to tell me that my mother was asking for me. That wasn't the case. Instead, they said she'd taken a turn for the worse and that I should get to the hospital within the next hour and notify any other relatives. I was just waking up. I got dressed when she called and I was out the door in three minutes flat. When I got to the bus stop, I realized that the bus had already picked up, and it was too far down the street for me to catch it. If it wasn't for that fuckin' bus…"

Sweet Pea took T-mack into her arms, but he was too weak to stand.

His ankles buckled, and he dropped to his knees, grabbing Sweet Pea around her waist, as if he were holding on for dear life. He repeated the same question over and over again: "Why her? Why her? Why her?"

All she could say was, "God called another angel home."

Between the two of them the tears steadily flowed and luckily little Deziray was content watching.

After a while, T-mack began to talk again. "Any other time, it would've taken me about twenty-five minutes to get to the hospital, but because I missed the damn bus and wasn't about to wait thirty minutes for another, I ran all the way to there. When I finally got to the ICU, I heard this machine going off, beeping like crazy, and I saw all these nurses and doctors scrambling around. I pushed past them to see what all the commotion was about. My mother was struggling, hovering between living and dying. I yelled to her, 'I'm here, Mama! I made it. Fight until you can't fight any more. You're not alone. I love you!' I saw her index finger rise up and point in my direction and then just drop. The machine started making this irritating buzzing noise, and there was a straight green line on the screen. She was just…gone."

"I'm so sorry it happened this way, but listen to me. God doesn't make any mistakes. When He called your mom home, He knew what He was doing. He stopped all her pain and suffering today. You don't see it that way now because the loss is still fresh, but you will realize it in the future."

"I can't take this right now. I just want to take it all away…all the pain and hurt. I want it all to go away. I need to use the bathroom. Where is it?" T-mack asked, gathering himself and getting up off the floor. He kept touching his pocket, as if he was trying to make sure whatever he'd stuffed in it was still there.

"Go all the way down this hallway and make a left. It's the first door on the right-hand side." Sweet Pea was beside herself. She'd looked forward to spending some time with T-mack, but now that time would be spent stricken with sad emotions.

Some thirty minutes later, he still hadn't come out of the bathroom. On one hand, she wanted to leave him be, but on the other hand, she wanted to make sure he was okay. Finally, she decided to go to the bathroom and check on him. When she first got to the bathroom door, she just listened. She heard some sniffling and sniffing, which brought back her tears, 'cause she knew his hurt. Just thinking about how much he loved and cared for his mother made her want to better her relationship with her own daughter.

"T-mack, is everything okay?" she asked through the door. "Well, I know everything isn't okay, but can you come out of the bathroom?"

He opened the bathroom door slowly. His eyes were bloodshot, bright red from what looked like something more than just crying. When he walked out of the bathroom, he kept swiping at his nose. He didn't say a word and found his own way to the living room. After a moment, he spoke again. "I have something to tell you, and I don't know how you're going to feel about it," T-mack said, continuously looking over his shoulder, as if someone was behind him or following him.

"Tell me. I ain't gonna judge you," Sweet Pea said.

"I do this to calm my nerves and relieve my stress," he said, then pulled out a baggie filled with a white, powdery substance. "I'm not addicted, so don't look at me like I'm some kind of powder-head, and I ain't no crack-head either. I only do this when I feel the need to."

"Is that what you were doing while you were in the bathroom?" Sweet Pea asked, her interest piqued.

During her time in prison, her cellmate had told her a lot about certain kinds of drugs and how they'd made her feel. She would say, "Girl, I didn't have a care in the world after I sniffed that shit." That woman's baby-daddy had introduced her to the drug, and now the same thing was happening to Sweet Pea.

"Yeah, that was what I was doing," he said with his head hung low in embarrassment. He opened the baggie and spread some of the powder on the table. Using a razor, he cut the powder into straight lines. T-mack then pulled out a $1 bill that was rolled up tight and proceeded to sniff a line of coke. When he finished, he leaned his head back and closed his eyes, as if savoring the feeling as the drug coursed through his body. He repeated that two more times. When he'd had enough and his high was just right, he dropped the $1 bill.

Sweet Pea's curiosity really began to get to her, and she wanted to try it for herself. *It can't be too bad,* she thought. She'd never experienced such a carefree feeling, and she was ready for it. "T-mack! T-mack? Wake ya ass up. How the hell you doze off that quick? Show me how to do this," Sweet Pea said, picking the rolled-up $1 bill off the floor and no longer focusing on her main concern... Deziray.

"Huh? I'm not 'sleep. I'm just relaxed. This shit ain't for you, baby. You don't need none of this. It ain't no game."

"Nigga, don't tell me what is and ain't for me. I said you best show me how to do this."

"All right. But don't say I didn't warn ya." He took her through the motions of sniffing the cocaine. He taught her that she should always hold one nostril closed and sniff with the other. He also told her that since it was her first time, she should take it easy and only do half a line. "If ya feel okay after that, you can do the other half," he said. "When you sniff your first line, your nose is going to be on fire. It'll feel like nothin' you ever felt before."

When Sweet Pea took her first sniff, she wondered when the good feeling of no worries would begin. All she felt was an excruciating pain shooting through her nostril and her entire head. Then, all of a sudden, it felt like she'd been thrown in an oven that was cranked to its highest temperature.

"You all right? I know you probably feel like you're on fire. That'll go away shortly. Go ahead and take another sniff. This shit is amazing once you get used to it."

"Turn the air up! Woo! I feel so warm and numb all over," she said, but that didn't stop her from taking another sniff. "Damn! Did you turn the air up? I'm starting to sweat." Sweet Pea couldn't take it anymore, so she removed her shirt and leggings. Her body was rather toned for a woman of her age. The first couple of years she'd spent in prison, all she'd done was eat and sleep, but during her last few years, she'd exercised, jogged, and lifted weights. That had really done her body good.

"Damn, man. Don't start that tripping shit and blow my high. I just turned the shit up."

"Am I hearing things? Did you hear that? Sounds like someone's at the door. Oh shit! What if somebody is at the door?" Sweet Pea said, overcome with paranoia and panicking.

Chapter Thirteen

Time To Get Back To Business

The past couple days had been good to Promise and Monica. They'd been putting in work, though not their typical kind of work. They'd gone to the club to dance but ended up not doing that after all. Before making their presence known as new dancers, they'd walked in the club dressed to be stressed. They decided to canvass the place and see what kind of guys were coming and going, to sort out the big spenders from the pretenders. As soon as they'd taken their seats at the bar, a man with a strong aura about him approached them.

"Hello, ladies. My name is Marcus Davidson, and this here's my friend Nathan Marshall. Sorry if we're bothering you. We just couldn't help noticing all that beauty when y'all entered the club."

"That's sweet, thank you," Promise said as she immediately checked out their dress code to calculate how much they'd spent on themselves. From what she could gather, Marcus and Nathan had to be businessmen of some sort; they were dressed in designer suits and shoes and even had diamond cufflinks, and they were definitely clean-cut, white-collar types.

"If y'all don't mind me asking, what brings y'all to a strip club?" Marcus asked, obviously the more outspoken of the two.

"We're just out looking for a good time in a more chill environment. What better place than one filled with beautiful naked women, drinks, music, and low lights?" Promise replied.

"I think y'all would have an even better time chillin' with us," Nathan spoke up.

"Well, time is money," Promise said bluntly.

"Money ain't a thing," Nathan said, feeling the ladies out as he pulled out a thick stack.

"Please spare us with your $1 bills. We like bank rolls," Monica stated, letting them know upfront that it was going to take more than what they thought to ride that ride.

"Dollar bills? We don't roll like that—or at least I don't. I don't know what kinda men y'all are used to, but that right there is a stack of twenties, and this right here is a stack of hundreds," Marcus said, pulling out an even bigger stack of money. "We're not in the business of faking the funk. We live this shit. I'm one of the top criminal defense attorneys in Boston. Most people like to assume it has something to do with my law firms, but I assure you it was my hard work that got me here. So let me reassure you ladies that this is chump change compared to what's in my bank account," Marcus chimed in.

"That's what I'm talking about! A man who's about his business. For the record, let me just say we've had our share of paid men, be they doctors, label owners, CEOs, actors, or professional athletes," Promise said, making sure they heard every word. She didn't want them to think they'd never been in the presence of money. At least she had, even if Monica hadn't.

Both the men smiled at them and Marcus called the bartender over. "Give these ladies another round of whatever they're drinking."

Monica was beginning to get a little restless. Tired of all the resume sharing that was going back and forth, she was ready to get on her mission. What she didn't know was that Promise was in no rush. She planned to play right along with them, keeping them in line every step of the way.

"Nathan, what is it that you do?" Promise asked.

"I'm more of a behind-the-scenes type of guy. I own a couple of businesses here and there," Nathan said, keeping his answer short and to the point.

"Two legit, upstanding black men? That's what's up! Oh! We've been rude, haven't we? My name is Monica, and this Promise. If you don't mind me asking, how old are y'all?"

"I'll be thirty in a couple months, and Nathan is thirty-one."

"I see your drinks are gone. What do y'all think about coming back to our rooms to have a little fun?" Marcus asked.

"Sounds like a plan, since we've all spent the past hour getting to know each other," Promise replied.

"Great. Let's all head out together and get the ball rolling," Marcus said, winking his eye at Promise.

As they headed toward the door, a pretty, thick chocolate woman stepped in their path, popping her gum and giving them major attitude. "Um, Marcus, is you leaving?" she asked, giving Promise a side eye, like she was standing a tad bit too close to him.

"MC, I don't need you questioning me. You see my friends and me heading toward the door, right? Move yo' ass on out the way," Marcus said, placing his hand on the small of Promise's back and sidestepping MC.

"I see how you niggas do! You get all high and mighty when you got a title to your name. You still ain't shit!" MC yelled.

"If I'm not shit, why are you sweating the fact that I'm leaving with somebody else?"

She had no answer.

"Exactly! You're embarrassing yourself. Now fall back, ma."

When Monica walked past the woman, she felt the need to taunt her. "Excuse me, hon'. You dropped something."

MC looked down around her feet. "I didn't drop nothin'."

"Your face! Now you best pick it up!" Monica said, and they all burst out laughing at MC.

"You bitch! I could—" But MC didn't get the chance to finish before a security guard came over and interrupted her.

"Do we have a problem?" he intervened.

"Yeah you do. A chocolate one!" Monica burst out laughing again.

They continued walking toward the door, sharing another laugh at MC's expense.

"Bitch, it's Milk Chocolate…and don't you ever forget that, you dry-ass ho!"

"Yeah, yeah," was all Monica said in response.

Once they made it back to their new friends' hotel, they split into pairs. Promise and Marcus headed off toward his suite.

Monica and Nathan stalled for a bit, both thinking about what they wanted to take from the other one. Monica thought about the things she could buy with the bankroll in his pocket, and Nathan was wondering about how wet her pussy would get.

As soon as they were inside the room Monica had made up her mind that she wasn't talking any more. "I don't see the need for all that talking like they were doing. Let's just get down to it," Monica finally said, going on a mental shopping spree with his money already.

"Damn! You're my type of woman—a take-charge, straight-to-business, no-time-to-play type."

"You got that right. So let's get busy, baby."

"I got no problem with that, ma!" Nathan said, obviously excited.

* * *

After that, the friends didn't do anything outside of each other. They fucked and sucked regularly, ate, shopped, and slept. Monica loved every minute of it because the money was flowing steadily. Promise, on the other hand, was quickly getting over the whole fuck-sleep-shop thing they had going. It wasn't anything new to her, but it obviously was to Monica, and she thought Monica was being too money-hungry. After all, Promise lived by the code: "Never milk a cow until it's dry. Just get a little, give it a rest, and then return for some more."

Finally, after another day passed of the same-old, same-old with Marcus and Nathan, Promise put her foot down. "I'm not hanging out with y'all today," she told Monica. "I've gotta focus on the reason I came here. I didn't plan on partying. Sure, I hoped to make a li'l money, but I wanted to find my deadbeat-ass baby-daddy in the process. Plus, I haven't talked to nor spent any time with Mike and that's not cool. Why don't you go ahead and chill with them today, and I'll hook up with y'all sometime or another."

"That's not a problem, chile. I know you came up here on a mission. That's why I'm not stressing over you having to focus on handling your business. I'll hang with them and keep 'em company until you can join us."

"Good," Promise replied. "Thanks."

"A'ight, I'm about to be out. Nathan is already down stairs waiting on me. How do I look?"

"You look good, girl. Those Steve Maddens would make the ugliest outfit look amazing."

"I don't know whether to take that as a compliment or an insult to my outfit. But anyway, I don't have the time to try and figure it out. See ya!" Monica said as she walked out the door.

If you ask me, it was both. The shoes were dope, but that outfit was a no-go, Promise thought.

After Monica was gone, Promise knew she had to get her mind on the right track. She was slipping too far off track and needed to put her game face back on. She hadn't even talked to her mom and daughter in a couple of days. The last time they'd spoken, it had seemed like Sweet Pea was trying to rush her off the phone, but she'd brushed that off, assuming it was just because her mother missed her.

* * *

"Hello, Sterling Kane Private Investigations. How can I help you?" the receptionist asked.

"Hello. This is Promise Brown. Is Sterling available?"

"He's not in the office this week, but I can transfer you to his cell. Please hold."

After a few clicks, Promise heard someone else pick up the phone.

"Sterling speaking. How can I help you?" the P.I. asked.

"Hi, Sterling. This is Promise Brown. We spoke over a month ago. I know it's been a while, but I'm calling to find out how your investigation is going."

"Oh, hi, Promise. It has been a while, hasn't it? Well, let me catch you up on what I know. I've found out a few things since we last spoke. Hold on," he said as he flipped through some papers. "Okay, well, when it comes to Dezman's professional basketball career, I haven't been able to find out much beyond a couple weeks ago, which makes since, because it turns out he was suspended when traces of enhancement drugs were found in his system during a random drug test. That explains why I've had difficulty finding his whereabouts. After he received word of his suspension, he went in hiding, you could say. After a little digging, I found out that he sold his mansion and a lot of his properties and traded his car in. A couple weeks ago, Dezman finally came out of hiding. I followed him to a couple clubs, and one day he went to an outside basketball court. I know he had a meeting with the commissioner of the NBA at the beginning of this week. At that meeting, he learned some upsetting news," Sterling said.

"What news?" Promise asked, afraid to hear the answer.

"Well, it turns out that the consequences of his use of performance enhancers were pretty steep. It cost him his spot in the league, and they even revoked his last MVP award," Sterling stated.

"What!? They let him go? Damn. I know he must be tripping right now. Well, that just goes to show, God don't like ugly…and He ain't too fond of pretty either," Promise said.

"Yes, they let him go. After that meeting, I tracked him to the airport. He booked a flight to Tampa, Florida. My investigation stopped there, of course, because I hadn't heard from you and had no idea if you two were back in good grace or not," Sterling replied.

"Oh my God! Tampa? How long ago was that?" Promise asked.

"He boarded the flight just yesterday morning," Sterling said.

"Well, thank you for continuing your search. Lord knows I wouldn't have gotten this far without your help. I got caught up in some other mess and lost my focus, but I'm refocused now. I'm gonna book my own flight to Tampa as soon as I can wrap up my loose ends here in Boston," Promise said.

"Okay. You handle your business. I'm actually flying there tonight. I'll keep my eyes on him until you're able to get here…I mean there. Silly me."

"Silly nothin'! You're a life-saver, Sterling. I will definitely give you a big tip when it's time for me to make my final payment."

"Anytime. I'm just doin' my job. I'm going to get going now. I've got to pack."

Promise didn't know how to feel. She was excited and mad at the same time. She had so many questions. First thing first, she sent Monica a text.

Promise: *Monica, "I'm out of here in a couple of days."*

Next, she dialed Rare Breed's number. When her call went straight to voicemail, she decided to send him a text as well.

Promise: *I need to see you ASAP!*

Then, Promise got a head start on packing, but she soon realized she'd accumulated far more new clothes than she had room for. Promise grabbed her purse and keys and headed out the door. "It's time to go shopping again—this time for luggage. It's time to go home!"

Chapter Fourteen

A Step Behind

Truth's meeting with Jelly had been the main thing for a while. He knew he had to tell his homie about Promise, but he didn't know how. *How can I possibly tell him that I've been hired to find the woman he's falling for?* The bad part was, he didn't even know how she was being set up or what Jelly planned to do to her once he informed her of Promise's whereabouts. He had a lot of questions of his own. *Why is Promise really in Boston? Maybe she came there to escape whatever danger was threatening her back in her hometown,* Truth thought.

"Yo, man, you know I dig what I do, but I thought this was going to be a work-hard-play-even-harder type of trip. Not a work-work-work-and-no-play trip. I know you hear me," Rare Breed said, trying to get Truth's attention.

"My bad, dude. Man, I got so much shit on my mind."

"Yeah? Like what?"

"Well, I actually need to run something by you, but I'll do that when I get to the bottom of the situation," Truth said, still thinking about what he was going to do.

"You know I'm an upstanding man. Whatever you need to tell me, you can tell me, Truth. It'll stay between you and me," Rare Breed replied, somewhat offended because he felt that he and Truth were closer than that. They'd been like brothers since they were young boys running around the projects.

"A'ight, then listen to this shit. My mans back in Tampa called me up and asked me to meet up with this girl he works with. Me and him go way back. Do you remember big Mark? He used to be with us stealing candy out the li'l bodega at the end of the block when we were jits"

"Yeah, I remember big Mark."

"Well, I told him I'd do him a favor and meet with this chick, and he said I'd get all the details from her."

"Okay. Well, quit beating around the bush and get to the point," Rare Breed said. "Did you meet up with her?"

"All right, man. Long story short, the chick's looking for your girl, Promise. I didn't let her know that I know Promise, but she said once I find her, she'll take it from there." When Truth finished, he looked at Rare Breed and noticed that his usual hardcore look had been replaced with a confused expression.

"What the fuck you mean she'll take it from there? I don't know this li'l bitch, but she can kill all that. Ain't nobody fuckin' with Promise. Over my dead body, Truth, and I mean that. In the short period of time me and her were with each other, I fell for her. She broke down my rough exterior and showed a nigga that I am capable of loving somebody," Rare Breed admitted.

"I feel what you're saying, but just hear me out. Let me find out what's going on before you jump to fuck-a-bitch-up mode."

"Yeah, I'll let you do what you have to do, but you better do it fast, 'cause I got a mind to go pick Promise up right now and not let her out of my sight till I find out what the hell's going on," Rare Breed said.

"I'm on it, man. Just trust me," Truth responded.

"Yeah, a'ight! Now I'm feeling some type of way. I can't go back in the booth right now. I guess I'll burn this pen and paper up with some new lyrics," Rare Breed said.

* * *

Saturday arrived in no time. They'd been doing all the essential things in the days leading up to it: putting in a rush order for new dancewear from a top dancewear designer, getting a Brazilian wax, and having their hair and nails done. They knew some people didn't think of stripping as a real job, but they knew better. Stripping was a job within a job, and it took a lot of hard work, preparation and dedication.

Jelly only brought up Dezman once and from the look on Black Ice's face, she knew to leave it alone for a minute. She was sure Black Ice would tell her what happened when she was ready.

Looking their best, Black Ice and Jelly entered the strip club and checked everything out.

"I know the owner, and I'm sure he won't have a problem with us dancing tonight. Just have a seat at the bar. I'm gonna go see what's up with him," Black Ice said as she strutted off down a discreet hallway next to the bar.

"Now that's more like the Black Ice I used to know. She wanted something and she made it happen. Ain't no whining and crying...just handling her business," Jelly said, smiling as she watched Black Ice disappear down the hallway.

The club was a nice, upscale gentlemen's club, and the atmosphere was very laidback. The bar ran all along one wall. As Jelly sat there, she wondered how Black Ice knew the owner of the club. Even more so, she wondered how Black Ice knew where his office was; from the bar, she couldn't even see that there was a hallway there, so she had to have some inside knowledge.

About fifteen minutes later, she emerged from the hall. "We're good, girl. Let's get dressed and get this night started off right."

"Eh, Poca, have a couple of screwdrivers with light ice waiting for us when we come back on the floor," Black Ice said.

Poca? She knows the bartender too? Damn! She must have visited this club a time or two when she was traveling to different states to dance, Jelly thought.

"Gotcha, Mama," the Puerto Rican beauty replied.

Jelly followed Black Ice into the dressing room, and the two instantly received dirty looks. As was the case in any club, the dancers who'd been there a long time hated seeing new dancers come in because they were sure the new chicks would try to take the spots they'd worked so hard to get.

"Suga, did I tell you about them two hoes that came in here the other night? They took one of my big-time clients, my main source of income. I ain't had to dance a day since I met him, up until a couple of days ago. Those two hoes pranced their little asses in here and sat down and just like that, my customer was gone, took, snatched up, or whatever you want to call it. The one that was with my customer had some pretty eyes. I noticed them because under the light, they were sparkling, and their strange color just popped."

"Strange color? What do you mean? What color were they?" Suga asked.

"I don't know. Hazel, I guess, with specs of green. That was the first thing I noticed about her, but I'm sure they were just some fake-ass contacts. Her hair was on point too. That shit looked so good I almost thought it was real. Her friend wasn't as on point as she was, but she was still a head-turner."

"Naw, you hadn't ran that by me, but I wish I would've been here that night. A bitch would've had to see me about dude," Suga responded.

"Even though Marcus wasn't a make-it-rain type of dude, he still spent straight cash very discreetly. Now he hasn't been around. I guess he's laid up. Nigga ain't called me or nothing.". Now look…here come two more hoes tryin'a come up in here and fuck up the rotation we done already established," the chick with the smooth brown skin said.

"Fuck them. It's plenty of paid niggas out there."

"Hold the fuck up! First of all, who the fuck you bitches callin' hoes? I been stripping for too long not to know the rules, and I don't fuck with another dancer's main customers," Black Ice snapped, no longer able to ignore their little conversation.

"I'm not even gonna take it there with you, chick. My bad, callin' y'all hoes. I just don't do too well with new faces, especially four new faces in one week," the smooth-skinned woman said.

"You gon' have to excuse Milk Chocolate. She doesn't know any better," Suga apologized on behalf of her friend.

"I can respect that. I never liked new faces at clubs I used to work in either," Black Ice replied.

"Hey, Milk Chocolate, can you describe in detail the female you say you saw with your customer? From what you said already, I think I might know her," Jelly asked.

Black Ice looked over at Jelly, confused, but when she thought about all that had been said, she began nodding her head in agreement. "Yeah, we might know her. Can you tell us more?"

"Well, there were two females, but the one who stole my customer was light-skinned and kind of tall, maybe about five-seven, with long, layered hair, a small waist, thick thighs, a phat ass, and full lips. She was dressed like she had just stepped straight off someone's runway. Does she sound familiar?" Milk Chocolate asked.

"Yep! That's her! Her name is Promise, and I believe every word you say about her, because I know she's a man-stealing, wannabe-boss bitch. In fact, that's one bitch I can't wait to get my hands on," Black Ice stated.

"She damn sho took my customer. I could've stomped her ass then, or her home girl's, since she seemed to like to joke a lot. Even though she didn't take my customer forcefully and he stepped to her, she outta know better in a strip club where bitches are tryin'a make money. I better never see her ass again. I was pressing Marcus for answers that night, but now that I know this Promise bitch is big on takin' other chicks' men, I'll kick her ass first and ask questions later," Milk Chocolate said.

"Fuck her! There's no need to waste time talking about her. Shit, it's time for us to get to the money," Jelly said, her mind wandering. *Where the hell could Promise be now? Seems we're always fuckin' two steps behind her!*

* * *

Dezman had made it to Tampa, and it felt like it had been forever since he'd been there. He had to use his rental car's GPS a few times just to get around. After checking into the downtown Marriott, he headed to the University Mall to pick up some clothes and shoes since he'd left Boston with only the clothes on his back. He tried to hide his appearance by wearing shades and pulling his fitted down over his eyes a little, but there was no way to hide his 6'6" frame. He tried to do whatever he could to keep from being noticed or recognized.

Once he picked up some boxers and socks, he tackled the next thing on his to-do list. He walked into a store called All Things Gold, in the middle of the mall, right by Macy's. "What's up, man? I don't want you to bullshit me, 'cause I know quality. How much of this stuff is real gold, platinum, and diamonds?" Dezman asked straight up.

"Hey, mister! Don't come up in this store and offend me! Everything we sell is real," the Arabian man said.

"I would hate to have to file charges against your store for false advertisement, so are you tellin' me that's your word and you're sticking to it?" Dezman asked as he slid the man a $100 bill. "Tell me the truth."

"All right," the man said quietly as he scooped the $100 up discreetly and placed it in his shirt pocket. "Some of this stuff is mixed gold or gold plated. Most of our 'diamonds' are cubic zirconia," the man whispered, making sure no one else could hear him since the store was busy.

"See? Now was that so hard? Thanks for looking out. So tell me where I can find the real stuff," Dezman asked, knowing he was pushing it.

The man discreetly pointed right across from his family's store, to a shop called Jahaun's Jewelry.

"Hmm. Do you know where I can find a Tiffany & Company or a Kay Jewelers?" Dezman asked. He knew he was pushing the man's patience to the brink, but he didn't want to get Promise's ring from University Mall after he'd found out they sold fake stuff.

"Are you trying to get me fired? Did my father hire you to set me up or something?"

"Naw, man! I'm not from here, and I've only visited here a couple times, so I don't really know my way around," Dezman explained.

"Okay. There's a Tiffany's over at International Plaza. I don't know the address, so you'll have to Google it," he whispered.

"All right. Cool," Dezman said, sliding the dude another $100 bill for his time.

"Sorry that we don't have what you're looking for, sir. Please come again," the Arabian man said, maybe a little louder than he needed too.

"Not gonna happen. Thanks again though," Dezman said, chuckling as he walked away.

Chapter Fifteen

Situation All Fucked Up

The cocaine made Sweet Pea and T-mack delusional. They began halluci-
nating and hearing things, like knocks at the front and back doors, crying
babies, and loud music.

Sweet Pea told T-mack, "I think someone's after my family—maybe an
enemy of Biggs's." She speculated that they knew she was out and possibly
wanted to retaliate for the deaths of their family member that had occurred at the
hands of Biggs.

T-mack tried to reassure her that no one would be on that after all those years,
but he was battling his own demons. He kept hearing voices, and they were
driving him crazy, though he only heard them whenever he started to come
down off of his high,

It seemed like days had passed while they were held up in the dark house,
with no lights, TV, or radio on and the shades drawn. Whenever Sweet Pea
began to sober up from her alcohol and drug induced state, she felt guilty for not
doing the things she'd been doing with her granddaughter before she'd become
a powder-head.

Now, poor baby Deziray had to stay in pissy diapers longer, she only ate once
a day, and she had no snacks or fun. She was stuck in darkness, and the whole
place reeked from the pissy and shitty diapers that Sweet Pea had thrown any
and everywhere throughout the house.

It had once seemed like things were on track and moving in the right
direction for Sweet Pea and her granddaughter, but that had quickly shifted into a
downward spiral after she sniffed that first line of powder. The seemingly perfect
life Sweet Pea had when she'd won her case and had been released from prison
was now a mere memory. All she knew was cocaine and alcohol. That was her
life, and nothing else mattered. She battled herself about the motives behind her
drug addiction, as Sweet Pea had always believed that everything happens for

a reason. Her mind constantly ran wild. *Was it the letter from the woman that finally pushed me over the edge that I've been trying to escape all these years?* She had never really grieved when her husband was killed because she knew she had to be strong and not show any softness while in prison. Sweet Pea believed tears were a sign of weakness, and she was far from weak—or at least that was what she pretended.

She sat in the dark with tears running down her face, dressed in a grungy oversized black t-shirt and stained tube socks. She felt sorry for herself. She had everything, but she felt that still wasn't enough. Although she'd chosen the life she'd led by marrying the man she'd married and accepting his job title and her position, she couldn't help but wonder what her life would've been like if she had followed her dreams of being an actress or celebrity hairstylist, but she'd never given herself the chance to find out.

Deziray lay on the floor next to her grandmother, still sticky from her food the night before. T-mack sat straight up on the loveseat, opening his eyes wide and staring into space. They both had developed swollen eyes and bags underneath them from the lack of sleep.

The house phone rang, which made Sweet Pea and T-mack jump. It wasn't surprising that it was ringing; it had been ringing a lot lately, but neither one of them had bothered coming out of their slump to answer it. When Sweet Pea's cell phone began to ring, it caused Deziray to wake up and cry.

"Shut up, girl. What are you crying for? Your ass is too spoiled as it is. Go back to sleep right now!" Sweet Pea yelled. She didn't mean to be so harsh, but she couldn't stop herself.

The strange impulse from her grandmother frightened the baby, and Deziray went from crying to a slight whimper.

Chapter Sixteen

Surprise! Surprise!

Another unanswered phone call? For a while, Promise had simply brushed it off as her mother being busy with Deziray doing the grandmother/granddaughter bonding thing or what have you, but she was beginning to get worried when her calls continued to go unanswered. She was thinking about getting in contact with Shad and having him stop by her house to see what exactly was going on.

A few minutes later, a call came through on her phone. She assumed it was her mother, so she didn't bother looking at the screen. "Hey, Ma. I've been calling and calling you. Is everything okay?" Promise asked as soon as she pressed talk on her phone.

"Sweet lady, I'm guessing you didn't look at your caller ID," the male voice said. "I ain't your mama, fo sho!"

"Oh shoot! Hey, baby. I thought you were my mother returning my call. I have been tryin' to catch up with you though," Promise said.

"Yeah, I know. I'm sorry 'bout that. I've been in the studio grinding hard, and I haven't even had a chance to catch much sleep. It's been nonstop. That's why I'm callin'. I think it's time to treat both of us to a li'l getaway," Rare Breed said.

"A li'l getaway, huh? Sounds good. I'm down! Where too?" Promise asked, a little too excitedly.

"If I told you, that would ruin the surprise, wouldn't it? Come on now, ma. We've been through this before," Rare Breed said.

Promise could tell he was smiling, and she imagined those lips of his, copped to the side and grinning. "Fine. Like I said, I'm down. When is this little getaway supposed to happen?" Promise asked, not mentioning that she was set to go back home in twenty-four hours.

"All you need to know is that you're going to need to pack for warm weather," Rare Breed stated.

"Hmm. I might have to do some more shopping for warm weather," Promise said.

"Do whatever you have to do. I'm just ready to have you all to myself," Rare Breed replied.

"You got it. Talk to you in a few. Muah!"

"I can't wait till I can get a kiss fo real! Back at you, bay," he said before he hung up.

That Rare Breed sho knows how to keep a woman on her toes! There's not one thing I can complain about when it comes to him. That man does something to me, and I ain't even sampled the dick yet. I wonder where we're going. Oh, I can't wait, Promise thought as she opened her suitcase to unpack everything and repack solely for warm weather. Since she had to change her plans, she sent a quick text to Monica:

Promise: *Something came up, so you can get comfortable for a couple more days!*

* * *

Promise met up with Rare Breed later that night. They went out to grab something to eat and went back to his suite to relax for a while until it was time for them to leave. They talked for hours. After Rare Breed received a phone call, he informed Promise it was time for them to leave. He once again, pulled out a blindfold.

Even though he'd been with her for hours, he still complimented her. "I see yo sexy ass got dressed up for this li'l getaway. You lookin' damn good, ma," Rare Breed said, admiring every inch of her. She was a special woman to him. In his twenty-five years of life, he never came in contact with a woman who could make him smile from the inside out. He felt like he was doing everything to protect her, even though he wasn't sure what or whom he was protecting her from.

"You know I like to keep it sexy around you. I have to keep you on your toes like you keep me on mine," Promise replied.

"Yeah, I know you do, and I'm not mad at you for doing it. Shoot! I gotta match you every step of the way. Turn around so I can cover up those beautiful eyes for a little while," Rare Breed said. "Watch your head stepping up into this truck," he coached as he helped her into the SUV.

It was a short ride to the airport. Once they got there, Rare Breed told one of the security dudes to go ahead and put the bags on the plane.

"Wait a minute. Did you say we're going on a plane? I thought we were just taking a little road trip or something," Promise said.

"Yes, I said we're going on a plane, our own private ride. Now shh! Just go along with me on this," Rare Breed said.

"I'm going to kick your ass, bay," Promise said, playfully swinging at the air in attempt to hit Rare Breed. "You got me about to get on a plane, and I don't even know where we're going."

"Don't worry about that. You're gonna have an amazing time. I wouldn't have it any other way. Now just sit back, relax, and enjoy the flight. If it'll make you more comfortable, I'll take your blindfold off, but only 'til we're about to land," he offered.

"Woo! Thank you. That thing was starting to squish my lashes. And yes, I'll have an amazing time with you anywhere, just as long as we're together," Promise spoke honestly, no longer thinking about Dezman and the fact that he's in Tampa.

Rare Breed told Promise he wasn't going to go back and forth with her. He planned to take a nap and suggested she do the same. She followed his advice, got as comfortable as she could, and dozed off.

* * *

A while later, Promise awoke to a sweet kiss.

"Wake up, sleepyhead. We just landed," Rare Breed said with that famous sideways smile.

"Oh my! It's daylight outside. How long have I been knocked out?" Promise asked.

"For a good minute. I guess you needed the rest," Rare Breed said.

"Yeah, I guess so. Now, are you finally going to tell me where you've whisked me off to?" Promise asked.

"Not just yet. I need to put the blindfold back on you, but only for a little while longer. We're almost to our destination."

"Wait a minute. Let me send this text to Monica. I told her I would text her when we got to where we're going. And after you put that blindfold on me this time, you're not going to use it anymore unless it's in the bedroom," Promise said, winking at him.

She pulled her cell phone out, but instead of finding Monica in her contacts, she found Shad and keyed in:

Promise: *Hey, I know it's been a minute, but I need you to do me a favor. Go by my house and see if everything's okay there. I'll explain later. Thanks in advance.*

Promise then shut off her phone and put in her bag.

When they finally came to a stop, Rare Breed removed the blindfold. Promise's eyes had to adjust to the sunlight shining through the windows of the Town Car. She saw palm trees and a beautiful blue sky, and she felt a warm breeze. "Are we in Miami?" Promise asked.

"Naw. We're actually in the Dominican Republic at the Casa de Campo Resort," Rare Breed said, proud that his surprise had gone off without a hitch.

Promise's mind immediately drifted to Dezman; he had, after all, been the first man who had ever taken her out of the States. She was speechless for a moment.

"You're not happy?" Rare Breed asked, sounding kind of disappointed. "Did I do something wrong, baby?"

"No, no. That's not it at all. I love your surprise, baby. Don't mind me. I was just remembering that I haven't been on an island in two years. I know this is going to be an amazing experience," Promise said as they made their way to the walkway leading to the main entrance while the staff took their luggage for them.

"Good, 'cause we're definitely going to have the time of our lives. I've got something set up for you."

"Don't you always?" she teased, loving how considerate he was. She looked around and took in her surroundings. "Wow, Mike! The villa is sitting right on the beach. It's amazing. It's so…peaceful. I love how open this is," Promise said, admiring the relaxing place Rare Breed had chosen for them to spend together.

"Oh, baby, this isn't all. Follow me," he said, leading her with his smooth swag up the winding stairs and out onto the rooftop of the villa.

"Oh my God, baby! The whole time we're here, I don't want to sleep inside. I want to sleep right up here. This is so beautiful. I can see everything from up here! We even have our own private pool?" she said, walking around and exploring every aspect of the rooftop.

"Can we just sit here for a while?"

"You relax, I'll be back in a few minutes."

"Okay."

Promise did just that. She sat and relaxed and enjoyed the cool air blowing off the water, the blue sky and the picturesque view. She was lost in the moment, not worrying about anything nor anybody. She thought about going to look for Rare Breed but decided against it. She knew he'd be back soon. She dozed off, not realizing she'd been sitting there long enough for it to be approaching dusk.

"Hey, are you okay out there?"

"Yes, why'd you let me sleep? I slept on the plane."

"You looked so peaceful that I didn't want to bother you."

"This view is absolutely gorgeous! I love it here!"

"So do I. Well, it's time to get on with our day. It's going to be dark soon."

"What's next?"

"Now you know I'm not going to tell you but I've got something else for you," Rare Breed said. He slid to the side, exposing a big green box.

Promise's eyes lit up. "Wh-what is it?" she asked.

"See for yourself."

She walked over to the box and opened it, only to find a smaller box in a different shade of green. When she opened the lid on that box, she found an even smaller box. She started to laugh, assuming Rare Breed was playing some kind of trick on her. When she got down to the smallest box, she expected to find just another box nested inside it, but instead she opened it to reveal a pair of canary-yellow teardrop earrings. "Oh bae! I love them. Thank you so much." She ran up to him and hugged him. "They're simply gorgeous. You're really trying to get me to fall head over heels for you, aren't you?"

"I don't have to do anything. You'll fall for me in time. When the time is right, I'll have you—mind, body, and soul," Rare Breed said.

"When I do give you some of this," she said, patting her hello kitty through her 7 jeans, "I'm going to please you just enough to make you beg for more," Promise said, licking her glossed lips.

"Shit! That sounds good! I'm glad you like this. I'll just continue doing what I can to keep that smile on your face," Rare Breed said honestly.

Promise couldn't help but smile.

"You overlooked something when you opened the first box. Check under the lid."

Promise looked under the lid and found an envelope. There was a letter inside, and she pulled it out and read it:

Are you ready to have a little fun? Here's a scavenger hunt. Look where you can find something warm and yummy for your tummy…

Promise knew where she could find that exact thing. When she turned around, Rare Breed was gone. Instead of going to look for him, she got started on her scavenger hunt.

As soon as she walked into the kitchen, she smelled shrimp pasta—her favorite. She repeated to herself, "Something yummy for my tummy?" *The oven!* she thought.

When she pulled the covered platter out of the oven, her stomach began to growl. She smiled at how thoughtful Rare Breed was. He knew she'd be hungry after their long flight, and she thought it was clever to add something to eat to her scavenger hunt.

She took the lid off of the food, grabbed a fork, and took a little taste. She didn't want to eat it all but it tasted so good. She could see something at the bottom of the plate, so she spread the food around the dish. She saw the next clue engraved there:

I hope you enjoyed that, baby. Now look in a place that's under my head, in a cozy bed.

She didn't bother to finish the food. Promise raced off through the open villa to find the bedroom. When she found it, she went to the king-sized bed and looked under the pillows. Under one of the pillows she found a long box with a bow tied to it. *Another gift! What a special man he is,* Promise thought.

She snatched the bow off and lifted the top of the box to find the most beautiful necklace she had ever seen, a canary-yellow diamond necklace that matched her earrings.

She felt special. Other than Dezman, no other man had ever taken the time to do anything like that for her. Every other man she'd come in contact with wanted one thing, and while she'd delivered that—at a price, of course—it felt good for someone to treat her for a change.

In the box was yet another clue:

Get dressed and meet me where there are seashells, clear water. and soft white sand. I'll be by the fire.

She sprang into action and ran to the front door where their bags were. When she got her luggage back to the bedroom, she pulled out a pure white, racer-back maxi-dress. *This will be perfect with my new necklace and earrings,* Promise thought. She pulled out her gold YSL sandals to finish the look. Before getting in the shower, she pinned her hair up so her fresh curls wouldn't be messed up.

Promise was dressed and on her way to find Rare Breed, whom she was beginning to think of as her man. When she reached the beach area, she didn't see him, but she did see a woman standing by a fire, dressed in a Casa de Campo polo shirt and khaki shorts.

"Hello. You must be Queen Promise. My name is Marcia, and I am here to take you to your king. He awaits your arrival," Marcia said in a very thick Spanish accent.

"Hey, Marcia, you say he's waiting for me…but where?" Promise asked, recalling the clue in her head. "He said he would be here."

"I'm not supposed to tell you where he is, but I will take you to him. Follow me," Marcia said, walking toward a boat. "Don't worry. It will only be a few minutes before you're in his presence."

Promise got excited again, eager to see Rare Breed and to thank him for all that he'd done.

The boat ride was a smooth one. When they arrived at Catalina Island, she was helped off of the boat.

She saw a figure standing at the end of the dock, but since it was now dark, she couldn't quite make out who it was. As she neared, she realized exactly who was waiting for her. She began to walk faster, trying not to trip. With tears in her eyes, she hugged Rare Breed. "Baby, nobody's ever done anything like this for me. The way you took the time out to think of all this…it just amazes me. Your swag is so 'hood, but yet you're just a gentle giant. I love you, Mike…I really do…already!'"

"True shit, ma. I tried to go all out for you. I want every experience you have with me to be better than your last. I know you were probably looking crazy on the mainland when I wasn't there to meet you by the fire, but I wanted to go the extra mile and bring you here for an even better experience. I like that your tears are happy tears. Ma, without a doubt, I-I love you too," Rare Breed said.

"I-I can't believe I'm crying," Promise said, covering her face to wipe the tears away. "I never cry!" She had finally given Rare Breed what he wanted most: her heart. Still, it wasn't her whole heart. Even though she wasn't with him and he hadn't been there for her daughter, Dezman was her first love, and he would always have a piece of her heart in some way, but this man had definitely stolen the other part—and fast!

"Believe it, baby. Are you hungry yet?" Rare Breed asked.

"No! I'm still full from that delicious meal you left in the oven for me."

"Okay, cool. I have a little entertainment set up for us, and then we're going to spend some private time under the stars, enjoying this warm, night air," Rare Breed said with a wink.

"Mmm! I love the sound of that."

The entertainment wasn't like anything they'd ever seen before. Being a dancer, Promise had thought she'd seen it all, but she couldn't have been more wrong. About twenty dancers, a group called Kandela, moved in various Afro-Caribbean rhythms. It was so sexual, so colorful, and it took them on an incredible musical journey. Promise even discovered some new moves to add to her routine when she hit the stage again. After a few minutes, the group pulled the couple onstage to join them. Promise fit right in, but Rare Breed struggled a lot.

After they danced a while and thanked the group for an extraordinary performance, they headed off to an open-top cabana, lit with candles and the humming of soft music.

"You're trying to make me cry again, aren't you?" Promise asked.

"As long as they're happy tears, let 'em flow, girl," Rare Breed replied.

They lay in each other's arms under the stars, listening to R&B oldies and talking about their pasts and their hopes for the future.

Rare Breed stared into her eyes. "You look stunning tonight. I just want you to know that since the night we met, I've known you'll be in my future."

"I want to be your future, and I want you to be part of mine and my daughter's," Promise said, then kissed him long and hard. She got up from the bed and slid the straps off her shoulders. Once she slipped out of her dress, she removed her diamonds. Left only in her thong and heels, she began to sway back and forth to the sound of the music.

Rare Breed licked his lips as he felt his dick rise. The smallest thing Promise did made him hard, but he never let her know that because he had too much respect for her.

"I want you. Do you want me?" Promise asked as she slid her thong over her phat, round ass.

A light mist of rain began to fall, but that only heightened the sexual tension between the two of them.

The thumping between her legs intensified. She pulled his slides off and removed his slacks. "Take your shirt off," she told him.

Rare Breed hurriedly unbuttoned his shirt.

She then straddled him and, inch by inch, eased down until every bit of his thick, nine-inch dick was inside her dripping-wet pussy. When she began to ride him, he searched for a rhythm; once he found it, they moved together, moaning in unison each time she came up and slid back down his shaft.

"Damn, baby. I coulda waited a lifetime to feel this. See how my man fit in her like a glove? It's meant to be!"

"This dick is so good I couldn't imagine waiting a lifetime."

"Ahhh! Fuck, this pussy is so good," he said as he flipped her over while staying inside of her. He started pounding her slow and then quickened his pace as his adrenaline grew. He spread her ass cheeks and plunged back into her wetness.

"Give me that dick, Daddy. Owww! This dick is the bomb."

"I thought you were gone turn out to be a track star, but you taking this dick. I like that."

He put his finger on her clit, and the friction from his stimulation and him going deep inside her made her cum hard. Her juices ran down her thigh and dripped down his balls. Promise then wrapped her hand around his pipe as he went faster and faster inside of her. It was hard for him to keep going without cumming, and his body began shaking and shivering. He pulled out of Promise and busted all over her ass cheeks. She had never felt anything like that in any of her sexual experiences. Her clit was still thumping, so she knew they had a long night of lovemaking ahead of them.

Chapter Seventeen

Tampa Bound

After working at the strip club for a night, Jelly was more determined than ever to find Promise. She wasn't trying to be dancing like that forever so she needed to make sure they ended Promise's search so that the next part of their plan could work. She hit Truth up, obviously catching him off guard. "What's up, sexy? I know it's kind of short timing, but I need to know if you've found out where Promise is here in Boston." Jelly asked.

"Actually, it's perfect timing. I'm glad you called. I found out a couple hours ago that she is no longer in the Boston area. I was gonna hit you up so we could get together and I could tell you about it, but you called me first," Truth said, purposely leaving out some of what he knew.

"What, nigga? Are you tryin'a play me or something? I just spoke to someone who said they saw her in a strip club the other night," Jelly said, heated and sure Truth wasn't living up to his name.

"Ma, ain't nobody tryin'a play you. I'm telling you the same thing my resource told me. She's not in Boston anymore," Truth replied, his temperature rising, though he tried to stay calm and keep his cool.

"Well, I'm telling you your resource is wrong. You can take it how you wanna take it. It is what it is," Jelly said very matter-of-factly.

"Yo, whatever, ma. I don't have no reason to lie to you. A nigga just tryin'a help you out. Since you know for a fact she's still here, how 'bout you find her yourself?" Truth said.

"Maybe I will!" Jelly said before she hung up. *Damn! If he woulda told me some good news, I would've given his ass the goodies. Why the fuck would Promise leave Boston without finding Dezman? Or maybe she did find him…* Jelly thought, knowing something wasn't adding up right. She quickly dialed Mark to give him an earful. "Hey, bay. Where did you find that dumb-ass nigga Truth?" Jelly scolded as soon as Mark picked up the phone.

"What chu mean? You know what? Never mind all that. Let me tell you what Tre just ran past me," Mark said.

Jelly immediately grew worried. *I hope his ass didn't tell Mark we been fuckin' this whole time,* Jelly thought.

"What did he run past you, boo?" Jelly asked sweetly.

"He told me he saw the nigga who used to fuck with Promise down here at the mall," Mark said.

"What? In Tampa? What the fuck is really going on? First Truth tells me Promise isn't in Boston anymore, and now you're telling me that Tre saw Dezman at the mall in Tampa?" Jelly asked, bewildered.

"Hold up. Promise ain't in Boston anymore? Well where the fuck is she? When Tre said he saw Dezman, he didn't say anything about Promise being with him, so I was assuming Dezman was alone," Mark said.

"That's what I'm wondering too. Listen, I know you were on your way up, but scratch that. I'm about to call Black Ice and put her up on the game, and then we'll be Tampa-bound. That's where it needs to go down anyway. Where she made her bed at is where she shall lie," Jelly said.

"Okay. Bet. I'm going to see if I can get Tre to put eyes on that nigga so we'll know his every move," Mark replied.

"All right, bay. I'll hit you back when we're headed that way," Jelly said.

"Fo sho," Mark said before he hung up.

This shit is getting way more complicated than I thought it would be, Jelly thought, but she tried to push that thought out of her mind while she called Black Ice. "Black Ice, what's up with you, chick?" Jelly asked, playing it cool.

"Nothing. Just lying here bored, trying to figure out something for us to get into. I'm thinking about going to the movies. Are you down? I haven't been in a while," Black Ice asked, sounding down.

"I don't know about that. Are you all right? You don't sound like yourself. How are you and Dezman doing?" Jelly asked.

Black Ice broke down and began to cry. "Girl, I'm a mess. Dezman and I aren't doing well at all. It's been a day or two since he's even been home," Black Ice revealed.

"Well, then I know me telling you this isn't going to make you feel any better, but Promise isn't in Boston anymore…and Dezman has been spotted in Tampa," Jelly said.

"What? I can't take this anymore, Jelly. I feel like I'm about to have a nervous breakdown or something. You're basically telling me, in not so many words, that my man went to Tampa to find her—or maybe they even left Boston together. I've lost him, Jelly! I've lost my man to that bitch after all!" Black Ice cried out.

"Girl, suck that shit up. You've gotta pull it together. I'll call the airport as soon as we hang up, and we'll head to Tampa to get your man back for good. Of course, that's never gonna happen if we don't take care of Promise first. Are you with me?" Jelly asked, trying to hype her up.

"Yeah, I'm with you. I'm packing my stuff right now, as we speak. Let me know when you've got our flight and shit set up. I want all this shit to be over," Black Ice whimpered, far from the strong woman she'd always been. Love had taken over her mind, body, and soul.

"Don't worry about it. I'll handle everything. Just be ready when I say it's time to roll." Jelly hung up, shaking her head. *If that's what love got to do with it, I don't want any part of it. Just give me all the money and send me on my way,* Jelly thought.

Chapter Eighteen

Blurred Lines

The lines between what was really going on and what the voices in his head were telling him had crossed. T-mack no longer knew where he was. He'd completely lost it, to the point where he wouldn't go outside anymore, not even to re-up on his drugs. Instead, he called the dope man and asked for delivery from him or one of his soldiers.

Once he put in the call to his drug dealer, he did what he always did: He dug in Sweet Pea's purse to get the cash to pay for the coke. This time, though, he didn't find any money in her wallet. All he saw was a couple of business cards, her driver's license, a bank card, and some receipts. That didn't sit too well with him, and the irrational voices in his head began convincing him that Sweet Pea had stolen from him. "You gotta teach her a lesson," he heard a voice say.

"You're an OG! You can't just let that bitch take from you. How are you supposed to get your fix without any money?" T-mack heard another voice in his head say.

"Shut the fuck up! I got this. Ain't nobody stealin' from T-muthafuckin'-mack! I'm that nigga! You hear me?" He started swinging at the air, as if he was in a heavyweight boxing match.

He walked downstairs and past the living room, where Sweet Pea was lying on the floor in a nod. Deziray sat up and pushed her all-American Barbie Dream Car along. She was only eleven months old and had no idea what her grandparents were up to; she was content with just playing with her toy.

When T-mack made it to the kitchen, he began to pace back and forth. He knew his shit was going to be there soon, and he'd have to pay up or walk around with a monkey on his back. He wasn't willing to deal with withdrawals, that constant sharp stomach pain, itching skin, and violent vomiting.

He looked all around the kitchen for anything he could give to the dope man in place of money. His eyes landed on the block of knives, and he pulled the biggest one out. It looked like it hadn't been used yet. The blade shined and when he ran his finger down it, he nipped himself with the tip. He knew the blade was sharp enough, but he wasn't sure what he would do with it. His mind wondered how he could come out on top of the situation.

Suddenly, a voice began to speak to him from somewhere inside his head. "Nigga, you know what you have to do. You either kill that nigga when he gets here or get that bitch who stole yo' money to find something in this house of value. No matter what, you can't go without."

T-mack went to the living room, stepped over Deziray, and snatched Sweet Pea up by her hair.

Sweet Pea came out of her nod, swinging. "What the fuck is going on? Let my hair go," she screamed, trying to get away from whoever was attacking her.

Deziray looked over at her grandpa and grandma tussling and started crying.

"It's okay, baby. Granddaddy is just playing with Grandma. See?" He shook Sweet Pea by her hair like a ragdoll. "Smile, bitch," he told her.

Sweet Pea smiled and found a way to laugh while tears filled her eyes. "It's okay, baby. Nana's okay. Play with your doll while me and your granddaddy talk, okay?" she said, trying to reassure the baby that everything was all right, which it clearly wasn't.

"Nana?" Deziray laughed as she said her name.

T-mack dragged Sweet Pea upstairs, his tall frame towering over her.

"Why are you doing this, T-mack? What did I do?" Sweet Pea asked.

"Bitch, you know what you did. You stole my money. I put you up on game, and you go and steal my fuckin' money! How am I supposed to get my hit?" T-mack asked, delirious. He slapped her so hard her neck jerked back.

"Ah! T-mack, I swear I ain't stole nothing from you. You've been buying our stuff with *my* money—the money Promise left for me to take care of Deziray. We can go to the bank first thing in the morning and get some more money," she pleaded as she wiped the blood off her lip.

"You lyin' bitch! That was *my* money. Where's the jewelry at? All this nice shit in this house, I know there's some jewelry somewhere," T-mack demanded.

"I think she took all her jewelry with her," Sweet Pea lied.

"You lyin' bitch!" T-mack repeated before he punched her square in her eye.

Her eye began to swell on impact, and her head started pounding, as if she's been hit with a two-by-four several times.

"You told me she didn't pack heavy 'cause she didn't plan to stay long and if she needed anything she would just shop for it up there. Now I'm going to ask you again. Where is the jewelry?"

"It's in her panty drawer, third one on the left," Sweet Pea mumbled reluctantly, with her hand pressed on her lip, where his slap had split her mouth open. "I can't believe you're doing this to me."

"Shut the hell up," T-mack said as he found all of Promise's diamonds, happy to see that she had quite a collection. The doorbell rang, and he knew his package was there. He grabbed a handful of the diamonds, over $25,000 in jewelry, and headed down to the front door.

"Yo! What's up, li'l nigga? The big man must be busy if he sent you," T-mack said, trying to make small talk with the young dude, who couldn't have been more than fifteen.

"Boss man doesn't make house calls anymore. Too much snitching going on," the young dude said, ready to get his sell and be on his way. *What the fuck is that smell, dude?* he wondered, wrinkling his nose. *Shit...literally!*

"True that! Check this out, I don't have no cash, but I got something better than money," T-mack said as he stepped out the door.

The boy's face screwed up, angry that he'd wasted his time and risked his life on a blank trip. "Listen, pops, I don't know what type of shit you on, but I'm not on that. If it ain't green, it ain't for me."

"Naw, young'n, I didn't mean it like that. I don't have no cash money, but I got some jewelry that's worth way more."

The boy looked at what T-mack had to offer, and his eyes grew wide. "Damn, pops! Who you rob? That shit's phat!" He pointed to a limited-edition, diamond-encrusted, big-face Gucci watch.

"You like that? How about I give you all this for whatever is in your pockets right now."

"Hell yeah! All this shit is dope. I got your word that none of this is fake? No knock-off shit?"

"Have you ever seen fake shit sparkle like this?" T-mack asked, shoving the jewelry up in the boy's face.

"You're right, man. My bad. Here," he said, pulling out eight baggies filled with white powder.

T-mack got excited at the sight of the cocaine, but he tried not to show it. The huge grin on his face and the twinkle in his eyes gave it away though. "Good lookin', young'n," he said. He snatched the baggies, shut the door, and stared at the coke in his hand.

A voice in his head spoke. "Now you got yo' shit, but you're gonna have to share it with that thieving bitch upstairs. I say you kill her so we can have this shit to ourselves."

T-mack thought about what the voice in his head was telling him and began nodding his head in agreement. He stuffed the baggies in his front pocket and pulled the knife out of his back one.

When he got back upstairs to Promise's room, he found Sweet Pea in the bathroom, looking at her injuries in the mirror. She didn't even notice him.

He approached her quickly, raising the blade and planting it in her body. The first strike hit her in the upper back. Blood began to pour down her back and drench the whole back of her shirt.

"Ah! Fuck! You…you stabbed me!"

Before she had a chance to defend herself, T-mack stabbed her in the neck with so much force that part of the handle broke off the knife. He pulled his hand back and swung it forward, this time catching her in the side of her neck and breaking the blade off in her neck. Blood squirted everywhere, all over the mirror and toilet, and Sweet Pea's body dropped to the floor. When she tried to breathe, more blood sprayed out. She began to twitch and struggle to say something, but T-mack ignored her, figuring it was all part of the dying process. Sweet Pea tried one last time to open her mouth, then gargled blood and fell limp.

T-mack turned around walked out of the bathroom and over to the desk by the window in Promise's room. He began to write a letter to his daughter, telling her everything, going all the way back to when he'd first met her mother. When he finished writing, he put the bloody pen down and pulled one of the baggies out of his pocket. He spread the powder on the desk, cut it into lines, and sniffed until he was where he needed to be; it didn't take much since he had all the cocaine to himself.

* * *

Shad received the text from Promise while he was heading back to Tampa from a run in Miami. He texted her back: "A'ight! Bet."

When he got back to Tampa, the first thing he did was take the drugs he'd just gotten from his connect to one of his trap houses so his main man could divide it up between all the workers. Once he took care of that business, he headed over to Promise's mini-mansion.

When he pulled up, something didn't feel right to him. It was dark outside, but it wasn't so late, and when he noticed that Sweet Pea's car was there and all the lights were off, he knew something was going on. Shad opened his glove compartment and retrieved his pearl-handle 9mm just to make sure he was strapped in case some shit was about to jump off.

Instead of knocking on the front door, he made his way around to the back of the house. He noticed that the light was on in Promise's room.

He pushed on the glass sliding door just enough to see if it was unlocked.

When the door moved, he quietly slid it open. As soon as he stepped into the house, his nostrils were invaded with the worst stench he'd ever smelled. *What the fuck is that? It stinks like rotten eggs and piss up in here,* Shad thought.

When he moved through the kitchen and walked down the hallway to the living room, he saw Deziray asleep on the floor, surrounded by dirty diapers. He rushed over to the baby and touched her to make sure she was okay. He knew Sweet Pea would never leave Deziray by herself, especially not on the floor in such filth. When he saw that the little one was breathing, he lifted her as gently as he could and placed her on the couch. *This damn girl is burning up, and her diaper is full. Man, what the fuck is going on?* Shad thought.

He left Deziray on the sofa and made his way up the stairs. When he reached the top step, he took his Polo boots off so the heaviness of his steps wouldn't be detected. When he got to the room, he looked in and saw a man sitting at the desk by the window, with his back facing the door. He was so busy snorting lines of coke that he was totally unaware of Shad's presence. He took another peek around the spacious room but didn't see Sweet Pea anywhere. *Who the fuck is this mu'fucka, and what the fuck is he doing in Promise's house all comfortable and shit?* He prepared to get some answers by cocking the barrel of the handgun, allowing a bullet to slide into the chamber.

T-mack heard the familiar sound of a weapon being cocked and immediately turned around in the direction of the noise. His heart was beating at a ridiculously fast rate from the drugs and the fear he felt when he saw a man coming toward him with a gun pointed directly at his forehead.

"Who the fuck are you?" Shad moved quickly toward T-mack, making sure he had a clear shot.

T-mack slowly rose from his seat. His nerves were shot. "Eh-yo, man! What's up with the gun? I don't got no…I don't want any problems," T-mack said, as his eyes darted around the room, looking for a weapon to defend himself or an escape route. "This is my daughter's house. Hell, take whatever you want, long as you get your ass outta here with that gun!"

"Nigga, quit lying. This ain't yo' daughter shit! I know the girl who owns this house, and I've never seen your ass before! I also know her father got killed damn near eleven years ago. Now, I'm gonna ask you again, who the fuck are you, and what have you done with Sweet Pea?" Shad asked, putting pressure on the trigger.

"I don't care what you heard. Sweet Pea was *my* woman, so like I told you, Promise is *my* daughter. Her mother just didn't have the chance to tell her yet."

"What the fuck do you mean, Sweet Pea 'was' your woman? Where is she, yo?"

T-mack thought about his words and cursed himself for not using them wisely. His head turned to the direction of the bathroom. The distorted vision of what he'd done popped in his mind, and a tear slid down his cheek. "I-I…oh, God, I don't know what I've done," T-mack said out loud.

Shad's eyes followed T-mack's stare, and he began to back up toward the bathroom with the gun still trained on T-mack. He leaned his head in the bathroom, and what he saw almost brought his lunch up from earlier that day. As long as he'd been in the game, he'd never seen such a gruesome murder scene. Without saying anything, he turned to T-mack and shot him in his left arm.

"Ah! Fuck, man! Why you have to go and shoot me? I-I didn't mean to do it," T-mack said, grabbing his wound to try to stop the bleeding.

"What the fuck did she do to deserve that shit, man?" Shad asked, his mind going crazy.

"It wasn't me, man. It was this cocaine. It's got my head all fucked up. We started out using it a little at time just to take some of our pain away, and it ended up being our downfall. Them voices told me to do it. I swear!" T-mack cried out in pain.

Shad didn't want to hear it. The barrel jumped again, this time hitting T-mack in his left knee, shattering the bones on contact. "You lyin' mu'fucka! Sweet Pea didn't do any drugs."

"Man, you wasn't here. She snorted powder with me. Man, fuck! Just kill me already. I'm a dead nigga anyway," T-mack said, wanting to escape the misery he felt, inside and out. There was such a pain shooting through the left side of his body that he couldn't bear it.

"You want me to put you out of your misery? How about I make that happen for you," Shad said, letting off a round in his right arm. Tired of torturing the stranger, Shad shot him once in the heart, causing blood to immediately spurt out. Then, just to be sure he was dead, he shot him twice in the head, turning Promise's bedroom into a bloody scene, even worse than the one in the bathroom.

Shad sprang into action, looking for anything that he knew he had to remove to protect Promise. He went to the desk where the man was sitting and saw the cocaine lines. Next to that, he saw a bloody pen and a pad with a letter on it. He didn't take time to read it and quickly tore all five pages of the letter off so there would be no trace of it for police or anyone to find. He folded the letter and stuffed it in his pocket, then got back to work.

After checking everything out upstairs, he ran downstairs, picked Deziray up off the couch, and hurried to his car. He knew the baby needed to get to a hospital and fast. Her little body felt extremely hot, and she was dripping with sweat. He didn't have any kids, but he knew it wasn't normal for a baby to have such a high fever. Her soiled diaper was so full and heavy that it was barely clinging to her small hips.

When he arrived at Tampa General Hospital, he took the sleeping baby out of the back seat. "I need a doctor now! I don't know what's wrong with her. Please help me!" Shad yelled as he rushed up to the front desk.

Some of the people in the lobby looked at him as if he was crazy, and others seemed worried about the child in his arms.

Seeing the poor condition of the child, the nurses sprang into action. One was on the phone behind the desk, requesting a doctor STAT. The other nurse came around the desk and took Deziray out of his arms.

"How old is she the?" asked the nurse behind the desk.

"Um, I believe she's one. Please take care of her. I'm going to try and get a hold of her mother now." Shad dialed Promise's number, but it went straight to voicemail. He hung up and tried again, but it went straight to voicemail again. This time he left an urgent message for her. "Eh-yo, some major shit went down at your house. When I finish leaving this voicemail, I gotta call the police and send them over there. I had to bring Deziray to the hospital. She's not feeling too good, and I don't know what's wrong with her. Girl, you need to hit me back ASAP! We're at Tampa General Hospital, and I'll stay here with your baby 'til you can get yourself back here. These people are going to start asking me questions that I don't—"

"To send, press one," the voicemail said, cutting him off.

"Damn!" he said out loud, then sent her a text: "Emergency! Call me NOW!!"

After that, he began to pace up and down the hallway like an expectant and worried father, completely beside himself. He didn't know whether he was coming or going, and all he could do was wait to hear back from the doctors or Promise. At that moment, he would have taken either one.

Chapter Nineteen

Reality Check

Afterr a night of passionate lovemaking, hot sex, and a lot of wetness, Rare Breed and Promise felt closer than ever, but Promise still wasn't all the way in the moment. While she enjoyed talking to him, her mind still wandered, either to her daughter, Dezman, or her future. She knew she didn't really have an excuse to be working as a dancer or an escort anymore. The money wasn't even enough; it had begun to feel like she was selling her soul every time she climbed a pole or slid into bed with a paying customer. It seemed as though Rare Breed truly wanted to give her more, but she'd believed that about Dezman too, and that hadn't gotten her very far in the end.

"What's wrong with you, baby? Everything has been perfect, but you just don't seem…happy," Rare Breed said as he noticed her looking into space.

"I'm really sorry. There's just so much going on in my head. I've enjoyed our time together. I'm here, but I'm really not, if that makes sense," Promise said, pointing between the two of them. "I haven't been able to contact my mother or talk to my daughter in a couple days." Promise went on to tell him the reason why she was in Boston in the first place. She told him what she did for a living and basically put it all out there, leaving it up to Rare Breed to decide if he still wanted to deal with her and all of her drama.

"Damn, ma. I didn't know it was like that. Shit is deep, but you know what? We're gonna get through this together. I'm gon' do my best to help you through this rough patch in your life. If you can't find that no-good-ass nigga, I'll step up to the plate and be Deziray's daddy," Rare Breed offered. "If she's anything like her mama, that girl must be a beautiful child."

"That's sweet, but I have to get through a lot of this on my own. I don't want to drag you into it. The reality of it is that I need to get back to Boston or Tampa to…well, to take a step back and figure all this out. I've enjoyed all this, but I didn't leave my daughter just to party. I left her because I thought it would benefit her in the long run if I'd been able to find her father. You do have a solid place in my heart, but I can't do anything about that until everything is settled. I need you to respect my feelings for now. Can we head back to the States so that I can get the die rolling? I guess they'll land where they will," Promise said. She was sad to cut their romantic trip short, but she was happy knowing that in the end, it might bring them even closer.

"Damn, ma. On the real, I can't do nothing but respect you for this. Ain't too many chicks I know who would keep all that real with a nigga after he done brought her to the Dominican Republic, spent thousands of dollars on jewelry, and given her the golden dick, but you did, ma. You're one of the rarest of the rarest. I'm not going to hold you up from doing what you have to do, 'cause the longer I keep you here, the longer you'll have to be away. Go ahead and get your stuff together. I'm going to make a few calls, and we can be out of here within a couple hours."

* * *

When they landed back in Boston and Promise got back to her room, she turned her phone on to call Monica and let her know it was time to head back to Tampa and find Dezman. Before she could call her, her phone started going off, alerting her of voicemails and text messages—all from Shad. The first text scared her shitless, and she wondered what was going on. Her heart began to race, sweat beads formed on her forehead, and all she could think was that the anonymous person who had sent all those letters to her must have made good on their threats to hurt her like she'd hurt them. Without opening another text or listening to a voicemail, she dialed Shad's number. She sat down on the edge of her bed in her suite and tapped her foot vigorously as she waited for him to pick up.

"Promise! Where have you been? Shit is all fucked up, man," Shad said as soon as he answered the phone.

"What happened? I'm just getting back to Boston from…well, never mind. I'll explain later. Just tell me what's going on. What did you find out when you went by my house?" Promise yelled, no longer able to contain herself.

"She's gone, Promise," Shad said.

"What do you mean 'she's gone' Shad? Who's gone? What are you saying?" Promise yelled.

"Your mom, Promise…your mom was killed."

"What the hell are you talking about Shad?" Promise's eyes filled instantly with tears. Where is Deziray…where is my baby?" She began to panic.

Shad attempted to explain the events that had unfolded after he'd arrived at her house but Promise interrupted him.

"Shad, you still haven't told me where my baby is. Please tell me nobody hurt my baby?"

"I brought Deziray to the hospital 'cause she looked so bad and was hot as hell and was unconscious. The doctors say she was malnourished, anemic, and severely dehydrated. That's why she was unconscious. I thought she was just sleeping. They keep asking me all these questions that I don't know the answer to. They wanna know where her mother is, who her daddy is, and how long she's been like this. The detective and social worker just hammered me, soundin' like they're accusin' me of lying. I don't know what in the hell to tell them!" Shad said.

Promise was silent on the phone, at a loss for words. Her daughter was laid up in a hospital, sick, scared, and probably feeling alone 'cause neither her mom or her grandma were there with her. Promise had lost her mother to a brutal stabbing, and a strange man who'd claimed to be her real father was the cause of it all. All she could do was cry. After she calmed down a bit, she answered, "I'm sorry, Shad. I'm on my way Shad. Thank you for everything you've done, and please stay with my baby. Tell her that her mommy's coming and that I love her. Oh dear God! I love her."

"There's more, Promise," Shad managed to get out. "After I shot and killed dude, I found a letter addressed to you. I think that's what he was doing before I found in him your room."

"A letter to me?"

"Yep, Also, CPS, the Department of Children and Families, has taken custody of Deziray. They said since I'm not a blood relative or legal guardian and none was available, Deziray will be taken into foster care when she's released from the hospital," he said, sounding like a broken spirit.

"Like hell they will! Over my dead body. I don't want that for my child, and I won't have it. I know what foster homes are like. I lived in them, and I'll be damned if my baby's going through any of that sick, twisted shit. I'm on my way," Promise said before hanging up.

Why is all of this happening? Haven't I suffered enough? Why!? Why can't I be happy for once with a good man who loves me, a family I cherish? Every time things begin to come together and build up to what I want out of life, everything seems to fall down at the snap of a finger. What am I going to do? I have to get home now! I don't have time to go through a search, security, baggage drop-off, and all that shit. Who knows how long the wait will be? On top of a three-and-a-half-hour flight, it's gonna take me six hours to get back to Tampa. That's far too long, Promise thought.

Then it hit her, and she called Rare Breed, who picked up on the first ring. "I need a favor. You know I would never ask you for anything if my life or family's life wasn't on the line, but is your private plane available? I need to get back to Tampa ASAP. Some serious shit has gone down there, and the county's trying to take my baby girl!" Promise said, all in one breath. No matter how much she wiped the tears, they still wouldn't stop falling.

Rare Breed could hear the distress in her voice, and he hated the sound of her crying. "Whatever you need, ma, I got you. I'll send a driver for you now, and I'll meet you at the airport, with a plane waiting for us."

"For *us*?"

"Absolutely. I'm going with you. It don't sound like you need to be alone right now," Rare Breed said.

She wasn't able to put up any kind of resistance about him joining her. "I can't thank you enough. I'll head downstairs and wait for your driver," Promise said before hanging up.

She looked around the room and realized she wouldn't have enough time to pack all of her stuff up. "Fuck it," she said. "I'll just have to have the hotel pack it up and ship it to me." In a hurry, she grabbed her purse and the still-packed luggage she'd taken with her to the Dominican Republic. She didn't even bother looking back as she exited the suite.

She decided to throw on her shades so no one would catch a glimpse of how distraught she was. She went to the front desk and tried to speak as calmly as possible. "I am sorry, but I need to turn in my key card immediately. You can take my name off of the room I'll pay for another day for my friend who was staying in the room with me. Give her a message telling her there's been an emergency I had to go back to Tampa! " she said. "I'd like all the belongings left in the room shipped to me in Tampa please, once she checks out. I'll leave you the address, and you can charge the shipping to my credit card."

The woman at the front desk informed her that they had never shipped a guest's belongings like that, but she could tell Promise was going through something major. "It's not our policy, but we'll make an exception for you this one time," she told Promise. Before Promise could walk away the woman called her, "Ms. Brown, it's not any of my business, but I feel your pain. Whatever is going on in your life, just leave it in God's hands. He'll take care of whatever burdens you," she said with a kind smile before she returned to her work.

Promise had never been very involved with church or religion. When she was younger, her parents had taken her to first Sundays, but that was about all she remembered. As she walked out of the hotel, she repeated what the woman at the desk had said: "Leave it in God's hands." *I'll try,* she thought.

A couple minutes later, a truck pulled up in front of her. The driver got out and assisted her with her bags, but before he could make it to the door to open it for her, she'd taken it upon herself to hop in. "I'm not trying to be rude, but can you step on it. I have an emergency back home."

"Your wish is my command," the driver said before he took off through the streets of Boston en route to the airport. Promise tried to call Monica, but her phone was going straight to voicemail. *This girl picks a fine time to have a dead phone or have the shit turned off. I'll just have to call her and let her know about everything that's going on when I get a chance.*

Rare Breed was at the airport waiting on Promise when she arrived. "I hope you're not upset I took it upon myself to have my driver pick you up since he was already on that side of town and by the way you sounded, I knew it was urgent. I drove my car here so I'll just leave it in the long-term parking lot. I'm here with you baby. Everything is going to be okay." He took her by the hand and led her to the plane.

Chapter Twenty

On the Hunt

After Jelly set everything up and booked the flights, she texted Black Ice to let her know their departure times, suggesting they meet up a couple hours earlier.

The flight went smoothly, and they made it to Tampa more quickly than usual. Jelly had little to say and remained quiet for the entire flight, anticipating what would take place next. Black Ice was nervous. More than anything, she just wanted it all to be over.

"Since we're staying at your apartment, we don't have to take our stuff straight there. Let's stop by Sweet Spot and see what's going on. Hopefully we'll get some more information on Dezman," Black Ice said.

"Sounds like being back in Tampa is bringing that old ruthless bitch back out of you," Jelly replied, laughing.

"Shut up! You know these were my stomping grounds for a minute. I just feel comfortable here, that's all," Black Ice replied.

"Well, then it sounds to me like you need to move yo' ass back to Tampa. Boston is making you soft."

When they got to Sweet Spot, they noticed something different about the gentlemen's club. There wasn't a very long line outside, and the lights were dim in some spots and out in others. The usually sweet aroma had been replaced by a stale musk.

"Damn, Jelly, Sweet Spot ain't lookin' or smellin' so sweet now, is it? You didn't tell me how bad it's gotten since I left. There's barely five customers in here—naw, scratch that. One just walked out the door," Black Ice said, astonished at the poor condition of the club.

"It must have just gotten like this since I been gone. Damn. The place has gone to hell, and I ain't never seen it like this in here. This shit is obviously bad for business, 'cause all the damn business is gone," Jelly replied, looking around in disgust.

"That bitch Promise was supposed to be holding shit down here, but instead she's been too busy out chasing my man. Where the hell are all the dancers anyway? Niggas sitting up in here like this is a chill spot instead of a spend-money-or-leave spot," Black Ice said.

Jelly couldn't help being offended. "Promise was supposed to be in here holding shit down? What!? Bitch, this is my club, and if anybody was supposed to be holding shit down, it shoulda been me. But no! I've been too busy helping you keep yo' nigga under wraps," Jelly snapped.

"Damn, all that! You didn't have to go! If you wanted to stay here, you could have. You're grown…remember! You should've just said no if it was messing up your dollars like that!"

"Whatever, it's done now. Let's just go up to Tre's office and see what the fuck is really going on around here," she said, leading the way.

When they got to the office, Jelly knocked politely, but Black Ice felt there was no need to knock and just opened it and walked right in. Tre's office was in disarray, just like the rest of the club. There was trash everywhere and clothes thrown all over the place, and the plasmas that had been hanging on three of the four walls were gone.

"Damn, Tre! What's going on around here? It doesn't look like shit's too sweet in your spot after all," Black Ice said, pointing around the room.

"Don't worry about what the fuck is going on around here. You don't work for me anymore," Tre said, clearly pissed. "What the fuck are you doing here anyway?"

"There's some shit I gotta handle, so I'm back. And you're right. I don't work for your ass anymore and from the looks of this place, I'm glad," she replied coldly, clearly wanting to spit fire at him.

"Whoa! Y'all best just chill out with all that," Jelly interrupted. "We didn't come here for that, Tre. I actually need your help. I need at least two guns, one for me and one for Black Ice. We have some shit that needs to be taken care of. I'll give you more details later, but for now, all you need to know is that somebody might be following us, and we need protection," Jelly lied.

Tre looked at Jelly and started shaking his head. "You don't know what I've been through over the last month and a half. One of my homies from high school came in from Texas and asked me for a favor. Of course I wanted to help him out, but homey or not, I started to get a little sketchy after I found out what the favor was. He told me he was pushing some weight and needed a place to stash it 'til the buyers got here. I eased up when I found out he was willing to pay me a storage fee. The extra money looked good for a minute, but then one buyer turned to two and then three. The next thing I knew, the fuckin' doors of my club were being kicked in, and the damn feds was runnin' all through my shit. I just got out of jail a week ago, and I think I'm being watched by them fuck-ass alphabet boys, so I can't get my hands on any guns. Hit that nigga Mark up and see what he can do for you," Tre said, looking Jelly over. "You know…since you fucks with him."

"What you talking about 'fucks with him', Tre?" Jelly asked, as if she didn't know what he meant.

"Don't play stupid now. You know what I mean and I'm glad I finally know. You were just another part of my fucked up past." Tre snapped.

"You know what, Tre? You ain't no fuckin' good. See how all this shit crumbling around you? Your position as that nigga has come to an end. I wish I'd never fucked with you. When they put yo' ass back behind bars, I hope you rot to death," Black Ice said, heated.

She turned to Jelly. "C'mon."

"Fuck you nigga. You're gonna get whatever is coming to you," Jelly said. I'm out this piece of shit. It stinks in here."

Black Ice was shocked as they walked out to the car. "Bitch, you never told me you was fuckin' Tre. If I'da known that, I would've told you to throw a cap on it ASAP! That nigga fuck any girl he feels can make him the most money at that particular time. He don't do nothing but test-drive chicks so he knows what client to set them up with. He's like some damn sleazy used car salesman, girl!"

"Sounds like you done had some of that *Mandingo* dick too," Jelly accused.

Black Ice looked at her coldly.

"Hey, don't look like that. I'm sorry, but that nigga is the pussy-pleaser. He gets it done in the bedroom," Jelly said, reminiscing about the last time they'd fucked.

Unbeknownst to Jelly, her phone had pocket-dialed Mark's while she'd walked up the stairs to enter the club, since he was the last person she'd talked to. Mark had heard every word and was beyond pissed. When he'd finally heard enough and was seeing red, he'd hung up the call. Full of jealous rage, and none to happy to have been used and made a fool of, he thought, *A'ight, so that's how it is with this bitch? Well, I'm about to get shit popping…or in this case blazing.*

"The dick was all right at the time, but it was never anything to brag about. I was young, and the money looked right. That was the only reason I did it. Although I got pleasured, for me it was never a pleasure thing with Tre. It was nothing more than a business deal, part of the game. Anyway, fuck all this talk about some dick that ain't even mine. Let's talk about the dick I'm trying to keep. Call Mark so we can see what he's found out on Dezman's whereabouts," Black

Ice said.

"I feel you. I'm about to get on that right now," Jelly replied. She picked up her phone and clicked on Mark's name, which was at the top of her list. She pressed talk, not even paying attention to the last call time next to his name.

"Yo!" Mark answered.

Jelly was caught off guard by his harsh tone, but she brushed it off as her being on edge and too sensitive. "Hey, baby. I'm just calling to let you know we made it," she stated, just to take it easy. "We're back in the Sunshine State."

"Oh yeah? That's what's up. That nigga moving around Tampa like he ain't got no worries," Mark said, getting straight to the point.

Jelly looked at Black Ice out of the corner of her eye. She then swallowed hard and asked, "Baby, are you mad at me?" The question caused Black Ice to pay closer attention to their conversation.

"Naw. What makes you say that? What I got to be mad about?" Mark replied, playing dumb.

"I don't know. It just sounds like something's bothering you, that's all. It's probably just me looking too deep. I'm a little tired from the long flight. Anyway, you say Dezman's running the town like he doesn't have any worries? We'll put a stop to that. Do you know where he is right now?" Jelly asked.

"Yeah. My li'l cousin Quay is following that nigga's every move."

"I need some of them thangs. We don't have to talk about it over the phone, but when the time is right, I'm gonna need two—not too big and just enough for me to handle."

"No sweat. I got chu, girl," Mark said, then hung up, barely able to control his anger.

Chapter Twenty-One

Back By Her Side

S had sat in Deziray's room on the pediatric side of the hospital and watched over her. Every couple of hours, she'd wake up and watch cartoons, but she turned her nose up at the hospital food. The only thing she would eat was a little fruit, and she was quick to fall back to sleep. Nevertheless, under the care of the doctors and nurses, she was getting better and stronger by the hour. .

Shad's phone had been going off nonstop, but there wasn't anything he could do about it. His business was being neglected. Of course he had people working for him, but ever since he'd been betrayed by Shirley, a woman whom was family and someone who'd been close to him but had committed the ultimate betrayal snitching on his father, he'd been unable to trust anyone except Promise. *Damn! I need to meet with my connect and pay him off for that loan. I shoulda done that shit first thing when I got back, but now I got this nigga blowing me up. Product needs to be moved. I got niggas calling me for re-up, and I can't do shit,* Shad thought. Still, he knew it was best to sit tight to show the social worker that although Promise wasn't present, Deziray was not alone.

About an hour later, Promise came bursting through Deziray's hospital room door with tears in her eyes and ran straight to her daughter's bedside. She couldn't hug the baby as tightly as she wanted to because of all the tubes and cords, but she kissed the little one all over her innocent face. "Mommy is here now, sweet angel. I love you so much! I'll never leave you again," Promise said.

A man walked in, dressed in casual street clothes.

Shad knew him from somewhere, but he wasn't sure if the man was actually who he thought he was. "Are you in the right place, bruh?" Shad asked.

Promise looked up. "I'm so rude! Shad, this is Rare Breed…or you can call him Mike. Bay, this is my friend Shad, the one I told you about. He's like a brother to me. We damn near grew up together. He's been here this whole time with Deziray."

"Yo, man. I knew I'd seen you somewhere before. You're that rapper, ain't you? That one who just signed to one of the top record labels, Big Money Entertainment? Ya shit goes hard," Shad said, excited to meet the rising star.

"Thanks, man. I appreciate the support. I'm nice with the mic," Rare Breed replied.

Rare Breed and Shad politely excused themselves to give Promise some time alone with her baby. They were engrossed in their conversation about the ins and outs of the industry as they walked out the door.

Promise turned her attention back to her sleeping beauty and, for the first time in a long time, actually prayed. She prayed that God would see her through the battle she was going to have to face with CPS, but she was ready every step of the way. She only wished that Dezman was by her side, fighting for Deziray along with her. That was when it dawned on her that she hadn't checked in with the private investigator in a few days.

Promise moved away from Deziray's bed and took a seat next to the window. She peered outside. Her mind wandered all over the place, but she had to hold it together. She dialed Sterling's number from the hospital wall phone.

A feminine but male voice answered, "Who is this?"

Promise pulled the phone away from her ear and then looked at the card in her hand, assuming she'd dialed incorrectly. "Uh, I'm sorry. I must have the wrong number. Is this Sterling Kane's Private Investigation?"

The person on the phone cleared his throat. "Sorry about that. This is Sterling. With whom am I speaking?"

Promise got a sour look on her face and replied, "Oh, okay. Hi, Sterling. This is Promise Brown. I know it's been a couple of days since we last spoke, but so much has been going on. I am back in Tampa, but I'm at the hospital right now."

"Hello, Promise. The hospital, you say? Sorry to hear that. Are you okay?" Sterling replied.

"Yes, I'm fine, but my daughter is in the hospital. She's okay now, but there's a lot going on surrounding the reason why she's here. Now, more than ever, I really need to find her father so I can fill him in," Promise said.

"All right. When I got to Tampa, it wasn't too hard to find Dezman. He was in seclusion for quite a while which made it much more difficult to track him but he's back to talking again. He posts a lot of his whereabouts on Twitter. He's staying at the Marriott downtown. As crazy as it sounds, he's in Tampa without any security, driving a modern car. I think he's trying to avoid bringing any attention to himself."

"Okay. I need another favor. Can you go to the Marriott and see if he's there? If he is, maybe you can tell him to come to the hospital immediately. You don't have to go into details. Just tell him it involves his daughter. If he's not at the hotel, leave a note at the front desk. That way, when he gets there, they'll let him know, and he can come straight here."

"I think it would be better for me to just leave the note at the front desk. If he's there, they can call him down to pick it up. If he's not, he'll get it when he returns to the hotel."

"That's fine," Promise said, not sure why he preferred to leave the note. "Thank you once again, Sterling. You've been a great help. That tip I will be leaving will be hefty."

"And that will be greatly appreciated. I'm just doing my job, though, and I don't mind going above and beyond for my clients. I'll see you once you get situated."

"Okay," Promise said, then hung up and exhaled a sigh of relief. It was one burden off of her back, but she still had plenty more burdens to face head on.

* * *

Monica had been wilding, going through each day as if she didn't have a care in the world. She never talked about her son, the one she'd put up for adoption, 'cause she didn't figure anyone needed to know about her sordid past. Her struggles went so much deeper than just living in the projects. She had a mother who threw her off on whoever she could, every time she got a new man. Her mother would tell her, Don't no man want no woman that already has kids 'cause he's not going to want to take care of another man's kids.'

Her father had been nonexistent in her life, so for Nathan to be willing to spend all his free time with her, giving her everything she'd ever wanted and all that attention, all she could do was soak it all up like a thirsty sponge.

At first, it had simply been an exchange of sex for money, but things changed when they began spending more time together. Falling asleep and waking up in each other's arms had altered their original agreement.

Monica was starting to feel that emotion she thought she would never have the pleasure of feeling. For her, love was finally in the air. Nathan and Monica balanced each other out. He was more reserved and observant most of the time, while Monica was loud, an in-your-face kind of person. When they were together, Monica brought his personality out, and instead of embarrassing him with her usual loud and sometimes obnoxious behavior, his demeanor calmed her and showed her she didn't have to be the loudest in the room to get the most attention.

Nathan couldn't deny that his feelings for her were growing rapidly. When he wasn't around her, he was compelled to text her constantly. For him, it was like some teenage kind of love that he just couldn't stop thinking about. He was considering a marriage proposal, but he didn't know if he was jumping the gun. When it came time to seek a second opinion on the matter, he trusted no one other than his right-hand man, Marcus. But when he went to Marcus with his thoughts, his friend shut him down just as quick as the words escaped his lips.

"Man, are you seriously thinking about making her your wifey? That ho was just tricking with you—or at least that's all it was supposed to be. Shit, you got the goods on the first night! It's just like that saying back in the day, bruh. You gotta pay to play, and when you do, just hit it and quit it. I knew something was up, 'cause y'all been spending too much time together, and that's not even like you. I call to hang out with you, but I gotta go through her 'cause you got the bitch answering your phone," Marcus said, hating the happiness Nathan and Monica had found in each other; after all, Promise had gotten what she'd wanted out of him and trashed him like a pair of out-of-season Louis Vuitton pumps.

"I don't want to feel like this, but do I hear someone hatin'? Nigga, if you see me dealing with Monica different than I've dealt with any other female, you oughtta be happy for me. That goes to show you she means more to me than those other chicks ever did. Now that I see how you feel, I'll just keep mine and my woman's business to myself from now on," Nathan said, pissed that Marcus, who was like a brother to him, would act that way.

"Hatin'? Nigga, I don't know what it feels like to be a hater. You've known me for too long, and you know I'm not hatin' on what you got going on. I'm just saying you best be careful. Whether you wanna admit it or not, all bitches have a motive," Marcus said.

"I'm about to bounce before this shit gets deeper than what it is you're trippin' about. I feel on the motives shit, but sometimes we gotta have some respect for women," Nathan replied.

"Okay, but let me just say this. Y'all are a nice-lookin' couple when y'all are together. She complements you rather than lookin' out of place with you like those ghetto birds you usually bring around." Marcus laughed.

"Humph. Ain't that the truth?" Nathan laughed too.

Chapter Twenty-Two

Seeing Her For the First Time

Dezman was in his room when he got a call from the front desk informing him that he had a message to pick up. He was stumped at who could be leaving anything for him, but he immediately headed to the elevator to ride down and find out. As far as he knew, no one knew he was in Tampa, and he hadn't talked to anyone before he'd up and left Boston in a hurry.

When he reached the desk and they handed him the letter, he curiously tore it open to read it before he was even halfway back to the elevator. The note didn't have a name written on it anywhere, which he thought was a little odd. His confusion quickly turned to excitement and then sadness. He was excited that he could finally see his daughter and the love of his life, Promise, but he was sad that it had to be under such circumstances. He didn't know what was wrong with his daughter, though he'd had the uneasy feeling since he'd touched down in Tampa that something just wasn't right.

Dezman passed the elevators and headed out of the hotel. He gave the valet his ticket and waited for his rental car to be pulled up. The whole time, he stared at the note.

Once he got to the hospital, his nerves started messing with him. He'd never seen his daughter before, but the anticipation of it all caused a light coating of sweat to swell on his forehead.

He stood at the closed hospital room door, contemplating whether or not he was doing the right thing by visiting. He wanted to find out what had happened to his daughter and to be sure she was okay, so he pushed those doubts to the back of his head and forged ahead into the room.

He stopped in his tracks when he saw Promise sitting in a chair right in front of him. He stared at her for what seemed like an eternity, taking in her flawless beauty. Their eyes pierced into one another, and they continued to look each other over, without saying a word.

Finally, a soft cough distracted him and caused Dezman to turn his head toward the bed, where his little girl lay. A tear rolled down his check at the sight of his baby, hooked up to all those beeping, cold, metal machines. Somehow he made his way over to Deziray's bedside. He wanted to say how sorry he was and tell her all the excuses for his absence, but no words would come out.

When Promise looked up and saw him, her words got caught in her throat. She couldn't believe Dezman was there…staring at her. At first, she thought she was seeing things, but it was him, in the flesh. Promise wanted to stop him from going near Deziray, but she couldn't. It was what she'd wanted all along: for him to be part of their daughter's life. Her only issue was she wanted him in her own life as well.

Promise broke their uncomfortable silence, "I know you want to know what happened to *our* daughter," she said. "So much has gone on and I know this may not be the proper time to ask you these questions but I need to know some things and then when we're done, I'll tell you everything. "

"I'm listening," Dezman responded.

"Why didn't you ever try to contact me again after you found out I was pregnant with our baby? Why haven't you ever tried to come see her? It was like you didn't even give a fuck," Promise said, just above a whisper and choking back tears. When he just looked at her and said nothing, she continued, "You promised you'd always be here for me, but in the end, you left, just like everyone else I've ever loved."

Dezman strolled around to the opposite side of the bed, grabbed Promise, and pushed her back against the wall, just enough for her to feel him both physically and emotionally. "Listen, Promise, I know I let you down. I did everything I promised you I wouldn't and then some. I've had to live with that. When we met for the first time at Sweet Spot, I never thought things would go anywhere. I had a woman back in Boston, but she traveled a lot. I wasn't expecting it but you and I grew into something. You brought the best out of me, and I tried to do the same for you, but when Bria found out about us, she went berserk You know I hate arguing, so I just agreed with her, whatever she yelled about. I didn't even really pay attention until a week later, and then it hit me. When she found out you were pregnant, the damn girl tried to get me to move halfway across the U.S., but that shit wasn't happening. To satisfy her and make up for my wrongdoing, I moved out of the mini-mansion and into a condo. At the time, I made everything about her. It was kind of like you and Deziray were out of sight, out of mind, but it only stayed that way for a couple months. She fucked me up when she said she had a miscarriage from all the stress that I had put on her. I couldn't believe that I was the cause of something like that happening. Then I started taking enhancement drugs because my performance on the court had all but vanished. I was told a couple days ago that I've been kicked out of the league, and when I heard that, I started wondering what else I have to live for. That was when I realized that I have a family that I've neglected. I knew I needed to be here with y'all, so I came here to find you…and to do this," Dezman said as he dropped down on one knee and pulled out a box.

When he opened it, it revealed the most beautiful piece of jewelry she'd ever seen, and she couldn't stop shaking. The waterworks began to flow between the two of them.

"I came to make things right with my family. Will you marry me, Promise?"

They turned their attention to the door when they heard someone walk in the room and took in the sight of Shad and Rare Breed.

Shad just leaned up against the wall 'cause he already knew shit was about to get real.

"What the fuck is going on in here?" Rare Breed said, but it dawned on him a second later. "Oh, wait. You must be the no-good-ass nigga who left Promise to raise a baby by herself. I don't know what you're doing down on your knee, and I don't give a fuck how much that li'l ring cost ya', butt she ain't marrying you. This…" Rare Breed said as he pulled Promise over to his side. "She's *my* woman now."

Dezman stood to his feet. "I'm really not trying to beef with you. She may have been with you once—or hell, maybe even twice—but I've always had her heart. That is *my* woman," Dezman said.

"Nigga, fuck! What you're talking about this shit—"

A knock came at the door, and a sigh of relief escaped Promise's mouth. The tension in the room could have been cut with a knife. "Come in," Promise said, finally finding the words.

The doctor was happy to inform them that Deziray could go home the next day, and he gave the baby's mother some more information and then left the room.

The room was silent for a few minutes before Promise spoke. "Look, it's been a long day for all of us. Shad, thank you for being here with my daughter. Only the Lord knows what would've happened if you hadn't gone to my house when I asked you to. You can go ahead and leave if you need to. I'll call you to keep you posted on what's going on," Promise said.

"No problem. I know you'd do the same for me. But before I go, I gotta give you this letter, the one ol' dude wrote, I guess before he started snorting that shit," Shad said. He pulled out the folded-up sheets of paper and handed them to Promise. "I didn't read it, but maybe this will give you some answers to the questions you have. I'm gonna leave now and head home. Don't forget to keep me posted," Shad said before he left.

Promise held the papers in her hand tightly. She wanted to read them, but for some reason, she wanted to be alone when she did.

Next, she turned to her new lover. "Rare Breed, I know the man you are, and I know you want to be here for me at a time like this, but remember what I told you. There are some things I need to handle on my own right now. I don't want you to leave Tampa, and I need a little time. I'll keep you posted on everything that's going on though. Thank you for all you've done and for being so understanding through this all," Promise said as she gave him a hug.

"No sweat, ma. Do what you need to do," Rare Breed said, sizing Dezman up and daring him to say something. "I'll stay here in Tampa for however long you need me to be here." Rare Breed kissed her slowly and walked out the door.

Promise turned toward Dezman, prepared to give him the same speech, but Dezman wasn't having it.

"Before you even waste your breath, I'm not going anywhere. As long as my daughter is in this hospital, I'll be here. When she leaves this hospital, I'll be there. I plan on being in my daughter's life. I want to be in yours too, but it seems like that won't be happening now, so just give me this time with my daughter."

Caught off guard, Promise agreed with him, but she told him to give her a little time to herself so she could read the letter and gather all her thoughts.

Dezman obliged and headed to the cafeteria.

Promise sat back by the window and began to read the letter…

"Hello, Promise. My name is Henry Treasure Mack, but everybody calls me T-mack. I am your real father. I'll explain that later in this letter. Your name was given to you by your mother because I used to make her pinky-promise everything…"

Promise continued to read, page after page. Some things surprised her, angered her, and even hurt her. She read about how her mother had played her father and T-mack, then left T-mack high and dry when he was sent to prison. She learned that he'd hoped and wished to meet her one day. He even wrote that her grandmother, his mother, had passed away a couple weeks earlier, but they'd been too high to even attend the funeral. T-mack also went on to explain to her how he'd killed her mother. When she finally finished the letter, she was at her wit's end. She felt like a nervous breakdown was right around the corner, and she didn't know if her heart could hurt anymore. She couldn't believe her mother had suffered such a brutal death. She was confused as to why Sweet Pea was getting high but that was confusion that would never be resolved. Tears for her mother flowed endlessly. Her heart hurt for her mother and she felt slightly guilty and responsible because had she been home, maybe none of this would've happened.

Dezman came back in the room ten minutes later and sensed something was wrong. He went over to Promise, pulled her to him, and just held her with everything in him while she cried.

Chapter Twenty-Three

Setting the Plan in Motion

Their plan was foolproof, and it was time to set everything in motion. If things turned out the way they hoped, Black Ice and Jelly would come out on top, and everyone else would be dead.

"We need to get this thing moving. I don't know what we're waiting for. Shit, it seems to me like we're just giving these muthafuckas more time to breathe, and I don't like the thought of that at all. I want them dead, and I want them dead now," Black Ice demanded.

"Damn, bitch! Are you PMSing?" Jelly asked.

"This ain't about me right now. We need to focus. If Dezman wants Promise, they can spend eternity together in hell. I know how to get Dezman to the meeting spot. All I have to do is send him a text saying some shit about that cheap-ass safe at home. I'll probably tell his ass I broke into it, took all the money and sold the jewelry. I bet his ass will want to meet up then. What we haven't figured out is how the hell we can persuade Promise to show up," Black Ice said, clearly thinking hard.

"From what Mark told me, Promise has a lot on her hands. Her daughter might be getting taken away from her because she was left in unfit conditions. You know Shad, right?"

"Yeah."

"Well, his fine ass is the one who saved her. If it wasn't for him, li'l mama could've died.

"How you know all that?"

"Well, you know, news in the 'hood travels fast," Jelly replied.

I wish the little bastard child would've died, Black Ice thought. "Fuck it. Let's just text her ass and fuck with her head about those letters we sent her. We can tell her ass if she wants to find out who sent them, she should meet us at the address we tell her," Black Ice said. "Just so you know, the bitch should lose all rights to her daughter so she won't grow up with such a poor example of a mother."

"That just might work. If not, we'll have to get her ass some other way," Jelly replied.

"I still have her number. I got if off our phone bill, since Dezman insisted on calling her ass. We're about to end this shit with a bang," Black Ice said as she slapped Jelly on the ass.

"You got me so hyped up that I can't wait to see how sweet victory tastes! Since you failed to inform me about that safe back at y'all's condo, we'll be taking care of that when we get back to Boston," Jelly said, thinking back to Black Ice's earlier words.

"There was so much stuff going on, that shit slipped my mind. Shoot, we can take a trip around the world once we hit that bad baby up," Black Ice said, unlocking her phone. She went to her contacts and found "Dead Man Walking," the listing for Dezman's name that used to say "Love of My Life." Once she clicked on it, she texted him:

Black Ice: *"I broke into your safe and got everything out of it. I'm thinking about selling the jewelry and keeping the cash for myself. Now do you want to see me, nigga? Ha-ha! I bet you do, but it's gonna happen on my time, when and where I say. Tomorrow night at 11:30. I'll send you an address soon…and yes, I'm in Tampa…#clown"*

She went back to her contacts and selected the name "Slut Bucket" from the list, then proceeded to send another text:

Black Ice: "Your best bet is not to mention this to anyone. If you want to know who's been sending you those letters, you need to be there. Hell, you might wanna show up at 11:29. Whatever you do, don't be late. I know something I'm sure you're gonna want to know."

"Well, I got the shit started. Now we need an address," Black Ice proclaimed.

"Ain't no need to wait. What about that abandoned warehouse in Ybor City? I think it's on Twenty-Third and Eighth. We can just Google the address and text it to them," Jelly said.

"Sounds good to me," Black Ice responded.

* * *

Their first stop was Mark's little apartment, and he quickly informed them that he had to meet with Tre about something. They told him that when they'd stopped by the club earlier that day, he'd been on to some funny-acting shit. For some reason, Mark didn't respond. He just handed them each a gun, then showed them to the door, without even saying a word.

Confused, they headed over to Jelly's modern condo. They needed to unload the guns they'd picked up from Mark. Jelly's gun was nothing major—just a little powder-pink .22. Black Ice had gone for something a lot bigger, with more power in its chamber: a Beretta Px4 Storm 9mm, chrome plated at the top and smoke black at the bottom.

"It's going to feel so good to see the looks on their faces when we stand there in front of them, raising our guns, ready to end it all," Black Ice said in a daze, staring off into space.

"Sometimes I think your ass be goin' stone-cold crazy," Jelly said as she watched a smile creep across Black Ice's face.

Chapter Twenty-Four

Have You Lost Your Damn Mind?

Promise ended up falling asleep in Dezman's arms, with her head resting on his chest. When she heard the knock on the door, she knew it had to be the doctor, ready to release them.

When the words came out of the doctor's mouth, Promise smiled. "You're free to go home, Ms. Brown, but..."

Her smile slowly faded as he went on.

"I'm sorry to say that Deziray won't be able to leave with you."

Dezman woke up when he heard Promise's voice rise. "No disrespect, Doc, but I already told one of your nurses that as long as my baby girl is staying in this hospital, so will I."

"Um, I'm afraid you misunderstood me. I have someone here who can explain better than I can. She's right outside the door. Just let me get her."

Promise turned and looked at Dezman. "Are these mu'fuckas serious? They can't be!"

The look Dezman saw on her face put him on guard. Promise looked as if she was out to kill.

The doctor walked back in with the woman Promise remembered from the day that had started the catapult of events that had sent her life into a downward nose-dive. It was the same freckle-faced, redhead with the same ugly wide-frame glasses. Promise tried to remember her name, but it just wouldn't come to her.

"Hello, Promise. I don't know if you remember me? Nicole Scott. What's it been? Six years? It's nice to see you again, though I'm sorry it has to be under the circumstances. I'm afraid Deziray will be leaving with me today. The child will stay with us until you have a court hearing and the judge finds you capable of properly caring for her," Nicole stated like she was reading from a script, showing no emotion whatsoever.

Nicole could've been speaking gibberish for all Promise knew, because the words that were coming out of her mouth made no sense. "You bitch! You just want to take my daughter and put her in those unstable homes with rapists, abusers, and monsters—like you did me? Well I'm not gonna let you!" Promise charged toward Nicole, who winced and closed her eyes tightly, preparing herself for a blow that she was sure was coming her way.

Dezman caught Promise just as she swung her fist. When he pulled her back, he saw that her eyes were filled with red rage.

Meanwhile, the doctor had radioed for security. Three toy cops came running through the door with one real officer in tow, looking very disinterested in what was going on.

Promise tried to calm herself, but she wasn't doing a good job. She knew if her daughter was taken away from her for good, she would lose her mind completely.

"Ma'am, we're going to have to ask you to leave," the real officer said, placing his hand on his weapon.

Dezman whispered in Promise's ear, "Let's just go. You don't want to make the situation worse. She'll put a whole bunch of bold things in her report if you do, and we'll never see Deziray again. Give us a fighting chance. Step away... for now."

Defeated, Promise walked over to the corner of the room, picked up her purse, and headed toward the door, crying uncontrollably. Halfway there, she stopped in her tracks, and Dezman squeezed her arm to let her know he had her back. "Let me just kiss my daughter before I go." After she kissed her baby goodbye, she walked past Nicole; it took all of the self-control she could muster.

"Oh, I forgot. Here's my card and some information you'll need if you decide to try to take your daughter out of the foster care system," Nicole had the nerve to say, handing Promise a stack of documents.

With clenched jaws Promise said, "I'll see you and whoever the fuck ordered this bullshit another time," and then she turned and stomped out of the room. She turned to Dezman. "You drove, right?" Without waiting for a response she continued, "You're going to take me to this CPS place listed on this paper. Hopefully, they don't give us the fuckin' run-around 'cause right now I could really blow a bitch's head off!"

This time, Dezman didn't even try to respond. He just led her to his rental car and got in, and then they rode off.

* * *

After filling out piles of paperwork and going through some careful screening processes, Promise slipped the front desk clerk a $100 bill and asked her to put her paperwork on top of the pile; she didn't want to wait in line for her day in court. It worked, and they were set to go to court in just two days.

"Let me save this wicked bitch Nicole's information in my phone. If anything happens to my angel, hers will be the first blood I shed. That's my word, Dezman," Promise said.

"Nothing is going to happen to our girl. After we go to that court hearing Wednesday, she'll be right back in our arms, where she belongs. But you've got to chill yo' crazy ass out until then," Dezman said.

For Nicole's sake, I hope you're right, Promise thought.

When she saw the text message alert at the top of her screen on her phone, she figured it was Rare Breed checking up on her. She opened the text, then realized it was a number she'd never seen before. The message told her to show up at midnight to find out who had sent the threatening letters. A second message displayed an address to a warehouse, and she knew exactly where it was. Instead of replying, she closed the message and opened a new one so she could inform Rare Breed of what was going on and let him know that in a couple of days, things would be back on the right track. She finished the text with: "I have something to handle tonight. If I don't make it out, know that I love you and that my feelings for you were real, but I have to do what I have to do alone." Then she turned to Dezman. "I need you to take me by Shad's house. You can be on your way after that. I'm sure you're tired and hungry," Promise said.

"Not really, but I'll drop you off. There's a lot on my mind, so sleep isn't on the schedule for me," Dezman replied.

When they arrived at Shad's house, she told Dezman she would be fine there. She said she was going to try to get a shower, something to eat, and a little shut-eye. "We can meet up tomorrow for lunch or something. I know you said you're ready to be in your daughter's life, but I need to know more before I agree to that. Here's your ring back. I think it's way too soon for all that. Yes, you still have a spot in my heart because you gave me a child, but my heart belongs to someone else," Promise declared before getting out of the car and placing the beautiful ring on the dashboard.

Once she was inside the house, thanks to her spare key, she yelled, "Shad? Are you in here?" When she didn't hear the TV on in the living room, she knew he had to be upstairs. She opened the door to Shad's master bedroom and saw a naked woman sprawled across the bed on top of the sheets and Shad lying comfortably on the other side of the California king bed. "Shad, get up. I don't mean to disturb you, but I need you to help me with a couple things."

Without making any movement, and in not even a blink of the eye Shad pulled a .45 from under his pillow and pointed it squarely at Promise.

She raised her hands and backed up. This nigga must be bugging! "What the fuck, Shad? Are you snorting that shit you're pushing?"

Shad opened his eyes and immediately put the gun down. "Fuck! My bad, Promise. A nigga was having a bad dream, and then I heard a muffled voice talking. I didn't know what the hell was said All I know is survival of the quickest."

Promise put her hands down. "Nigga, don't you ever point a gun at me again. Remember what you taught me? You shouldn't ever point a gun at anyone unless you plan to use it 'cause that same mu'fucka will be the one to come back and kill you later. Now get up. I'll meet you downstairs in the kitchen."

When Shad stood, Promise's eyes slowly scanned his toned physique. "Nigga, if you wasn't like a brother to me...woo! Naw, I'm just kidding," Promise lied. "Hurry up though. I'm crunched for time."

Shad smiled that sexy smile of his.

His naked jump-off woke up, saw Promise standing there, and immediately went on the defensive. She looked between the two of them and started poppin' off. "Uh-uh! Who the fuck is she, and why the fuck is she in here? I don't play that gay shit," ol' girl said, rolling her neck.

She didn't know who she was talking to, though, because at that very moment, she had the right chick. "Hold up, bitch. First, let me set you straight. If I was a full lesbian, you wouldn't be my choice. Ho, you wouldn't even touch my top twenty, and from the looks of it, you don't have enough to pay me to eat your box. What you shoulda done was wake your ass up and be glad that a bad bitch like myself is even standing in your presence," Promise said, undeterred by the jump-off's attitude.

"Now, Shad, you best get rid of your little dick-hacker and meet me in the kitchen. I got some shit I need you to do for me. And don't ask any questions. I can handle mine." She blew him a kiss, smiled wickedly, and winked at the chick, who was obviously fuming, mad that Promise expected Shad to handle a mess she created. Promise didn't care, because as far as she was concerned, little mama was way out of line. *When you know better, you do better...or at least you play your role.*

About fifteen minutes later, Shad came strolling into the kitchen with a white towel wrapped around his waist. The print of his dick was very evident, and Shad was definitely working with a monster. His dreads were still dripping; he'd clearly just gotten out of the shower.

"I thought you were up there begging the bitch to stay, as long as it took you to come down here."

"Naw. I got rid of that trick as soon as you left the room. I threw her shit out the window and told her ass to fetch it through the balcony exit. I told her next time she felt like opening her mouth to family like that, she'd think twice, and then I told her to step. I don't even know why she tripped. She knows her role. Anyway, fuck that. On to the business at hand. What's going on?"

"I need some things—a black hoodie, black sweat pants, and a gun like the one you pointed at me," Promise said sarcastically. "Lastly, I need a ride, preferably black."

"I see it's that time again. Somebody has to feel the wrath! I'll take care of all that for you. All I ride in is black on black, so that won't be a problem. Pointing the gun at you was a mistake. I told you I was having a bad dream."

"I hear you, but that's not all you ride in. Remember that all-white truck you used to have?"

"True, but that was my old swag. Now I'm on that black-on-black-everything swag."

"Okay. I can dig it. Are you going to let me get the keys to a ride? After I take a shower, I'll be ready to roll out."

"Fo sho. I got chu. The keys are in the front room on the table. Since this sounds like some illegal shit you're about to get into, you can take the new Max with the paper tags? It's in the bitch name that just left."

"Good looking out!"

"I only look out for my family. Everything you need will be in one of the guest bedrooms when you get out of the shower. I'm heading out. I got some cash I need to pick up and shit I need to handle myself. Be safe out there, Promise. I don't want to have to bust a nigga or bitch head over you," Shad said before he gave her a kiss on her forehead.

Promise sat at the table a little while after he had walked off and took his scent in. She wondered why they had never tried anything, but then she figured it was probably best. They had such a great relationship on the family end of things, and anything more would have probably fucked it up.

Promise was out of the shower in no time. As Shad said, everything was sitting neatly on the guest bed. She put on the clothes, which went perfectly with the all-black Coach sneakers she'd worn to Shad's house, grabbed the gun and extra clip he'd left on the nightstand, and headed downstairs. Once she had the keys and her purse, she was set to go. *Somebody's set to die tonight, whether it's me or the mu'fucka who's been toying with my mind.*

* * *

Dezman headed back to his hotel with Promise's ring in his hand. He kept thinking about the words she'd said and finally decided to call her so they could talk more. He loved her and figured she would most likely be spending time with that rap nigga, but he thought he could persuade her to drop those plans and spend time with him. When he turned his phone on, he saw a ton of text messages and voicemails from his former agent and a couple friends and old teammates; he assumed they'd just heard the news about him being kicked out of the league. He only had two texts from his ex, Bria, which was surprising since she usually blew up his phone and filled up his voicemail with threats to break his stuff or kill herself if he didn't come home. When he opened the text message from her, he realized she'd actually done it this time.

Shit! *This bitch done broke in my shit and brought her dumb ass to Tampa to bribe me with my own shit and 'cause more drama than I care to deal with. This bullshit ends tonight. I don't care about the tears or sob stories,* Dezman thought as he pulled into a Subway/gas station. He made up his mind that once he finished grabbing something to eat, he would head over to meet Bria at the address she'd given him. It was time to end things once and for all.

Chapter Twenty-Five

It All Comes Down to This

A little while before Black Ice and Jelly were to meet with Dezman and Promise, they went to the abandoned warehouse and broke in. Black Ice took a brick and threw it through the low-level window. Once she cleared all the jagged pieces of glasses from the window frame, she climbed through. The sun was going down outside, so she had to feel her way around the wall to the find the light switch. She ran her hand across a couple of filing cabinets and realized she was in some kind of office. Even after she flicked the light switch a couple of times, no lights came on.

"Go to the car and get the duffle bag. There isn't any power in here. I'll find my way to the front door with the little light from the window," Black Ice said.

Jelly headed to the car as instructed.

Meanwhile, Black Ice continued trying to get a feel of the warehouse. She wanted to see where all entrance and exits were, just in case they needed a quick escape.

Jelly pushed through one of the rusted side doors. She took a candle out and lit it so she could see. She needed to chain all the doors closed, except for the front and back.

After checking out the warehouse, Black Ice decided it was best to have the meeting in the main space instead of a back room.

They placed candles around the border of the room. There were enough to give some light, but not so many that the room was bright.

"When we get back here, I'll come in the warehouse. You stay in the car and serve as a lookout. I want you to let me know whenever anyone arrives. Just send me a text message. That way, when my phone vibrates, I'll know someone is here. Sit across the street in the parking lot that faces the front door of this place."

"Are you sure you'll be able to handle the situation with Dezman and Promise by yourself? You're emotionally attached to all of this, and I'm not so sure. Maybe it would be better if I stayed I here with you. We don't need you focusing all your attention on Dezman, leaving Promise free to sneak-attack yo' ass. You know the bitch is kinda gutta. She had a hand in killing Shirley from around the way. Word on the street is that she orchestrated the whole thing. If we really need a lookout that bad, I can have Mark come be our lookout," Jelly replied.

"I got this shit, man. We don't need to involve Mark in what we've got going. If nobody but us knows anything, then nobody can give anything away. Now come on! We've been here long enough. What took you so long anyway? You must've been in the car for ten minutes, like you couldn't find the damn bag. Let's go get ready for these fools," Black Ice said.

Unbeknownst to Black Ice, while Jelly was in the car retrieving the duffel bag, Mark had called and she had given him the rundown on everything, thinking Black Ice wouldn't mind him serving as their lookout. Jelly knew if she told Black Ice that now, she'd flip out. She shot Mark a text really quick to tell him they wouldn't need him after all. She didn't see anything wrong with it, because Mark had been rocking with them all that time, and as far as she knew, he had no reason to turn on them.

* * *

Dezman arrived at the warehouse without a minute to spare. He would've been early, but while eating his sandwich, he'd gotten caught up in thoughts of him, Promise, and Deziray living as a real family. He drove past the warehouse a couple times just to survey the place. He knew Bria couldn't be trusted, and he was sure it would only be a matter of time before she'd do some petty shit like she'd just pulled. The thing that was a little off to him was the fact that there was not one car parked at the warehouse. *Fuck! This bitch better be in here,* he thought.

* * *

When Jelly first saw the Chrysler 300 pass by, she didn't really pay it any attention because the car didn't slow down or stop. She sat in the driver's seat of her car, parked directly across the street, giving her a perfect vantage point to see everything that was going on. Not even a minute after the Chrysler had passed by, a Crown Vic came cruising by. The car slowed down and made a turn, startling Jelly at first, but that quickly went away when she saw that the Crown Vic was headed to the back of the warehouse, where there was a side street that led to a residential area.

A couple minutes later, the Chrysler drove up in the parking lot, backed up, and parked. She knew then that it was Dezman. She did as she was told and sent Black Ice a text:

Jelly: *Dead Man Walking has arrived." She did her best to shield the light of her phone from being seen.*

Dezman was clearly looking around for anything out of the ordinary. He looked nervous as he got out of the car and slowly made his way to the front door. He peeked in and then walked all the way inside.

All Jelly could do was laugh. *Ain't no need to be nervous now, nigga. You're finally gonna get what you want—to be with your precious Promise,* Jelly seethed.

* * *

The driver of the Crown Vic had another plan. Instead of making their way right to the warehouse, they drove around back to the side street that led to a residential area, but that wasn't their destination. This driver quickly turned around and turned off the headlights so they wouldn't be seen when they pulled up near the back of the warehouse. The driver got out, shut the door very quietly, and hurried in the back door. There was a good reason for taking such drastic measures: The car across the street with a female in it, trying to play I Spy, had been easily detected.

Inside the warehouse, the uninvited guest decided to hide until the party officially began. Only then would he or she make their presence known.

* * *

When Black Ice saw Dezman walk into the warehouse, she tried to stay calm and wait for Promise to arrive, but she couldn't. Jelly was right. She was too emotionally attached and would be overcome with pure emotions once she saw Dezman.

"So you came back to Tampa to see your whore, huh? You just couldn't stay away? I don't understand what she has that I don't, Dezman. Her pussy is good. I can go for that, but is it better than mine? Hell naw! I'm the one who can make that jump-man in your pants go to work for hours. All I had to do before was blink, and he would come alive," Black Ice stated, knowing that he couldn't see her, even if she could see him.

He looked around, trying to figure out where Bria was, but it wasn't until he heard her coming down the creaky steps that he saw her. "I don' know what the fuck you're talking 'bout when you say you can admit her pussy is good. Save those mind games for someone else. I already told you what time it is. There's no need for us to stand here and go back and forth about something that ain't going to change. I didn't come to this little meeting to work things out with you. I came to get my shit and move on. Yo' ass didn't have any right to break into my safe."

Black Ice met Dezman in the middle of the room and admired the sexy man who stood before her. Under the candlelight, he looked even more tempting. She was quickly losing control of the situation. "Never mind all that shit you're talking about. I'm in control. Four years, Dezman. I gave you four years of my life, and what thanks do I get? You settling down with your home-wrecking whore and her bastard child. If I didn't love yo' ass, I would dead you right here and now, but all that can wait, 'cause I have a surprise for you." As soon as she said that, her phone vibrated. "Looks like your surprise is right on time."

* * *

Promise was ready to get the shit over with. She pulled up on the side of the warehouse, threw the car in park, and stepped out, taking note that there was one car parked in front—a Chrysler that looked quite similar to the one Dezman had been driving earlier. *Ugh! I hate those cars. They must be on sale or something, 'cause it looks like they're becoming quite popular*, Promise thought. She tried to pull on the side door, but it wouldn't budge. *Damn! Just my fucking luck. Now I have to walk around to the front.*

Promise checked her surroundings as she headed toward the front of the building, making sure to keep her purse clutched tightly at her side. Inside the warehouse, she heard two voices; it sounded like a male and female were arguing. There was minimal light in various parts of the room, coming from the flickers of candles. There wasn't really anywhere for Promise to hide, so she kept as quiet as she could and made her way into what she figured was the main room of the warehouse.

"Nice of you to join us, Promise!" Black Ice said when she heard Promise trying to tiptoe into the room.

When Promise heard the voice clearly, that she was now a couple feet from the man, who had his back facing her, and the woman, who was obviously standing in front of him, her hand automatically balled into a fist. "Black Ice? So we meet again!" Promise said.

The look on Dezman's face when he turned around was epic. He looked as if he'd seen a ghost.

"Dezman, you have five seconds to tell me what the fuck you're doing here and why the fuck are you with this bitch!" Promise said. She was so mad she could feel her body heating up.

He just stood there speechless, looking back and forth between the two women who'd each played major roles in his life. He only had feelings for one of them now, that woman wanted answers.

"What the fuck? Cat got your tongue? You were talking just fine a minute ago, arguing with this scandalous bitch," Promise said between gritted teeth.

Black Ice began to laugh and smile in a most sinister way. When Dezman tried to explain, she cut him off. "Uh-uh-uh! *I'm* running this show," she said, walking around Dezman so they could both face her. "Y'all just couldn't leave each other alone. I tried everything I could to keep y'all apart, but I guess y'all are connected on a much deeper level. You think you're just gonna dump me to be with this bum bitch? She doesn't even amount to half of me," Black Ice ranted.

At that point, Dezman's mind was doing all types of flips, and he was confused as to what exactly was transpiring. "You mean to tell me y'all know each other? Bria, you left Sweet Spot before Promise started working there, so how do you know her?" Dezman asked.

"Wrong! The day you called me and told me it was time for me to quit working there and come to Boston, where I supposedly belonged, I told you I would, but I just couldn't up and leave. I had to tell Tre that I would no longer work there. I met this bitch when I went to tell him that night," Black Ice explained.

"Okay. I got that. But why all the animosity between y'all? This shit seems like it goes deeper than me. Bria, you never once told me you knew Promise," Dezman said.

"If you're going to tell the story, tell him the whole damn story," Promise said, damn near piercing a hole in Black Ice with her glare.

"This she-devil met me the first night I worked at Sweet Spot. She made me feel as though she cared. She helped me through my first exotic dance onstage by giving me some x, took me out to eat, and told me she would tell me everything I needed to know to survive and make something out of myself in the entertainment industry. While we were out eating, I must've been so gone on the pill she'd mixed in my alcohol that I passed out. Next thing I knew, I was waking up later on that morning at my aunt's house, and that bitch was nowhere to be found. That's not even the worst part. On top of this grimy bitch raping me, she stole money from me. When Tre, Shad, and I went to her house, the shit was cleared out and up for sale. I haven't seen the trick again until now," Promise said, sizing Black Ice up.

"So you're nothing but an ol' sheisty-ass bitch. I remember that night like it was yesterday. I went out to celebrate with the team. After I got in I called, but you didn't answer. The next morning, you texted me with some lame lie, talking about getting some rest before your early-morning flight, saying that was why you didn't answer when I called. I let it roll 'cause I wasn't trying to be on some arguing shit," Dezman said.

"So what? I fucked you and took your money. You wasn't nothing but a naïve little girl who probably would've splurged your money and spent it on some bullshit. I felt like I was teaching you a lesson. No one is to be trusted in this business," Black Ice said, justifying what she'd done.

"Just shut up, Bria. The more you talk, the more you make me wanna knock you the fuck out. I can't believe you did her like that. I knew I should've listened to ol' boy when I met yo' ass at that club. He told me just to hit it and quit it, but naw. A nigga had to listen to my li'l head." Dezman turned to the woman he still loved, the mother of his baby. "Promise, I need you to believe me when I say I didn't know anything about y'all history," he pleaded.

"Since everybody is laying everything out on the line, I have something to say."

Everyone turned around to see where the voice was coming from. It was supposed to be a closed meeting, and Black Ice wasn't familiar with the voice. In the blink of an eye, the tables had turned, and out from the shadows walked a woman—or at least what looked like a tall woman with brown skin, a long, jet-black, curly wig, and dressed to a T in a purple Roberto Cavalli mini-dress. "My name is Olivia, but Promise, you know me as Sterling," he said.

Promise was stunned. The man she'd spoken with on the phone had seemed so manly. Never in a million years would she have imagined that the private investigator she'd found in the Yellow Pages would look like that. The only reason she'd chosen him was because he was based in Boston.

"Hello, Dezman. You know me by Olivia, so I don't need to go over that. I've missed you, Daddy," Sterling said in a seductive, raspy, female voice, then blew Dezman a kiss.

"As for you," he said to Black Ice and waving her off, "I really don't see a need to acknowledge you, since you're irrelevant, a non-muthafuckin'-factor."

Now the two people with the confused looks were Promise and Black Ice.

Why in the hell is the private investigator I hired calling my baby-daddy Daddy, and who the hell is Olivia? Promise wondered.

"I didn't know what type of meeting he was attending, but I knew if your crazy ass was involved in it, shit was bound to get violent. Let me explain to y'all my role in this little sexcapade. I was hired by Promise as a private investigator to find you," he said, pointing at Dezman. "When I found you, I lost contact with Promise for a little while, so I decided to continue following you. I admit that in the beginning, you were hard to find, seeing as though you never went anywhere. Usually when I'm on the job at night, I dress as a woman. That makes it easier to follow a man without him suspecting anything. Besides, I like getting all glammed up," Sterling said, shifting his weight from one side to the other. "The more I followed Dezman and watched how you moved the more, intrigued I became with you. I bugged your phone, put a tracking device on both of your cars, and just watched and followed you until I finally got my chance one night. You exited the club very drunk. After your boy made sure you made it to your car safely and dapped you up then left, I came along and slid into your passenger seat. It didn't take much for me to sweet talk you, rub on ya pole and you were down to get busy. Once we checked into the room, I requested that we keep the lights off, and from there it was an all-night fuck fest. I enjoyed every minute of it. Drunk dick is the best dick, 'cause the mens go all in. Now Dezman is *my* man. I'm hooked, and he's going to be with me. Isn't that right, Dezman?" Sterling asked.

Dezman couldn't take it anymore. The Subway he'd eaten not even an hour earlier came up, and he bent over and vomited. The thought of the events that had taken place that night were just too much for him.

"Dezman found out the next day that I'm a man underneath all this. I guess he sobered up and thought about everything. I wouldn't stop blowing up his phone. I even threatened to expose him to the world if he didn't see me again. From that day on, Dezman and I have been an item," Sterling blatantly lied.

Promise didn't believe a word of it. Dezman tried again and again to make someone listen to his side of the story, but every time he started, he stuttered and choked up. Promise tried to calm him down, and he was finally able to explain his side of things to her.

Black Ice flew off the handle and pulled her gun from the small of her back. She pointed it at everybody, but her temper flared when her eyes landed on Dezman. She trained the gun on him while he was down on his knees, begging for forgiveness and understanding from the mother of his child and love of his life.

Dezman and Promise stared each other in the eyes. Promise was looking for even a bit of a connection between them, but there wasn't one. She was no longer connected to him.

Black Ice flipped out in a rage at the sight of Dezman begging and pleading with Promise, and she shot him continuously, until his body lay lifeless and her clip was empty.

Promise shed a tear not for herself, but for her daughter. She knew her daughter would now never get the chance to know her father as a person.

The next thing Promise saw was Sterling aiming a gun at Black Ice's head. "Wrong move bitch! How dare you kill my man? He was mine!" Sterling yelled, shaking and clearly no longer in control. His eyes looked glossy, and tears poured from them.

Promise pulled her 9mm out of her bag. "Sterling, don't do anything stupid! This meeting wasn't for you or about you. Black Ice and I have some unresolved issues that need to be sorted out. Your services are no longer needed. And I've still got that tip for you!" with that said, Promise sent one shot to the back of his head that dropped and killed him on impact.

Black Ice stood there like a wild woman, staring in space, talking gibberish to herself.

Promise began to rant at her about how she'd treated her that first night at Sweet Spot, when she'd stolen her money and left her that little cute note. "You like notes? Huh, bitch?" Promise asked as she walked around Black Ice, keeping her distance. "I guess you thought I'd never catch up to you. I really don't need to kill you, considering I've been getting you back in more than one way this whole time, unbeknownst to me," Promise said gloating in the moment.

Black Ice snapped back to reality and pointed her gun at Promise. "Game over!" she said as she pulled the trigger. She heard the *click*, but nothing came out, and she knew then that she was in hot shit. She'd fucked up by acting on her emotions again.

Promise began to laugh, and her laughter grew louder when she saw the expression on Black Ice's face turn from evil to scared. "Looks to me like your game is the only one that's over."

Pow! Pow!

Two to the chest were the last gifts she gave her. "Black Ice, it was nice to meet you again, bitch!" Promise said as she stood over her dead body.

Next, Promise heard a noise that sounded like a gun being cocked, but by the time she turned around, she already felt a bullet ripping through her left shoulder. She dropped her gun to find Jelly standing there with the smoking gun, the other bitch from Sweet Spot who always hated on her and wanted to be on her level.

"It's all your fault! I've been working on this plan for four years, and you come in the picture and fuck shit up. We were only supposed to get Dezman to marry Black Ice so she could take him for all his money and we could finally be together, but that plan took longer than we thought. It went out the window when he met and fell for you. That was supposed to be my way out of the game. No more fucking, sucking, and shaking my ass just to get by. I had to fuck and suck that fat fuck Mark, that slim-dick nigga Tre, and lose my baby Black Ice because of this shit. Now it's time I come out on top for a change. It's time for you to die," Jelly said, breathing hard. When she heard all the gunshots, she jumped out the car and hurried inside. She'd burst in just in time to see Promise putting two bullets in Black Ice.

Promise closed her eyes. She was not willing to beg. If it was her time to die, she would go out like the only father she'd ever known—like a G. She heard the deafening shot but didn't feel any pain other than her shoulder throbbing. When she opened her eyes and looked over to where Jelly had been standing just a second ago, she saw Mark standing over her with a gun in his hand.

He yelled at Jelly as she lay there clutching her leg. "Ain't shit bitch made about me! You thought shit was sweet, running around here fucking that man, not even knowing he had AIDS, spreading that shit to every Tom, Dick, and Harry, including me! Your time has expired, bitch! I know every-fuckin'-thing. I picked up that nigga Tre's prescriptions at the pharmacy, you dumb bitch!" He riddled her body with more bullets. He put the gun to his head, turned to face Promise, and said, "I'm sorry for my part in all of this." Mark said one last prayer and shot himself in the head. Unwilling to live with the pain, Mark died immediately and fell next to Black Ice, Jelly, and Dezman, dead on the filthy warehouse floor.

Damn. Mark too? Promise thought.

She rolled over on her back, still in excruciating pain, pulled her phone out of her pocket, and called her savior. Although Rare Breed hadn't wanted her to go to the meeting alone, he'd respected her wishes when she'd told him it was something she needed to do by herself.

Rare Breed arrived at the abandoned warehouse in less than five minutes. Instead of taking Promise to the emergency room, he called a 'hood doctor. He was really a doctor in a hospital, but for the right price he made house calls. The doctor determined that the wound was through and through. He did a little minor procedure and stitched her up, then gave her a couple of prescriptions. "You're gonna hurt for a while, but you'll heal up in no time," he said to Promise. He also let her know she was lucky that the bullet hadn't hit any arteries, or she wouldn't have made it.

Epilogue

A month later...

After all of the traumatic events in Tampa, Promise didn't want any part of that city anymore.

The police had found Tre stinking in his office at Sweet Spot, and Promise heard that a bum who usually got money from him was the one who found him slumped over, but the officers made a case and had picked up that same bum as their main suspect in what they called a robbery/homicide. Promise, of course, knew what really happened. Mark had killed Tre and made it seem like a robbery. After all, in some way, Tre had given him AIDS. *I guess he'd made up his mind not to die slow, and he wanted to get revenge on everyone who had a part in giving it to him*, she reasoned.

Monica finally got what she'd always wanted: a husband who loved her for her. She never left Boston again, and she began keeping in touch with her son, whom she'd given up for adoption. Nathan wanted a child, and surprisingly enough, Monica was willing to give him one, though she seemed to enjoy the baby-making process far more than she did the thought of actually having a baby. That was Monica! She finally had what she'd set out to get: real love and a man with money enough for her to afford the life she wanted.

When her case was finally cleared with CPS, Promise departed Tampa quickly, leaving all the bad memories behind. She relocated to New York City to make a life for herself with Deziray, Rare Breed, and her soon-to-be second child; she was now five months pregnant. Things were going great for her. With the money she'd saved up from stripping and escorting, she opened up a heels store called So You Fancy, Huh?, and the shoe shop quickly became popular amongst residence in New York and also people who visited. Rare Breed blew up and became one of the hottest young cats in the rap game. Later that year, he even won two awards—one was the BET Hip Hop Award for Rookie of the Year and Rookie of the Year at the MTV Music Video Awards for his debut album.

Everything was finally on the straight and narrow. Promise was happy with her life and also happy for those closest to her, even though Shad wouldn't get out of the game like she'd asked him to before she left. It was cool; 'cause she sympathized with the fact that, unfortunately that was all he knew.

So what's the moral of this story?

Simple. Broken Promises don't always end the way you may think. Sometimes they do a 360 and show you that when life throws you lemons, you have to do whatever you can to make lemonade.

G STREET CHRONICLES

~A NEW URBAN DYNASTY~

We'd like to thank you for supporting G Street Chronicles and invite you to join our social networks. Please be sure to post a review when you're finished reading.

Facebook
G Street Chronicles Fan Page
G Street Chronicles CEO Exclusive Readers Group

Twitter
@GStreetChronicl

Email us and we'll add you to our mailing list
fans@gstreetchronicles.com

George Sherman Hudson, CEO
Shawna A., COO